Lyric's List

Carrie Rachelle Johnson

Copyright © 2017 Carrie Rachelle Johnson
All rights reserved.
ISBN-10: 1982093978
ISBN-13: 978-1982093976

DEDICATION

I dedicate this novel to those who believe in true love.
.

CONTENTS

Acknowledgments	
Prologue: Leap of Faith	1
Chapter 1: Complete Control	3
Chapter 2: Fashion Crisis	10
Chapter 3: Shocking Report	19
Chapter 4: Crushed Heart	25
Chapter 5: Forced Job	30
Chapter 6: Rural Visit	36
Chapter 7: Amusing Fun	43
Chapter 8: Facing Fears	55
Chapter 9: Magical Attraction	61
Chapter 10: Giant Brawl	68
Chapter 11: Sentimental Swim	77
Chapter 12: Hovering Heights	85
Chapter 13: Drowning Sorrows	91
Chapter 14: Unlimited Love	103
Chapter 15: Dark Hearts	114
Chapter 16: Frozen Fears	120
Chapter 17: Melting Truths	129
Chapter 18: Determined Rescue	134
Chapter 19: Abandoned List	142
Chapter 20: Shared Sorrows	147
Chapter 21: Hasty Decisions	154
Chapter 22: Uncertain Hearts	160
Chapter 23: Harsh News	170
Chapter 24: Dangerous Choices	183
Chapter 25: Fearful Odds	189
Chapter 26: Perfect Bliss	196
Chapter 27: Seeking Miracles	212
Chapter 28: Shaken Faith	220
Chapter 29: Shocking Discoveries	225
Chapter 30: Returned Life	231
Chapter 31: Familiar Moments	248
Chapter 32: Unbreakable Love	255
Epilogue: New List	260
About the Author	262

ACKNOWLEDGMENTS

    First and foremost, I would like to thank God for being my Inspiration, my Guide, and the One and Only Lord of my life. I thank Jesus Christ who died for my sins not because I deserve it, but because of His great love for me.

    I would like to thank my family and friends who have constructively advised and encouraged me. I also thank my readers who have entered and experienced the various worlds of my novels.

PROLOGUE

LEAP OF FAITH

Lyric Sinclair held her breath as she ducked under the turquoise water of the city pool. She opened her eyes seeing the blurry movements of the other swimmers. The ten-year-old girl resurfaced sucking in fresh air. Her nose wrinkled at the chlorine smell that wafted off the water.

"Are you ready to go home yet, Mermaid?"

Lyric wiped wet red hair out of her face as she smiled up at her father. The redheaded man was beaming at her from the side of the pool.

"A little longer please, Daddy?"

Her father crossed his arms looking uncertain. Lyric held her breath hoping that he would agree. She didn't have to worry as she saw the twinkle in his eyes. *He's pretending to think about it.*

"Okay. Ten more minutes."

Lyric thanked him before swimming backwards from the concrete wall.

"Lyric!"

The high squeal caused the girl to glance up. She smiled at a dark-skinned girl waving down at her from the high diving board.

"Harper!"

Lyric's best friend hopped fearlessly off the diving board falling into the deeper water with a splash. The other girl waited as Harper swam toward her.

"Did you see me jump, Lyric?"

"Yes. That was so brave, Harper."

"You try it."

Lyric frowned as she moved her gaze to the high diving board which towered above her. Her heart pounded as fear filled her.

"Come on, Lyric. You can do it."

The redheaded girl swam toward the pool edge before climbing out. She glanced over at her father who was drying off with his beach towel and talking to a couple he knew. A woman laughed at something the man said. Lyric sighed sorrowfully wishing that she still had a mother. *She left us. At least I still have Daddy.*

Lyric approached the high dive line wishing that her father would see her and forbid her from doing it. However, he was distracted by his friends.

The girl took hold of the two metal rails that were stationed beside the diving board ladder. She took a deep breath as she moved her feet up each step.

At the top, Lyric's bare feet touched the white plastic diving board. Her eyes widened at how high she was from the water. The girl's heart thumped violently as she considered going back down the ladder.

"Lyric!"

The deep voice drew Lyric's attention down to the water directly below the diving board. She smiled at her father who was treading water.

"Come on, Mermaid. I'll catch you."

The frightened child shook her head unsure that it would work. She thought about how her father always kept her safe.

"Trust me, Lyric."

Lyric took a deep breath jumping off the diving board before she could change her mind. She squeezed her eyes shut tightly awaiting the splash. The girl hit the water. She kicked her feet knowing that it was useless since the bottom of the pool was far below her.

Suddenly, strong arms grabbed the child pulling her upward. Lyric gasped as she came out of the water. She breathed several times.

"It's okay, honey. I've got you."

Lyric smiled at her father. She nodded to show that she was okay.

"I'm proud of you, Lyric."

The daughter whispered, "That was scary, Daddy."

Her father hugged her closely, "That's why you had to do it, Mermaid. You'll never live if you don't take a leap of faith."

CHAPTER 1

COMPLETE CONTROL

Lyric Sinclair tapped away on her cell phone as the taxi cab trudged through rush hour traffic. Impatience swamped over her as her mind raced with all the things that needed to be done. The thirty-year-old fashion designer scrolled down the list on the screen of her cell phone. *I still need to go over the music selection for the fashion show. Also, I better check the labels on the clothes. I don't want the models to wear the wrong outfits. Of course, Harper can help me.*

Suddenly, the cab lurched to a stop. Lyric's body jerked forward. She glared at the driver who was yelling at another man who had pulled in front of them. The woman swiped a curl of strawberry-blonde hair that had fallen into her view. She pushed her designer sunglasses up her nose with a huff. *I should have hired a driver. Incompetent taxi driver.*

"Sorry, ma'am. It's a mess out here."

Lyric snorted, "Well, try to hurry. I have a lot to do."

A low grumble from the front seat caused the woman to stare at the driver with raised eyebrows. The rugged man noticed her attention in his mirror. He straightened up in his seat.

"Yes, ma'am."

Lyric returned her gaze to her cell phone. She hated these moments when she wasn't in control. The designer spent most of her time making lists and organizing her life. *That way there are no surprises. I hate surprises.*

The woman rubbed her head as it began to hurt. She knew that her busy life provided her with many headaches. *It's just stress.*

"We're here, ma'am."

Lyric handed the amount of money that she owed to the taxi driver. She could see his disappointment at the lack of tip. *He gets what he deserves.*

With her cell phone in hand, Lyric grabbed her Chanel purse. She stepped out of the cab slamming the door before strutting toward the building where her fashion show would take place. *McAlister's Banquet Hall. I wish we could have reserved something better.*

The fashionista had made several calls trying to find a more exquisite place for the show. However, everything had already been booked for the summer season. *I should have scheduled sooner.*

Lyric cringed at the classical music that resounded around the vast banquet hall. *That will not be playing during my show.*

The young woman froze as she saw the beautiful stage that she and Harper had decorated the day before. Her eyes narrowed at the rustic wooden chairs that were lined up on both sides of her perfect runway. *No way.*

"Harper!"

Lyric's shriek rang out over the music. She placed her hands on her hips.

Movement came from the curtain that divided the backstage from the performance area. A tall woman with caramel brown skin and short curly hair stomped into view.

"You bellowed, Your Highness?"

Lyric rolled her eyes aware that her lifelong friend was teasing her. She lowered her hands from her hips with a sigh.

"Did you see the chairs?"

Harper raised her hands to her face as she looked around the room.

"Oh, my! I can't believe these horrible chairs have dared to be in the presence of Miss Lyric Sinclair. Whatever shall we do?"

"Very funny, Harper. You know that tomorrow night has to be perfect."

The other woman stepped carefully off the stage approaching her friend.

"Sorry, Lyric. You just get so edgy before one of these things. Yes, I saw the chairs. I have already talked to the custodian who is going to move them back into storage. I called Mercy's and they are sending over a hundred of their best velvet chairs which will match our décor. So, do us both a favor and chill out. Okay?"

Lyric nodded, "Okay. Sounds like you've got this. Let's see what else is on the list."

The redheaded fashion designer ignored Harper as the other woman rolled her eyes this time. *She hates my lists, but my life would be chaotic without them.*

Harper Raines squealed loudly as she saw a blouse that would look stunning on her.

"Harper, you startled me. It's just a shirt."

The other woman smiled over at Lyric who was scowling at her.

"Please, Lyric. I have seen how you react to a pair of shoes or a jacket."

The redheaded fashionista shook her head.

"Not in public. You don't want to embarrass yourself."

Harper laughed glancing around. She noticed that no one was paying any attention to her.

"Trust me, Lyric. There is not a woman here who hasn't squealed over a good buy. We all do it."

Lyric rolled her eyes before approaching a rack of fancy scarves. She touched each one examining the quality of them. Harper picked up the tangerine blouse holding it up to herself as she spun toward a mirror. She loved coming back to the shopping mall that had been practically their home during their teen years. The woman knew that Lyric preferred to shop in more prestigious and expensive places, but Harper thought that it was good to remain close to their roots.

"What do you think, Lyric?"

The excited woman turned toward her friend. She frowned at the sight of Lyric rubbing her forehead. *Again?*

"Does your head hurt again?"

Lyric shrugged, "It's just stress. I'll feel better once the show is over. Maybe we can rest for a few days."

Harper snorted knowing that her best friend would never stop to rest. *She'll have a new list for us by the end of the show.*

"I think the blouse is perfect, Harper. You should get it."

"Yes, I think I will."

Lyric Sinclair marched toward the high-rise apartment building with her hands full of shopping bags. She would never admit it to Harper, but she loved shopping in the mall that they had grown up in so many years ago. The woman nodded slightly to the door attendant as he held the door open for her. She smirked as a portly man with a mustache who approached her.

"Good evening, Miss Sinclair. May I help you with your bags?"

With her nose raised in the air, Lyric passed by the manager.

"No, Harold. I have them." *An independent woman needs no one. Besides, I can't trust him with such valuable merchandise.*

The elevator door opened with a ding. Lyric entered without a word. She noticed that the elevator operator was watching her with a smile.

"Eighteenth floor."

"Yes, Miss Sinclair."

The woman faced the door as it closed. She stared hoping that the elderly man would not speak to her. Lyric had always hated small talk. She didn't understand why people wanted to fill the silence with inconsequential chatter. *Why can't we just ride up without talking?*

"How was your day, Miss Sinclair?"

Lyric stayed silent pretending that she didn't hear the man's question. She was relieved when he didn't say anything else for the rest of the ride up to the eighteenth floor. When the door opened, the woman strutted out of the elevator heading down the hallway to her apartment. She pulled out her key gently putting it into the lock before entering.

Lyric sighed happy to be home though she knew that there was a lot that she could work on during the night. Her body ached with exhaustion, but the woman was not ready to rest for the evening. Dropping the shopping bags on the red velvet sofa, Lyric tapped on her cell phone opening her list. She scanned what she still had to do before the fashion show.

With a sigh, the fashion designer headed into her bedroom to put comfortable clothes on before beginning the night shift. She kicked her high heel shoes off. Lyric changed into a pair of blue sweatpants and a light blue T-shirt. She pulled her strawberry-blonde hair into a ponytail before moving to her vanity to remove her make-up. *That's better.*

The young woman returned to her living room snatching up her laptop from the coffee table. She plopped down on the sofa turning the computer on. Her head hurt though Lyric tried to ignore it so that she could concentrate on her list of tasks. *It will be worth the work. Everything must be perfect.*

Aiden Wilder leaned back in his recliner eager to relax after another long day of driving the rich and the entitled around New York City. He was relieved to be away from his last employer. The thirty-five-year-old man had survived the snotty remarks and superior glances of an elderly socialite who had insisted on him driving her to a dozen businesses.

"Rough one, Aiden?"

The exhausted man snapped his attention to his twin brother who was entering the living room of their rundown apartment. The men were identical with their tan skin and short black hair. In fact, the only difference in their appearance was their eyes. Aiden had green eyes while Desmond's were blue. *He should have driven that chick around.*

"You have no idea, Desmond. That old bag wasn't happy with anything that I did. She had a gripe for every second of the day. I pray that she never calls on us again."

"Don't pray for that, bro. We need the money. We can't be picky about who we work for."

Aiden sighed, "I know, Des, but I am so sick of these spoiled rich people. Nothing makes them happy and they act like they are so much better than us. Snobs."

Desmond crossed his arms.

"I know. I know. But playing driver and bodyguard pays the bills. Besides, it's good to be able to use our military skills protecting people."

The other man chuckled, "Oh, yeah? When have we been able to use our skills, Des?"

"Well, never so far, but if someone ever comes after one of these elites, we would be able to stop them."

Aiden closed his eyes with a shake of his head. He knew that Desmond was right about needing to pay the bills. The man wished that there was another way.

Suddenly, the phone rang alerting both brothers to the possibility of work. Desmond picked up the portable receiver.

"Hello? Yes, ma'am. We have a driver available to help you tomorrow."

Aiden waited as his brother became silent listening to the speaker on the other end of the phone.

"Yes, ma'am. That will be fine. Your driver will meet you outside your apartment building at nine o'clock tomorrow morning. He will stay with you in and out of the car providing you protection as needed. Thank you, ma'am."

Desmond hung up the phone scribbling something on the notepad that the two men left beside the phone charger. He smiled at Aiden before plopping down on the couch.

"Well?"

Aiden frowned as his brother remained silent. He had a sinking feeling who was going to be the available driver.

"Des, please tell me that you are the driver tomorrow."

Desmond sighed dramatically, "Oh, I wish that I could, Aid, but I already have a job tomorrow."

"Ah, Des. Come on, man."

"Sorry, bro, but you have to do this. I already told the customer that you would."

Aiden growled under his breath aware that he was going to lose the fight.

"Fine. Give me the details."

Desmond smirked, "You are going to play driver-bodyguard to fashion designer Lyric Sinclair as she prepares and implements her summer fashion show which is tomorrow night. Doesn't that sound like fun?"

Aiden rolled his eyes.

"Oh, yeah. Loads of fun." *Another day of being tortured by a pampered princess. Terrific.*

Harper Raines sipped on a glass of wine as she stared at the television. She could feel her body relax though she felt slightly guilty. The woman knew that Lyric was at home working away to make sure that the fashion show would be flawless. She had offered to help, but her friend had quickly declined. *Lyric must do everything herself. She doesn't trust anyone else to do it her way. Girl needs to slow down.*

Harper set her wineglass on the side table making sure that it was stable on the coaster. She glanced at her cell phone expecting to see missed calls or text messages from Lyric. However, nothing showed on her screen. *Of course not. She won't let me do anything. Oh, well. Lyric likes to stay busy.*

Harper smiled as she thought about the lists that helped her best friend remain organized and controlled. *I like surprises. Maybe Lyric needs a few surprises in her life.*

The woman's smile faded into a frown as she snapped her attention to a picture on the living room wall. She saw herself and Lyric as children standing at the city pool with Lyric's father in the middle with his arms around the girls. The memory of that day caused the smile to return to her face. She had always felt like Connor Sinclair was her dad. He had filled in the void that her real father had left in her heart.

"You'd be proud of your girl, Mr. S. She has worked so hard. I wish you could have been here tomorrow for the fashion show. I know that she would have loved it too."

CHAPTER 2

FASHION CRISIS

Lyric Sinclair tapped her foot on the sidewalk impatiently. She scowled up and down the street as she waited for her ride to arrive. The redheaded woman mumbled under her breath about lazy drivers with her fury growing by the minute. *I have too much to do. I can't stand here wasting time all day.*

Suddenly, a black limousine pulled up to the sidewalk of the high-rise apartment building. Lyric glared as a tall man in a black suit exited the driver's side. She was stunned by his handsome face and muscular physique.

"Good morning, ma'am. Are you Miss Sinclair?"

Lyric shook the feeling of awe at the man's appearance away at the question. She crossed her arms with a frown.

"Yes. You're late."

The man glanced down at his watch.

"It's 8:45. I was told to pick you up at nine o'clock."

Lyric knew that the man was right. However, she was not going to admit her own mistake.

"It was supposed to be eight o'clock. Perhaps your answering service is confused."

The man bit his lip. His green eyes hardened at her reply.

"I will let my boss know, Miss Sinclair. Shall I open the door for you?"

Lyric snorted, "Of course. What do you think that I'm paying you for?"

Aiden Wilder's temper fumed at the snotty tone of the young woman. He had dreaded the job since the night before certain that he would be stuck with another snob. The man had driven up to the sidewalk sure that the lady with the green summer dress was his client. He cringed as he opened the door knowing that it was going to be one of those days.

"Close the door. I'm in a hurry." *Hang in there, Aiden.*

The driver-bodyguard stomped toward his side of the car watching for other vehicles before climbing into the limousine. He closed the door before glancing into the rearview mirror.

"Where to, ma'am?"

"1225 Park Avenue." *Of course. Snob Street.*

Aiden turned the key in the ignition bringing the limousine to life. He stared at the street ahead hoping that the pampered princess wouldn't resort to small talk or lectures. *Let's have a quiet ride.*

Lyric Sinclair scrolled through her lists on her cell phone as the driver drove her toward Park Avenue. She was thankful that the man wasn't making small talk as they travelled. The woman could tell that he was not thrilled to be working for her. *Who cares? Drivers are easy to come by. I have bigger things to dwell on today.*

"We're here, Miss Sinclair."

Lyric rolled her eyes.

"Then open the door."

The woman placed her cell phone into her purse as the driver slammed the door. She frowned at his unprofessionalism as he stormed around the car slinging the passenger door open.

Lyric climbed out before straightening her mint green dress. She slung her matching purse on her shoulder before gliding toward the entrance to a restaurant. The woman could see the driver following her in the reflection of the windows. She was pleased that she didn't have to tell him everything about his job.

Lyric waved at Harper who was sitting at a table near the back of the restaurant. She motioned to the driver.

"You can wait over there."

The man mumbled something before walking over to stand guard where she had indicated.

Lyric hung her purse on her chair before sliding onto the leather seat. She opened her mouth to say something to her friend. However, Harper was staring over at another part of the restaurant.

"Who is the fox?"

Lyric rolled her eyes at her boy-crazy friend.

"My driver. He's not going to make it long. I must tell him everything. He must be a complete idiot."

Harper flicked her eyes over to Lyric.

"Girl, with those green eyes and muscles, he can be the stupidest man alive. What's his name?"

The other woman picked up her menu with a shrug.

"I don't know."

Silence filled the other end of the table. Lyric looked up at her friend confused by the stern expression on her face.

"What?"

Harper grunted, "Lyric, really?"

"What? I don't have time to become buddies with my bodyguard. We have a show to put on."

The other woman pulled her fingers through her curly black hair.

"I'd like to be more than buddies with him."

Lyric sighed, "Harper, please. Focus. There are more important things to talk about than the driver."

Harper shook her head.

"Oh, no. There is nothing more important to talk about than that fine-looking man."

The redheaded woman set her menu down with a scowl. Harper giggled as she raised her hands up.

"Okay. Looking at eye-candy time is over. What do we still need to do for tonight?"

Lyric smiled before pulling out her cell phone. She tapped on her list.

"Plenty."

Aiden Wilder clenched his teeth as he was ordered to stand over by the wall like a statue instead of a human being. He glanced around the restaurant hoping that someone would try to attack the snotty woman so that he could get some of his aggression out. The man sighed at the peacefulness of the place. He leaned against the wall crossing his arms. *At least she is focused on someone else for the moment.*

Movement drew Aiden's attention to a man hurrying toward Miss Sinclair. He frowned as the stranger reached into his suit jacket. Dread filled the bodyguard as his military training came to mind. He rushed forward to intercept the man.

Suddenly, Miss Sinclair's friend waved at the approaching man. Aiden halted in surprise. He watched as the two women motioned for the man to sit down. The tension in the soldier's body faded into relaxation as he backed up toward his wall again. *Get a grip, Aiden. Who would want to attack this brat?*

Miss Sinclair moved her gaze toward him with a scowl. She flipped her reddish hair before returning to her conversation with her friends.

Aiden snorted at his earlier question. *Probably anyone who has met her.*

Lyric Sinclair turned her attention toward her driver. She had seen the man move out of the corner of her eye. The woman wondered what he was doing. She glowered at him as he took his place against the wall. *What was he up to?*

"Lyric. Harper. I have terrible news."

Lyric returned her attention to her sound manager.

"What's wrong, Miles?"

The blond man swiped a hand through his spiked hair nervously.

"I went by the hall to make sure that the technology was all working for the show. I received a call from the modeling agency. They said that two of the girls are sick and won't be able to model tonight."

Horror swept over Lyric at the unexpected news. She swallowed hard hating the surprise.

"They are sending replacements, right?"

Harper's question mirrored her own. Hope filled her at the thought. However, as soon as she saw Miles' distraught face, the woman knew the answer.

"No. They didn't have anyone available."

Lyric leaned forward placing her head in her hands. Her head hurt though she tried to ignore it. *I don't have time for this.*

"Forget brunch, Harper. We must get to the hall. We need a plan."

Harper stood up with a nod.

"We'll figure it out, Lyric. We just need to regroup."

Lyric snatched her purse up and motioned toward the driver. She wished that it would be that easy. Her mind raced with ideas of how she could solve the shocking problem. *There must be a way to fix this.*

Aiden Wilder followed the fashion designer and her friends into the McAlister's Banquet Hall. He was surprised at the lowly venue that the wealthy woman had chosen for her fashion show. The man stared at the main room that had been decorated for the event. He was impressed by the beauty of it. *They did pretty good for what they had to work with.*

"Driver, you stand over there out of the way."

Aiden grimaced at the woman's commanding screech. He nodded slightly as he walked over to another wall which had been assigned as his station. The man watched as the three adults went backstage. He sighed in relief glad to be alone for a moment.

Seeing that he was truly alone, Aiden pulled out his cell phone. He tapped a message to his brother.

You owe me big time, Des.

A reply beeped seconds later. The man smirked at Desmond's response.

It could be worse, Aid. You could be stuck in a country club with a bunch of old men smoking cigars and talking about the country's downward spiral. At least you have beautiful women to watch tonight.

"Driver!"

Aiden jumped startled at the shriek. He dropped his phone which clattered on the hard floor. The man grumbled under his breath as he picked it up before turning his attention to the stage.

Miss Sinclair stood at the end of the runway with a hard glare on her face. She placed her hands on her hips.

"Don't just stand there. Make yourself useful. Unstack those chairs and line them along both sides of the runway."

Aiden mumbled, "Yes, ma'am."

The woman spun on her heel before marching back past the curtains that led to the backstage area. *Sure, beautiful women, but venomous ones too.*

Harper Raines swiped the dark apricot lipstick across her lips expertly as her heart raced with excitement. She puckered her mouth with a smack before grabbing a tissue to blot the excess make-up away. The woman bounced a hand onto her short black curls before standing up to admire her outfit. She loved the honey color of her sleeveless summer dress.

"Harper, I can't do this."

Harper spun around to Lyric who had come out of the bathroom. Her eyes widened in surprise before a warm smile spread on her face.

The other woman was wearing a knee-length dress that was an enchanting cobalt blue. Her strawberry-blond hair was piled up on the top of her head in a messy bun. She wore matching blue heels that were higher than what Lyric would normally wear.

"Lyric, you are rocking that dress."

Lyric sighed, "I think we need a different plan, Harper. I can't go out there."

Harper nodded her head understanding her friend's fear.

"There's no time, Lyric. We must do this. Take a deep breath. You'll feel better."

The confident woman watched as her friend took several deep breaths. She frowned realizing that she had never seen Lyric look so pale. *She looks sickly.*

"Are you okay, Lyric? You look like you are going to puke."

Lyric Sinclair closed her eyes trying to breathe the pain in her head away. She had thought through every possible solution to their problem of the two openings for models. The woman had realized that only one option worked for them.

Now, Lyric was sick at the idea of stepping out on the runway dressed in one of her summer dresses. She wanted the guests to see her new line of clothes. However, the fashion designer hated that everyone would be staring at her.

"Are you okay, Lyric? You look like you are going to puke."

Lyric's eyes snapped open at the question. She shot a disapproving glance over to her friend who was staring at her with concern on her face.

"Harper, please don't say puke. It makes me want to even if I don't need to. I'm fine. We just need to get this over with." *Then everything will be back in my control.*

Aiden Wilder stifled a yawn as the announcer droned on about Miss Sinclair's summer collection. He didn't mind seeing the glamourous models strut down the runway gesturing to the crowd and showing off the clothes. The man wished that they could skip the descriptions in between.

"Now, ladies and gentleman, let me direct your attention to Harper who is displaying a honey colored dress that is fashionable no matter where you are going this summer. Head on down to the beach in this cool dress or add a silk scarf and go out for a night on the town."

Aiden smirked as Miss Sinclair's friend bounced down the runway like a professional. He held back a chuckle as she blew a kiss toward him before spinning to walk back toward the backstage curtain. *She is certainly enjoying herself.*

"Thank you, Harper. Ladies and gentlemen, I have a real treat for you this evening. Our final piece will be modeled by the highly talented fashion designer herself. Ladies and gentlemen, Miss Lyric Sinclair."

Aiden rolled his eyes as the curtain parted. He crossed his arms not really wanting to see the haughty woman who had hired him. However, as the redheaded woman stepped onto the stage, the man stood up straighter. He blinked in surprise at the beauty of his employer. Her blue dress seemed to flow around her like magic as she glided down the runway.

Aiden frowned leaning forward as he noticed that Miss Sinclair stumbled slightly in her high heels. He examined her from head to toe with his eyes as she reached the end of the stage. Applause filled the air as the audience rose to their feet praising the young designer.

Aiden cocked his head in confusion as he saw Miss Sinclair's body shake for a second. He wondered if he had imagined it as she smiled brightly at the crowd. The young woman reached up placing a hand on the side of her head. Her eyes seemed to scan the audience though not in an admiring way.

Aiden shook his head as he rushed toward the runway. *Something is wrong.*

Lyric Sinclair took a deep breath as she strutted down the runway. Her legs felt shaky, but she refused to let anything ruin her perfect night. The fashion designer smiled at the audience as they rose to their feet to give her a standing ovation. *It's a success!*

Suddenly, Lyric's body shook. It was only a slight jerk, but she had never felt anything like it before. The woman pasted on a smile to keep anyone from noticing the fear that was spreading throughout her. *What is wrong with me?*

Lyric's heart thumped loudly as she noticed that the music didn't sound right. It seemed muffled or skewed. She frowned wondering how Miles had messed it up at the last moment. The fashionista hoped that the guests wouldn't only remember a sour moment of music when they thought about her fashion show.

"Thank you, Miss Sinclair. I am sure that everyone is looking forward to buying from your new collection."

Lyric blinked in confusion as her vision blurred and the announcer's conclusion came out in a lower voice than before. The frightened lady opened her mouth to beg for help. Yet, no words came.

Suddenly, Lyric felt herself falling off the end of the runway.

Harper Raines giggled in excitement as she watched the fashion show audience jump to their feet to celebrate Lyric's triumph. She clapped her hands pleased that her best friend's night had turned out perfectly after all. *She deserves to be happy.*

Suddenly, Lyric fell forward at the edge of the stage. Horror swept over Harper. Kicking off her yellow high heel shoes so that she could move quickly, the startled woman pushed the curtain aside. Her heart pounded as she rushed down the runway toward her falling friend.

Relief filled her as Lyric's driver-bodyguard caught the woman before she hit the floor. A gasp of shock rose up in the banquet hall followed by the guests' chatter. The music silenced at once. Harper held her dress to the side as she hopped down off the stage.

"Lyric!"

The man gently placed the unconscious woman on the floor. He kept her head propped as he tried to wake her.

"What's wrong with her?"

The hero shook his head.

"I don't know. She just didn't look right."

Harper nodded disliking Lyric's unresponsiveness.

"Harper? What happened?"

The distraught woman held her friend's hand as she snapped a desperate glare to Miles who was hovering nearby.

"Call an ambulance!"

CHAPTER 3

SHOCKING REPORT

Lyric Sinclair winced in pain as she opened her eyes. She blinked at the bright light that flashed into her view. The confused woman glanced around recognizing that she was lying in a hospital bed. She tried to sit up, but found her arm pinned down.

Lyric smiled as she saw Harper asleep with her head on the side of the bed and her hand glued to the patient's arm. She used her other hand to tap a finger on her friend's head.

A groan came from Harper before the woman sat up. Her brown eyes filled with tears which confused the redheaded woman more.

"Oh, Lyric. I thought you were going to die."

Lyric rolled her eyes as her best friend hugged her tightly.

"I just fainted, Harper. I'm fine."

Harper pulled back with a shake of her head.

"No. The doctor thinks there was more to it. He is running some tests."

Lyric sat up in surprise.

"That's ridiculous. I overdid it. That's all. There is no need for tests."

Her friend's eyes hardened as her frown deepened. Harper raised a finger in the air.

"Now you listen to me, Miss Lyric Daisy Sinclair. You will do exactly what that doctor tells you. We are not leaving here until we know what caused you to fall off that stage."

Lyric winced at her full name which she hated people knowing. She glanced around hoping that no one had overheard Harper. The woman was relieved that the nurses and orderlies in the hallway seemed too busy with their own business to eavesdrop on hers.

Suddenly, Lyric's eyes narrowed at the sight of her driver-bodyguard asleep in a chair at the far wall of the room.

"What is he doing here?"

Harper's voice lowered back into a tender tone.

"His name is Aiden. He caught you when you fell off the stage. He refused to leave until he knew that you were okay. We have been here for hours."

Lyric snorted, "He probably just wants to make sure that he gets paid."

Silence followed her statement. The redheaded woman returned her gaze to Harper who was staring at her with her arms crossed.

"That's cold, Lyric. Aiden seems to really care that you are okay. Why do you have to be so hard on people?"

Lyric waved a hand in dismissal.

"Never mind him. How long until this doctor gets done? I want to go home."

Harper sighed, "I will go check with the nurse."

As her friend left the hospital room, Lyric patted her hands onto her hair wishing that she had a mirror. She hated that anyone would see her not looking her best especially the incompetent driver. The woman glanced back over him. *Maybe Harper's right. He saved me from a nasty fall.*

Lyric shook her head. *Well, that's what he gets paid for.*

Aiden Wilder stretched his arms as he yawned. He opened his eyes immediately remembering that he was at the hospital. The man moved his attention to the hospital bed. He sat up from the chair that had been his bed for the night.

"You're awake."

Miss Sinclair snorted as she tapped on her cell phone.

"Good eye, detective."

Aiden frowned at the woman's snotty tone. He bit his lip hoping to keep the words he wanted to say trapped inside. The man had been worried about Miss Sinclair when she had fallen off the stage so weak and sickly. Now, he regretted helping her. *No. Mom always said to treat others the way that you want to be treated. Not that the princess would ever help me.*

"Well, I'm glad that you are awake."

Aiden waited for the fashion designer to speak again. However, she remained silent as she stared at her phone.

"Miss Sinclair."

The redheaded woman dropped her phone to her lap with a sigh.

"Your services are no longer needed. You can go. I will have the check delivered as soon as I get out of here."

Aiden's face flushed in fury at the dismissive nature of the rude woman. He stood to his feet eager to leave her in the hospital.

"Yes, ma'am. That will be fine."

The man stomped out of the hospital room grumbling under his breath as he passed the nurse's station.

"Aiden? Where are you going?"

Aiden stopped as Harper hurried to his side.

"My job's over. She told me to leave so I'm leaving. Good luck, ma'am." *And good riddance.*

Harper Raines watched Aiden storm down the hospital hallway. She grunted before turning toward Lyric's room. The woman opened the door. She sighed at the sight of her friend texting on her cell phone.

"So, you told Aiden to leave?"

The redheaded woman narrowed her eyes in confusion.

"Who?"

Harper approached the bed snatching the cell phone out of Lyric's hand.

"Hey! Give it back, Harper. I have to make a new list."

Annoyed, the other woman pocketed the cell phone. She crossed her arms.

"No, you don't. You need to rest, Lyric. That may be what caused all of this. Now. Why did you tell Aiden your bodyguard to leave?"

Lyric glared, "Because his job is over. I don't need him. What is he going to do here? He will receive what is due to him."

Harper smirked, "Oh? And what did he earn by keeping you from needing plastic surgery?"

Her friend rolled her eyes.

"I will make sure that he gets a good tip. Okay?"

The other woman snorted, "I hope so. He has earned one dealing with you."

Harper raised a hand to stop any protest from Lyric.

"Dr. Nash is coming to talk to you in a few minutes. Let's try to put on our Sunday manners for him."

Lyric Sinclair held her breath as the hospital room door opened. She bit her lip as a male doctor with brown hair and glasses came to her side wearing his white coat. He carried a clipboard that must contain her medical records.

"Miss Sinclair, I am Dr. Nash. How are you feeling?"

Lyric swallowed hard wishing that she felt brave and confident.

"Do you know what is wrong with me?"

Dr. Nash nodded slightly with a frown on his face. Lyric glanced over at Harper who smiled weakly back at her. *She's scared too. I'm not used to Harper being scared.*

"Miss Sinclair, your sister gave us permission to do a CT scan and MRI."

Lyric raised an amused eyebrow at Harper who shrugged unapologetically.

"The results for the MRI will be available in the morning, but I can tell you about the CT scan. It shows a mass on your brain. We won't know more until we get the MRI results tomorrow, but I think you should be prepared for the possibility that this is a brain tumor."

Lyric froze feeling like her heart had stopped. She stared at the doctor waiting for him to explain the joke. The woman's throat choked causing her to wonder if she could speak enough to ask any questions.

"Dr. Nash, if it is a brain tumor, what can we do?"

The doctor turned his attention to Harper.

"It depends on what type of brain tumor it is. Surgery can be performed if the tumor is in a reachable part of the brain. There is also chemotherapy and radiation treatments. We really won't know the full options until we get the MRI results."

Lyric's mind raced at the information. Tears threatened to come though the controlling woman blinked them back.

"How long do I have?"

Both Harper and Dr. Nash turned their attention to the patient.

"We won't know until we have more information."

Lyric shook her head.

"Worse-case scenario."

Harper interrupted, "Lyric, I don't think we need to talk about that right now."

The redheaded woman scowled at her friend, "I think we do. Am I dying, Dr. Nash?"

Dr. Nash frowned, "I don't know, Miss Sinclair. Many brain tumor patients live for years after diagnosis with surgery and treatment. Stage 4 patients usually about a year."

Lyric gasped for breath at the thought of having only a year left.

"That may not be you, Lyric. You need to rest. We will find out more in the morning."

The distraught woman stared at her friend in shock.

"I'm not staying here tonight. I will rest better at home."

Dr. Nash cleared his throat.

"Miss Sinclair, I think that it would be best that you stay in the hospital so that we can monitor you."

Lyric shook her head vehemently.

"No. I am going home."

"Lyric."

"It's my choice, Harper. You all can't keep me here. I want to go home now. I will come back tomorrow for the MRI results."

The determined patient focused on the doctor who was concentrating on the clipboard now.

"We can't keep you here, Miss Sinclair, but know that this is against medical advice."

Lyric nodded, "I understand, Dr. Nash. If you need me to sign something, then I will. Just let me out of here now."

Aiden Wilder opened the apartment door with a sigh. He shot a glare at his brother who was lounging on the couch with a bowl of cereal.

"About time, brother. How's the customer?"

Aiden snorted, "As ornery as ever."

Desmond chuckled as he lifted a spoonful of cereal to his mouth.

"Well, that job's done. You're free now."

The other brother plopped down into the recliner knowing that he should head to his bedroom instead. Exhaustion pulled on him.

"And I'm glad to be free, Des. That woman was a piece of work." *At least I don't have to worry about her needing a driver or bodyguard any time soon.*

CHAPTER 4

CRUSHED HEART

Harper Raines stared at the elevator floor trying to think of what to say. She was irritated with Lyric for insisting to leave the hospital. The worried woman didn't think that it was wise for her friend to go home without all the answers.

"Just say it, Harper."

Harper snorted, "Say what?"

"Whatever you are sulking about."

The frustrated woman turned a scowl toward her friend who did not look at all concerned about her health.

"You should have stayed in the hospital. There are people there to help you if you need something."

Lyric's eyes hardened.

"You know I hate hospitals, Harper. I wouldn't get any rest there. Here I can sleep in my own bed."

"Well, at least let me stay with you."

The redheaded woman shook her head.

"You hate sleeping away from home. You've already lost a night's sleep because of me. You aren't losing another. Go home. I'll be fine."

The other woman returned her attention to the elevator floor. She thought through what Lyric had said. *It's true I hate sleeping anywhere besides my bed.*

Harper glanced over at the elderly elevator operator who was staring straight ahead at the blank wall. *I guess she won't be completely alone. The building's full of people. It's only until tomorrow morning. I'll be back to drive her to get the results from Dr. Nash.*

Harper nodded with a decision, "Okay, Lyric. I'll go home, but you have to promise me that you will go straight to bed and keep your phone in reach in case you need something."

Lyric smiled, "You'll have to give it back to me first."

The confused woman cocked her head. A wicked smirk rose on her face as she remembered taking the cell phone and shoving it in her pocket.

"Right."

Harper reached into her pocket pulling out the phone. She handed it to Lyric with a raised eyebrow.

"Only for emergencies."

Lyric rolled her eyes.

"Yes, Mom."

Harper released the phone with a chuckle. The elevator dinged before the door opened on the eighteenth floor.

"Thank you, sir."

The operator answered brightly, "You're welcome, ma'am."

The two women exited the elevator heading for Lyric's apartment. Harper waited as the other woman used her key to open the apartment door. She crossed her arms.

"So, you are going to be okay until morning?"

"Yes, Harper. Go home and rest."

The woman turned toward the elevator with a teasing smile.

"Yes, Mom."

Lyric Sinclair closed the apartment door behind her. She took a deep breath before releasing it loudly. The woman dropped her purse on the floor not caring where it landed. She trudged into her bedroom wondering how she would be able to sleep with a medical diagnosis hanging over her head. *I'm fine. It's nothing but a shadow. Dr. Nash will find nothing on the MRI.*

Wishing that her thoughts were true, Lyric removed the T-shirt and khaki pants that Harper had brought to the hospital. She pulled on her comfortable blue pajamas before sitting down in front of her vanity. The woman picked up her silver hairbrush. She gently slid the brush through her strawberry-blonde hair staring at herself in the mirror. *It's only a shadow. I don't have a brain tumor.*

Suddenly, a twinge of pain came to her head. Lyric winced seeing her expression in the mirror reflection. Fear, anger, and sorrow swamped over her in a flood of emotions. The distressed woman shrieked as she hurled the hairbrush at the mirror. The glass shattered with a loud crack.

Lyric rose to her feet before pacing back and forth across her bedroom. Her eyes fell on a stack of papers and books on a desk under the bedroom window. The woman stomped to the desk swiping her hands across the top of it. She fell to her knees with a scream as the papers and books rained onto the floor.

Lyric clenched her hands into fists as she leaned her head toward the carpet. Tears came to her eyes. For once, the tough woman allowed them to fall. She sobbed violently as she thought about the possibility of her life being over. Her mind reeled with places that she had always wanted to go and things that she had always wanted to do. *I haven't even lived yet.*

When she had no more tears, Lyric sat up placing her hands on her lap. She stared at the floor unsure of what to do next. The devastated lady sighed at the mess that she had made. She reached for some of the papers stacking them neatly.

Under one of the pages, Lyric saw a picture of her father. She picked it up relieved that the frame and glass had not been damaged in her tantrum. The daughter rubbed a tender finger over her father's face missing him more than she had in two years.

Pain wrenched Lyric's heart as she thought about the months of anguish that her father had experienced with his "treatment" of chemotherapy and radiation. *And it didn't work. You're gone now.*

Lyric sighed remembering how wonderful her father had been before the cancer had sucked the life out of him. She recalled his final hours where he could barely talk. The daughter had told her father that she would be fine. With her last loving goodbye, she had watched the man who had always loved and protected her die. *I can't go through what you did, Daddy.*

Lyric closed her eyes as a memory that she hadn't thought of in years came to mind. She had jumped off the high diving board at the city pool where her father had been ready to help her. The woman smiled weakly at the words that the man had spoken to her that day and many afterwards.

"You'll never live if you don't take a leap of faith."

Lyric opened her eyes before standing up and placing her father's picture gently on the desk. She sat down in the chair pulling her cell phone out of her pajama pocket. The organized woman tapped on the screen frantically as she made a new list. *This could be my last one. I need to make it the best.*

Aiden Wilder startled awake at the loud ring of the phone. He rolled over with a growl listening for Desmond to answer it. The man opened one eye as the phone continued to ring. A piece of paper blocked his view.

Aiden pulled off the paper squinting to read it as all remnants of sleep faded away. It was a note from Desmond who had left on a job. The other brother grumbled as he reached for the portable phone which his twin had left on the area of the bed next to him.

"Wilder Protection Agency. How may I help you?"

Aiden knew that Desmond would be proud of his professional phone greeting.

"This is Miss Sinclair."

The man forced back a groan at the voice of the haughty woman who had treated him so badly.

"I am going on a trip and I need someone to go with me."

Aiden rolled his eyes glad that Desmond wasn't here to accept the job. *There is no way that I am going through that again.*

"I'm afraid that we don't have any bodyguards available, Miss Sinclair. I'm sorry."

"Wait please. I would really like the man that I had yesterday." *She doesn't even recognize that it is me.*

Aiden sighed, "Okay, Miss Sinclair. When do you need him?"

There was a slight pause. The man waited curiously.

"I know that this is short notice, but can he meet me at Bergdorf Goodman in an hour?"

Aiden glanced at his watch surprised to see that it was three o'clock in the afternoon.

"I suppose. How long will you need him?"

Another pause came as the response. *What's the deal?*

"The trip will take a few days. I'm not sure exactly, but I will pay all expenses including gas, food, and anything else that comes up. Please. This is very important."

Aiden wondered what could be so immediate since the woman had just gotten out of the hospital. *I guess she wasn't as sick as we thought.*

"Okay, Miss Sinclair. I will have Aiden there in an hour."

"Thank you."

After the woman hung up the phone, the man sat in bed surprised by how she had talked. He couldn't believe that she said please and thank you. Miss Sinclair seemed almost desperate. *She must be planning a shopping spree. Oh, well. It's money. I just hope that I can stand her for a few days.*

Lyric Sinclair dragged her wheeled suitcase down the hallway toward the elevator. Her mind raced as she thought through all that she had packed. The traveling woman wondered if she had forgotten anything. She decided that she could always buy it on the way if something came up.

The elevator door opened with a ding. Lyric ignored the elevator operator as she rolled the suitcase inside. She stared at the closing doors.

"Lobby please."

"Yes, ma'am."

Lyric took several deep breaths certain of what Harper would say if she knew what she was doing. *Sorry, Harp. I can't just sit around waiting for the bad news.*

In the lobby, the determined woman strutted toward the front doors of the apartment building. She could see the taxi cab waiting out front.

"Do you need help, Miss Sinclair?"

Lyric shook her head at the manager.

"No, Harold. I can manage." *Here we go.*

CHAPTER 5

FORCED JOB

Aiden Wilder leaned against the black limousine waiting for Miss Sinclair to make her entrance. He had arrived before the designated time hoping to keep a rude repeat of the other day from occurring. The man had texted Desmond who was amused by the turn of events. He had also packed a bag for the extended trip that he was about to begin. *I doubt this will be worth the money.*

Movement drew Aiden's attention. He saw Miss Sinclair dressed in a floral summer dress climbing out of a yellow taxi before pulling a black suitcase out of the car. The man frowned wondering why the woman would want to meet him at the prestigious store with luggage instead of her apartment building. *It doesn't make sense.*

Aiden took a deep breath before moving toward his employer. The scowl on her face caused the man to regret accepting the job. *When will I ever learn?*

"Let me take that, Miss Sinclair."

Miss Sinclair pulled the suitcase away from Aiden's offered hand.

"We need a regular car."

The man frowned in confusion, "What?"

"We can't take a limo. We need a normal car. Don't you have a car?"

Aiden wanted to snap at her that he had a rundown old Chevy that had belonged to his father. However, he knew that it wasn't the kind of car that she was talking about.

"I guess we can rent one."

Miss Sinclair passed the suitcase toward the man. She put her sunglasses on before gliding toward the passenger door. Aiden hurried to open the door giving the lady access to her seat. He waited for her to get settled before he shut the car door. *Here we go.*

Lyric Sinclair leaned back against the black leather of the limousine. She felt anxious about the adventure that she was about to begin. The fashion designer examined her manicured fingernails pleased that they were blemish-free.

"There's a car rental place around the corner. What kind of car do you want to rent?"

Lyric glanced up at the driver before moving her attention to the passenger window.

"I don't care. Nothing too flashy. Maybe an SUV. You pick and I'll pay."

"Whatever you say, Miss Sinclair."

The woman snapped her gaze to the driver not liking his patronizing tone.

"I don't appreciate your unprofessionalism."

The driver snorted, "It's Aiden. Aiden Wilder. You could at least have the professionalism to learn my name especially if we are going to be traveling together for a few days."

Lyric glared at the man.

"Very well, Mr. Wilder. We need a car. Let's go and get one."

"Yes, ma'am."

Aiden Wilder scanned the line of cars on the rental lot. He had selected three cars now which had all been rejected by the picky woman. *She's found something wrong with all of them. There's no pleasing her.*

"How about this one, Miss Sinclair?"

Aiden smirked at the persistence of the car rental agent. He knew that the woman had to be as annoyed with the fashionista as he was though she hid it well behind the smile that was clearly pasted on her face.

"No. I don't like the color."
Aiden rolled his eyes.
"What color do you want?"
Miss Sinclair shot him a scowl.
"I don't care. Just pick a car."
The man threw his arms into the air dramatically.
"Apparently, you do care since none of the cars that I have picked have satisfied you. I think that you have decided to waste this poor woman's time as well as my own."

Aiden waited for the retort from the haughty woman. However, she remained silent. Her eyes softened before she turned to the hunter green SUV that the rental agent had chosen for them.

"This one will be fine."

Aiden frowned in confusion as Miss Sinclair and the rental agent headed for the office to sign the papers. He couldn't believe that she had given up so easily. The man had expected to be fired. Yet, the wealthy woman had not said a word to him about his tone or professionalism this time. *She probably didn't want to say anything in front of the agent. She'll have plenty to say when we hit the road. Lucky me.*

Lyric Sinclair scribbled her signature on the packet of papers that the car rental agent had printed for her. She had wanted to argue with Mr. Wilder who insisted on using an insubordinate tone with her. However, his mention of time brought the sick woman to her senses. *I don't know how much time I have. We must get going before it is too late.*

"You're all set, Miss Sinclair. Here are the keys. I hope you enjoy your trip."

With mumbled thanks, Lyric headed for the office door. She held the keys tightly thinking about the adventures that her rental car was going to take her on. The woman tossed the keys to Mr. Wilder who caught them surprised. She reached for the front passenger door opening it before climbing into the SUV.

Lyric could tell by Mr. Wilder's expression that he was shocked that she could open her own door. She ignored him as he climbed into the driver's seat. The man adjusted his seat and the mirrors before putting the key into the ignition.

"Where are we going, Miss Sinclair?"

Lyric tapped her phone reading her list. She smiled weakly at the first item on the list. The woman knew that they wouldn't make it by nightfall.

"There is a Bed & Breakfast outside of the city where I have reserved two rooms. We can stay there tonight and then head out in the morning."

Lyric recited the name of the inn and the address. She watched as Mr. Wilder typed the information into the GPS. The woman turned her attention to the window watching as the SUV began its trek out of New York City.

Harper Raines yawned as she glanced at her digital alarm clock. She reached for her cell phone eager to check it in case Lyric had contacted her while she was asleep. The woman had always been a sound sleeper.

Harper tapped around on the phone screen narrowing her eyes at a text message from Lyric. She opened it quickly hoping that her friend was okay.

I'll be out of town for a few days. Don't worry about me. The driver from the fashion show is with me.

Harper's heart wrenched at her friend's message.

"Oh, Lyric."

Aiden Wilder followed Miss Sinclair as the duo walked toward the quaint cottage that served as a Bed & Breakfast. He couldn't believe that the wealthy woman had chosen such a modest inexpensive place for them to spend the night. *She probably didn't want to spend much money on my room.*

"What's the plan for tomorrow?"

Miss Sinclair stopped walking before turning back toward him. She tapped on her cell phone.

"I have a list of places where we need to go."

Aiden frowned at the lengthy list of cities and states that the woman was planning on visiting. He had thought that they would visit a few places close to New York, but obviously Miss Sinclair had other ideas. The man wondered why she wanted to go to all these places. *This will take forever.*

Lyric Sinclair held her breath as she waited for Mr. Wilder to respond to their agenda. She could tell that the man did not like the list of places that she planned to go over the next few days.

"Sorry, Miss Sinclair. I work for a local business. Most of these places are out of my jurisdiction."

Lyric released the breath. Her mind reeled as she tried to think of a way to convince the man to continue the journey with her.

"I will double your pay, Mr. Wilder."

The man's expression seemed uncertain. He turned away from her as he stared around the Bed & Breakfast property. After a moment, Mr. Wilder returned his attention to her.

"Fine, Miss Sinclair, but know this. Money can't buy everything. I will go for now, but I have the right to quit at any time."

Lyric's temper flared at the man's lecture. She bit her lip forcing herself to remain silent. The woman didn't want to change the man's mind about helping her on the trip.

"I understand, Mr. Wilder. Let's get checked in. I'm sure we both could use some rest." *Paying double? Talk about throwing money away. Oh, well. I may be dead soon. I can't take my money with me.*

Dr. Nash sipped on his coffee as he settled down in his office chair. He scanned his appointments for the day stopping at the name Lyric Sinclair. The doctor snatched the file folder that held the results from the woman's MRI. He opened it reading over the information.

Dr. Nash's heart sank at the MRI results. He reached for the phone dialing the number that his patient had left as her cell phone number. The doctor waited eager to have Miss Sinclair come in earlier for her appointment. *This can't wait.*

Lyric Sinclair brushed her teeth thinking about the day's activities that she hoped would be successful. She smiled at her fresh appearance feeling better than the day before. The woman glanced down as her cell phone buzzed. She recognized the phone number as the doctor from the hospital.

"Dr. Nash."

Lyric tapped the decline button on her phone ending the call. She didn't want to hear from the doctor yet. The patient was not eager to learn the results of the MRI. *I must do this first. I must do this before it is too late.*

CHAPTER 6

RURAL VISIT

Dressed in jeans and a green T-shirt, Aiden Wilder waited outside the Bed & Breakfast for the princess to join him. She had informed him the night before to dress normally since he wouldn't blend well in a suit where they were going. *Let's get this over with.*

The front door of the inn opened with the inside bell ringing. Aiden glanced over at Miss Sinclair. His mouth fell open in surprise.

The fashionista was dressed in a pair of blue jeans and a pink T-shirt. Her strawberry-blonde hair was pulled back into a ponytail. She was wearing sneakers instead of her designer shoes. Her face did not have the usual make-up. *She looks like a normal person.*

"Good morning, Miss Sinclair."

The woman frowned, "You can call me Lyric, Mr. Wilder. I don't want anyone to know who I am."

Aiden nodded, "Okay, Lyric. You can call me Aiden."

Lyric's frown transformed into a weak smile.

"Very well. Good morning, Aiden. Let's get going."

The man gestured toward the hunter green SUV amazed by the change in the woman. He wondered what was going on. However, Aiden decided not to rock the boat as his grandma used to say. *I need to keep her happy. It will make things better for both of us.*

"Where's the first stop?"

Lyric tapped on her cell phone.

"Calhoun's Farm. It's only thirty miles from here."

Aiden stared at her as she spouted off the address. He couldn't believe that the city girl wanted to go to a farm.

"Is there a problem, Aiden?"

The man shook his head as he started the car. He typed the mailing address into his GPS before following its directions. *This should be interesting.*

Lyric Sinclair stared anxiously at the Calhoun's Farm sign that towered over the entrance to the property. She hoped that the farmer would allow her to fulfill her purpose, so she could mark it off her list. *My bucket list.*

Sorrow filled the young woman at the thought. She wished that she didn't know anything about her health or brain tumors. However, Lyric had searched the Internet for information about her condition. She had read about different types of brain tumors and the stages. All the information seemed to fill her with a deeper urgency than before.

Suddenly, her cell phone vibrated in her hand. Lyric frowned at Dr. Nash's name and phone number that flashed on the screen. She tapped the decline button before shoving the phone into her purse. *No time for that now.*

"Now what?"

Lyric turned her attention to Aiden who had parked the car near the farmhouse. The man leaned back in the seat waiting for her instructions.

"Let's go and talk to Mr. Calhoun."

Lyric opened her car door hopping out. She scanned the farm area marveling at the beauty of the property. The woman turned toward the house as a screen door slammed.

"Can I help you, folks?"

Lyric smiled warmly at the farmer who had stepped out onto the porch. He was a middle-aged man with thick arms and tan skin. His clothes were worn out overalls and a plaid shirt. Brown work boots were covering his feet.

"Yes, sir. My name is Lyric, and this is Aiden. We are from New York City."

Mr. Calhoun cocked his head curiously.

"New York City? That's a long way from here. You all lost?"

Lyric shook her head.

"No, sir. We were hoping to tour your farm and interact with the animals."

The farmer frowned, "Why?"

"I've always wanted to see the workings of a farm and be a part of the experience. Please, Mr. Calhoun. We don't plan to stay long."

Mr. Calhoun shook his head.

"No, ma'am. I don't think that's a good idea."

Lyric lowered her head in disappointment. *I knew I should have called ahead. I shouldn't have been in such a hurry with my planning.*

"Oh, let her do it, Huck. They can't cause too much trouble."

The fashionista blinked in surprise at a middle-aged woman who had come to the screen door. The farmer's wife wiped her hands on a towel as she stepped out on the porch. She was a short woman with brown hair tied up in a bun. A yellow apron guarded her blue dress from her work.

"I don't know, Myra. A farm is no place for city folk."

Mrs. Calhoun put her hands on her hips.

"Huck Calhoun, you were just saying at breakfast that you wished that more people would spend time on a farm, so they could appreciate what we do. Now you let these folks experience the farm."

Mr. Calhoun mumbled, "Yes, dear."

Lyric smiled warmly at the farmer's wife.

"Thank you, ma'am. We won't disturb anything."

"Oh, I'm sure you won't, honey."

Aiden Wilder followed Lyric and the farm couple into the barn. The group had already seen the chicken coop and the pig sty. Now they were coming to see the cow which Huck Calhoun had announced was the pride and joy of the farm. Aiden didn't know how a cow could bring such feelings to someone, but he didn't say anything.

"Here's our cow Sophie. We use her milk for all of our dairy products."

Aiden nodded at Huck's explanation. He had to admit that the farmer was a good tour guide. The man could tell that Huck was enjoying himself.

"Can I milk her?"

Huck cleared his throat.

"I don't think so. She is very testy. She doesn't like strangers."

"Huck, stop lying to that girl. You know Sophie gets along with everyone. She is the gentlest soul there is in the whole world. Let Lyric milk her."

Aiden crossed his arms with a smirk as Huck mumbled in understanding before gesturing to the wooden stool that was set beside the cow. Lyric sat down on the stool before leaning forward to grab Sophie's udders. *Well, at least she knows the basics.*

Suddenly, the black and white cow mooed loudly and shifted. Lyric fell back off the stool. Aiden chuckled at the startled yelp that burst from the woman.

"I don't think that is quite right."

Lyric shot a glare at the amused man though it was not as harsh as times before.

"If you know so much, why don't you milk her?"

Aiden shrugged, "Okay. I will."

The man offered a hand to Lyric who ignored it while getting on her feet alone. He put the stool back upright before sitting down on it. Aiden gently took the udders into his hands. He squeezed them expertly glad that his aunt and uncle had let him visit their farm when he and Desmond were children.

The milk squirted into the metal pail. Aiden turned toward Lyric who was watching him with her arms crossed.

"Want me to show you how?"

The woman nodded, "I guess."

Aiden surrendered the stool to Lyric. He squatted next to her. The man showed her how to milk the cow correctly. He smiled as the woman caught on quickly.

"I bet no one has ever seen a fashion designer milking a cow."

Lyric smirked before squeezing an udder in Aiden's direction. The warm milk hit the man in the face. Both adults laughed.

Aiden noticed Lyric's warm smile. He realized that she looked very pleasant when she wasn't scowling at people. *Maybe she isn't so bad after all.*

"Wasting good milk."

"Hush, Huck."

Lyric Sinclair's eyes widened at the beautiful chestnut brown horse that was saddled by the corral. She was thrilled that Mrs. Calhoun had convinced her husband to let them ride their horses around the property. The woman had only ridden a pony at a fair when she was a child, but she was sure that she could do it. She patted the horse's neck marveling at the size of the beast.

"Her name is Lady Aurora. She'll be kind to you."

Lyric smiled warmly, "Thank you, Mrs. Calhoun."

"You're welcome, honey. Have fun."

The young woman put her foot in one stirrup before raising herself up into the saddle. She glanced over at Aiden who was waiting in the saddle of a black horse. Lyric nodded at the man that she was ready.

"Don't worry about getting lost. Lord Philip and Lady Aurora know the way back."

The two adults waved at the farmer and his wife. Lyric gave a gentle kick to Lady Aurora's side moving her into action. She was pleased at the smooth flow of the ride. The woman noticed that Aiden was also able to ride his horse.

The riders were carried into a peaceful meadow that was near the farmyard. The warm breeze caressed Lyric's face. She closed her eyes trusting her horse to keep her safe. The woman enjoyed the exhilarating feeling that swept through her body. She wished that the carefree moment could last forever. However, Lyric knew that there were many more things to do on her bucket list.

Suddenly, pain came to the woman's head. She winced at the discomfort before opening her eyes. Lyric rubbed her head while taking several deep breaths. *I'm running out of time.*

Aiden Wilder halted his horse as he approached a fence that formed a perimeter around the Calhoun's Farm. He snapped his attention to Lyric to ask what she wanted to do now. The man frowned as he saw that the woman was rubbing her head.

"Are you okay?"

Lyric lowered her hand as she focused on Aiden.

"I'm fine. It's so bright out here. My sunglasses are too weak for countryside sunshine I guess."

Aiden cocked his head trying to decide if he believed her. The woman had easily kept up throughout the tour without any problems. *Maybe it is only the sun.*

The man stared at Lyric seeking out any other symptoms. He didn't see anything of concern.

Suddenly, the woman pulled out her cell phone before tapping one part of the screen. She shoved it back in her pocket.

"Let's head back. We have several miles to drive before our next stop."

Aiden nodded, "Where are we going next?"

Lyric smiled weakly, "A motel. I reserved us two rooms at the Green Lion inn. It is closer to our destination than the B&B from last night. You did load our luggage into the car, right?"

The man restrained himself from rolling his eyes at the question.

"Yes. I followed all your instructions. You didn't tell me where we are going next."

The fashionista swiped a loose red hair from her face tucking it behind her ear.

"It doesn't matter right now. I'll tell you in the morning."

Aiden opened his mouth to protest. However, the woman suddenly took off on her horse.

"Race you back to the farm!"

The young man couldn't help but smile at the challenge.

Myra Calhoun sat on the porch steps as Huck helped the young couple put the horses back in the stables. She had watched them as they rode across the meadow enjoying themselves. The farmer's wife loved the life that she saw in the young adults' faces as they explored the farm. *It's so nice when you are young.*

"Myra, the city folk are leaving now."

The woman gave her husband a scowl. She shook her head at his rudeness. *Was he raised in a hole?*

Myra stood up shaking Lyric and Aiden's hands.

"I hope you found what you were looking for here."

Lyric nodded, "Yes, ma'am. We did. Thank you for letting us experience your farm. It is lovely."

The other woman smiled brightly, "You're welcome, dear. Safe travels."

As the young couple drove away in their hunter green SUV, Myra leaned against Huck who placed an arm around her shoulders.

"We did a good thing here, Huck."

"How's that?"

The wife sighed, "Those young folks needed a peaceful day without the hustle and bustle of city life. We were able to give that to them."

Huck chuckled, "Well, it was fun to watch them with the animals."

Myra watched as the SUV moved out of sight. *They have so much life to live.*

Dr. Nash dialed Miss Sinclair's phone number for what seemed like the hundredth time. He had tried to contact the sick woman all day in between his other appointments. The doctor was worried about the lack of response from Miss Sinclair.

Dr. Nash waited as the phone rang five times. Then the call was dropped on the other end. He sighed loudly before hanging up the phone.

"Ms. Benson?"

His receptionist entered the office with a smile.

"Do you need something, Dr. Nash?"

"Yes. I need the phone number of Miss Sinclair's sister."

"I'll get her contact form." *Maybe her sister can help me find her.*

CHAPTER 7

AMUSING FUN

Aiden Wilder plopped down onto the bed in his motel room. He was exhausted from the day on the farm and driving to the Green Lion Inn. Their trip had taken them out of New York. They were in some small town in Pennsylvania though Aiden had no idea why they were there.

Aiden groaned as his cell phone ringtone began to ring. He tapped the screen seeing that it was his brother. The man touched the accept button before putting the phone to his ear.

"Hey, Des."

"How's it going, Aid? Has the princess beheaded you yet?"

Aiden rolled his eyes.

"Yes, Desmond. I'm a zombie."

"Cool."

The twin brothers laughed at their mutual silliness.

"Seriously, Aiden. How are you?"

Aiden sighed, "Not too bad actually. We spent the day at a farm."

Desmond's snort brought a smile to his face.

"Yeah right."

"It's true. We milked a cow and rode on horses. Lyric has a list of weird places that we are planning on going."

There was a pause in the conversation. Aiden wondered if the signal had been lost.

"Des?"

"Lyric? Since when do you call a customer by their first name?"

The other man explained, "She told me to call her that because she didn't want people to know she's famous."

"Oh. Well, be careful, Aiden."

Aiden frowned, "Of what?"

"Just remember how this spoiled brat has treated you. I don't want you to get hurt, bro."

The other man snorted, "You don't need to worry, Des. I have no interest in her. Besides, I am too poor for her."

"Okay, Aid. Keep me posted on your adventures."

The two brothers ended the call. Aiden stretched before heading toward the bathroom to take a shower. *I need to get the farm smell off me.*

The man stared into the mirror recalling how happy Lyric had seemed at the farm. *I wonder what she has planned for tomorrow.*

Harper Raines wiped her tears away with a tissue. She took a deep breath attempting to steady herself. *I love romance movies.*

The young woman turned the television off ready to go to bed. She tapped the screen of her cell phone seeking Lyric's number. Harper sighed as she clicked on it dialing her friend. She hoped that the other woman would answer her call.

"Hi, Harper."

"Lyric Daisy Sinclair, how could you leave here without talking to me?"

A soft sigh came from the other end as if the young woman had known this was coming.

"I'm sorry, Harper. I should have talked to you about it, but I knew you would talk me out of it. You are such a mother hen sometimes."

Harper's temper flared.

"Well, you act like you are the only person in the world. You happen to be putting my best friend's life in danger by not finding out what Dr. Nash found on the MRI. I don't take that lightly."

Silence followed the woman's outburst. Harper took a deep breath attempting to cool her anger.

"I am sorry, Harper."

"At least tell me what you are doing, Lyric."

Another pause caused the woman to wonder if her friend would say anything else. She waited as patiently as she could.

"Do you remember when my dad was sick?"

Harper's heart sank as memories washed over her. She knew that this was a delicate subject for both women.

The woman whispered, "Yes."

"After his last chemo and radiation treatment, Dad was so weak and sickly. We all knew that he wouldn't make it much longer. Do you remember?"

"Yes, Lyric. It was horrible."

Lyric replied, "Yes. It was. I was sitting with Dad while you were off getting some groceries. He could barely talk, but he told me that he had made a big mistake."

Harper frowned, "What mistake?"

"Dad told me that he had made a bucket list when he first got sick. He said that he should have gone through the list while he was still strong enough to do it. After the treatments, it was too late. He was too weak. He knew that he would never get another chance."

"Where is this going, Lyric?"

Her friend sighed, "I don't know how sick I am, Harper, but I am not going to wait until I am almost dead to do the things that I have always dreamed of doing. I am checking off the items on my bucket list now before it is too late."

Harper bit her lip wanting to say that it was crazy what the other woman was doing. However, she could tell that the plan meant a lot to her. *Maybe she should do this.*

"I understand, Lyric. I'm just worried. What if you collapse like you did at the fashion show? You should have let me come with you."

"I'll be fine, Harper. Besides, Aiden is with me."

Harper raised her eyebrows in surprise. She knew that the man was with her friend. However, the woman had never heard Lyric use his first name. *Or any name at all.*

"Aiden? Since when do you know his name?"

An unladylike snort came from the other end of the line.

"We thought it would be best to learn each other's first name while we are traveling. We need to appear to be friends."

Harper smiled at the thought of Lyric and Aiden being friends.

"So, you two are getting along now?"

"Yes, Harper. Don't sound so smug. It's just a business arrangement."

"Okay, Lyric. Just treat him nicely. You want him to get help if you need it. If you tick him off, then he may let you just lay there."

Silence returned to the phone as the conversation had unintentionally taken a serious direction. Harper tried to change the subject back to something lighter.

"So, what's the plan for tomorrow, Lyric?"

"Oh, something very exciting."

Lyric Sinclair stared up at the cartoonish sign feeling like a child. Her heart pounded in excitement at the plans that he had for the day. The woman glanced over at her bodyguard who had a confused expression on his face. She smirked knowing that the odd location didn't fit his view of the fashionista. *He probably thinks that I'm a snob.*

Lyric returned her attention to her bucket list location with a shrug. *Well, who cares what he thinks. I'm paying for his services. My thoughts are what matter.*

"What are we going to do here?"

The annoyed woman tossed her strawberry-blonde ponytail over her shoulder.

"Whatever I want." *I'm in charge not him.*

Aiden Wilder glared at Lyric's back as she marched into the flashy amusement park. His temper flared at the rudeness of the woman. He had thought that she had changed her attitude toward him. However, the spoiled princess was back. *I can't believe I was starting to see her as a human being.*

"Are you coming?"

Aiden grumbled, "Yes, ma'am."

The disgruntled man trudged into the amusement park. He glanced around taking in the colors and sounds. Under normal circumstances, Aiden would have found the theme park exciting and fun. *But not with Her Highness.*

"Let's do the bumper cars."

The hired man rolled his eyes.

"You go ahead."

Aiden stared at Miss Sinclair who had planted herself in front of him. He bit his lip as the redheaded woman placed her hands on her hips.

"I am paying you a great deal of money, Mr. Wilder. So, if I say that we are trying the bumper cars, then we are both doing it."

Aiden opened his mouth eager to protest and give her a piece of his mind. However, the words of Desmond filled his thoughts. *We need the money, Aid. Don't blow it.*

The offended man took a deep breath before answering.

"Yes, ma'am. Let's do the bumper cars." *At least I can vent my frustration by hitting her bumper car.*

Lyric Sinclair smirked feeling smug as she entered the bumper car gate. She climbed into a red car strapping herself in. The woman watched as Mr. Wilder sat down in a blue car. She could tell that the man was angry with her. *Maybe I shouldn't have been so ugly to him.*

Lyric shook her head. *No. This is my bucket list. He must do it my way.*

The bumper car ride began as bouncy music floated through the air. Lyric grabbed her steering wheel excitedly. She moved it causing her car to head toward an orange car driven by a woman she didn't know. *This is going to be so fun. Dad loved the bumper cars.*

Sorrow ached in the woman's heart as she thought about her father. Her own illness plagued her. *I may suffer like him.*

Lyric shook her head refusing to allow it to happen. *I will live before I suffer. I will find true happiness.*

Suddenly, the red car jolted forward with a crash. Lyric gasped as she turned her head. She was surprised to see that Mr. Wilder had bumped into her car with his own. The challenging expression on his face angered her. *How dare he bump into me.*

As the man backed up, Lyric had a sinking feeling what he was planning to do next.

"Don't you dare!"

The man sped forward crashing into her again. The red car slammed into the wall that formed a perimeter around the ride. Fury filled Lyric as she glared at the man.

"What are you doing?"

With a smirk, Mr. Wilder shrugged, "Playing bumper cars."

The man backed his blue car away again. Lyric spun her steering wheel desperate to escape from the wall before he came back for a third strike. She moved faster zooming around the area. The woman smirked as the blue car came in view. She swiveled her red car around before heading toward Mr. Wilder. The man expertly dodged her attack.

Lyric chased him with a laugh. She loved the exhilaration that filled her as the two adults attempted to hit each other's cars. The woman's heart pounded with delight as she crashed into the man's car surprising him.

Suddenly, a bell ringing signaled that their turn at the bumper car ride was ending. Lyric waited for her car to become still before climbing out. She walked over to Mr. Wilder who was standing near the gate waiting on her.

"I guess we are even, Miss Sinclair."

The woman raised an eyebrow at the man.

"Oh? I believe you hit me twice, Mr. Wilder."

"I know, but you deserved the first one."

Lyric opened her mouth to protest. However, she closed it realizing that the man was right. *I have been hard on him.*

"You're right, Mr. Wilder. I deserved it."

"Truce, Miss Sinclair?"

The woman smiled warmly, "Yes. If you will call me Lyric."

"Okay, Lyric. What do you want to do next?"

Lyric glanced around the amusement park.

"Why don't you pick, Aiden?"

Aiden Wilder smirked at the stunned expression on Lyric's face. He had been surprised when the woman had suggested that he pick the next ride. The man had scanned the amusement park map before finding the perfect form of entertainment.

"Paintball? You can't be serious."

Aiden shrugged, "You said I could pick. I want to play paintball."

Lyric glanced down at her stainless green T-shirt and white Capri pants.

"Don't worry, Lyric. They have coveralls to keep your clothes clean."

The fashionista crossed her arms.

"I know that. I just don't think I want to give you a chance to attack me again. Bumper cars are one thing, but paintballs are another."

Aiden chuckled, "Okay. I promise to only shoot strangers. We can be on the same team."

Lyric cocked her head with a thoughtful expression on her face.

"Okay, but you better not shoot me."

The two adults put their gray coveralls and clear goggles on before picking out their paintball guns. Aiden nodded toward another couple who were preparing for battle. He examined their enemies wondering what strategies to use for victory.

"Have you ever fired a gun?"

The man rolled his eyes. He was amused by the question. *Only a million times in training and combat.*

"I was in the military."

"Oh."

Aiden turned to regard Lyric who was staring at her chosen weapon. He smiled at the huge size of the paintball gun knowing that there was no way that the petite woman could manage it. The man reached for the weapon.

"I think that one is too heavy for you, Lyric. Here try that one."

Aiden pointed to a smaller rifle that he knew would be light enough for the woman to carry through the battlefield.

"Oh. Thank you. Will you show me how to use it?"

The soldier nodded as he handed the rifle to her. He sighed as she held the lengthy weapon in one hand stretching her arm out like a cowboy in an old western movie. Aiden moved to stand by her side. He showed her how to hold it closely to her body for support. The man also placed her other hand on the front handgrip. He was close enough to smell her perfume which was intoxicating. Aiden swallowed hard.

"Hold it like this."

Lyric Sinclair blushed as Aiden stood next to her guiding her hand to the handle of the paintball gun. Her heart pounded nervously though she knew that it had nothing to do with the weapon that she was learning to shoot. The woman held her breath as he leaned closer to adjust her other hand so her index finger was ready at the trigger.

Suddenly, the two adults met gazes. Lyric swooned at his green eyes that seemed to bear into her own. She backed up with a sigh.

"I think I've got it now, Aiden. Thank you."

The man nodded, "Right. Let's go."

Harper Raines growled as her cell phone rang with an unknown number. She was fed up with all the reporters and elite who kept calling to get the scoop on Lyric Sinclair's condition. The woman wouldn't have minded if she knew that the callers were concerned about her friend. However, it was obvious that they were searching for gossip. *Vultures.*

Harper sighed as the voicemail message icon popped onto the screen of her cell phone. She typed in her passcode before waiting to hear who was bothering her.

"Ms. Raines, this is Dr. Nash."

The woman's heart sank at the doctor's name. She wondered why he was calling her instead of Lyric.

"I have been trying to call your sister, but she hasn't answered or returned my calls. I really need to see her immediately. I can't tell you any information without her permission, but it is crucial to her health that I talk to her. Please let me know if you have another number I can try. Thank you."

Harper's hand shook as she set the cell phone onto her lap. She leaned back in her chair feeling the life drain out of her. The woman ran a caramel hand through her black curly hair nervously. She didn't want to jump to conclusions, but it didn't sound good.

Harper picked her cell phone back up. She searched her contacts until she found Lyric's name. The friend tapped on the name dialing the number. She waited as the phone rang several times. Then it went to voicemail. Harper cringed as she listened for the beep.

"Lyric, call me now."

The concerned woman ended the call with a sigh. *She needs to come home now.*

Aiden Wilder stepped silently through the hay maze listening for any sounds of his prey. His eyes darted back and forth through the plastic goggles that protected him from the possible threat. The soldier cringed at the loud breathing that was coming behind him. He knew that his comrade could get them both caught.

Aiden slowly turned to look at Lyric who was clinging to her weapon tightly. He smiled weakly enjoying the look of fear that was in her eyes. The man raised a hand to capture her attention. He kept his voice low as he gave his sidekick a new plan.

"We need to split up. Up here is a fork in the maze. You go left, and I'll go right."

"Are you sure?"

Lyric's voice was raspy. Aiden placed a hand on her shoulder.

"Don't worry. They'll be tracking me since I am the expert. Just keep moving and shoot anything that moves."

The woman nodded as she tightened her grip on the gun. She stepped forward toward the fork in the maze. Aiden followed her slowly listening again for their opponents. He stopped as Lyric glanced back at him. The man raised a thumb up in encouragement. He knew that she would be destroyed if the other players found her. *Sometimes you must make sacrifices to win the game.*

As Lyric moved out of sight, Aiden stepped toward the fork in the maze. He glanced around making sure that no one was sneaking up behind him. Satisfied by the lack of movement, the soldier froze at the end of the stack of hay. He took a deep breath before heading toward the right.

Suddenly, movement from behind caused Aiden to spin around. He yelped as a goggled player slammed into him knocking him to the ground. *What in the world?*

Lyric Sinclair's heart thumped loudly as she moved down the left side of the fork in the hay maze. She didn't like the idea of separating from Aiden. The woman hated to admit it, but she needed the experienced bodyguard's protection. *I shouldn't have agreed to this. I'm in charge here.*

Lyric shook her head knowing that she was being ugly again. She didn't want to experience another conflict with Aiden.

Suddenly, rustling footsteps coming from ahead caused the woman to pivot around and hurry back toward where she had left the man. She panted as her feet flew down the dirt path. Lyric glanced back to see if the threat was still chasing her.

Pain came to the woman's chest as she ran into something hard. Her body fell to the ground. Lyric shrieked until she saw who she had collided with. She sighed in relief.

"Lyric! What are you doing?"

The woman took several deep breaths. She closed her eyes steadying her nerves.

"Aiden, thank goodness! I was so scared."

The man chuckled, "Of what? We're in a paintball field. Nothing can really hurt us except maybe colliding with each other."

Lyric opened her mouth with a retort. However, she swallowed it as Aiden closed his eyes laughing. The woman giggled picturing how silly she must have looked running through a maze with gray coveralls and plastic goggles. Her laughter increased as she dropped her forehead to the man's chest feeling foolish.

"You should have seen your face. You looked like a grizzly bear was chasing you."

Both adults continued to laugh at the hilarious situation.

"Wow! You two are bad at this game."

Lyric snapped her head back up at the unfamiliar voice. She frowned at the presence of their opponents standing over them with their paintball guns ready. The woman glanced down at Aiden who had also stopped laughing. The two adults met gazes before starting to laugh again.

"I guess you guys win. Congrats!"

Lyric nodded at Aiden's words. She watched as the other players shook their heads in confusion before moving away to look for new opponents.

The woman stared back down at Aiden who was watching her with a smile. She realized that she was still lying on top of the man. With a blush, Lyric rolled off. She lay on the ground staring up at white fluffy clouds that slid slowly across the sky.

"Should we go?"

The pleased lady nodded as she noticed that Aiden was towering over her now. She took the offered hands before being pulled to her feet. Her heart swooned at the happy look in the handsome man's eyes as they stood face to face. *I feel like I am on a date.*

Suddenly, Lyric let the smile fade into a frown. She averted her gaze searching for her paintball gun. *I can't become attached to him. I may be dying. I can't give him false hope that we could be together if I may not be around for long.*

"We should go."

Aiden Wilder continued smiling as Lyric's face turned red before she rolled off him. He stood up knocking the stray pieces of hay off his coveralls. The man extended his hands toward the woman who was staring peacefully at the sky.

"Should we go?"

Lyric took the offered hands instead of attempting to get up on her own. She smiled at the man who had a sudden urge to pull her closer. However, he restrained himself as the two adults stared at each other with smiles on their faces. *She is so beautiful when she smiles like that.*

Suddenly, the redheaded woman's smile sank into a frown. She snapped her eyes to the side before moving away to retrieve her paintball gun.

"We should go."

Aiden was confused by the sudden change in the woman. He frowned as Lyric removed her goggles before releasing her ponytail. Her strawberry-blonde hair fell to her shoulders. She tossed her head making the hair fly around her. The woman strutted toward the changing area.

Realization hit Aiden hard causing his heart to twinge. He picked up his own weapon as he trudged after her. *I get it. I'm beneath her. She would never want to be with me.*

CHAPTER 8

FACING FEARS

Harper Raines bit her lip in frustration as she dialed Lyric's phone number for the tenth time. She had waited for an hour for her friend to return her call. Finally, the annoyed woman began to call her every ten minutes hoping that Lyric would give up and answer.

Fear filled Harper at the thought of how severe her friend's condition could be. She wished that Dr. Nash had given her more information though she understood why he couldn't legally do so.

As Lyric's voicemail asked her to leave a message, Harper shrieked in anger. She ended the call tossing the cell phone onto the couch.

"Just call me, Lyric!"

The fearful woman took a deep breath as her eyes fell on the pool picture that included Connor Sinclair and the two girls. She sighed as tears formed in her eyes. Harper remembered how the man who was like her father had taken both girls to church every Sunday. She had never really believed the whole God thing. However, as hopelessness swamped over her, the young woman could see no other help.

Harper moved her chocolate brown eyes to the ceiling of her apartment. She stared at the popcorn bubbles on the white paint.

"Lord, I don't know if You are real, but Mr. S always believed in You. If You are real, please take care of Lyric for me. Please keep her safe and bring her to her senses. Thanks. Amen."

Aiden Wilder followed Lyric halfheartedly around the rest of the amusement park rides that the woman wanted to experience. He participated in each activity, but the fun had faded in the paintball field. The man wished that the day would end so they could go back to the Green Lion Inn for the night. His heart was heavy that the woman he was beginning to like didn't think that he was worthy to date her. *I keep forgetting that she is a spoiled snob.*

Aiden grumbled, "Are we done here yet?"

Lyric shook her head.

"One last thing. I have been building up to it all day. I'm a little nervous about it."

The man cocked his head curiously.

"Okay. What is it?"

The redheaded woman pointed up into the air. Aiden followed her finger. His eyes widened as he saw the tallest rollercoaster that he had ever seen.

"You want to ride on that?"

The man swallowed hard not liking the fear that he could hear in his voice. He didn't want the woman to know that he was afraid. Aiden and Desmond had both been afraid of heights since they were small children. Their mother had blamed it on their uncle who had shoved them off the barn loft on his farm when the boys were only three years old. *Mom tore into Uncle Tim that day.*

"Yes. I want to ride on The Widow-Maker."

Aiden gulped at the dark name of the rollercoaster. He shook his head vowing in his mind that he would never ride on that monster. *She can do it if she wants, but I won't.*

"Are you coming?"

The man flicked his green eyes to the woman who was watching him with a faint smile. He couldn't tell, but it looked like Lyric's pale white skin was paler than normal.

"I don't think so." *There is no way that I'm going on The Widow-Maker. I don't care what she says.*

Panic filled Lyric Sinclair as Aiden refused to ride The Widow-Maker. She had hoped that the man would be willing to ride it with her, so she would have the courage that she needed to face her fear. The woman didn't think that she would be able to ride the rollercoaster without his help.

"Please, Aiden. I really need to do this, but I don't want to do it alone."

Lyric hated to sound like a damsel in distress. However, fulfilling everything on her bucket list was important to her. *I could be running out of time.*

A long sigh drew the woman's attention back to the man. She could see that he was fearful of riding on the tall rollercoaster though she found it odd since he was usually so tough. Lyric waited for Aiden to decide.

"Okay. Let's get this over with before I change my mind."

Lyric smiled warmly, "Thank you, Aiden."

Aiden Wilder smiled warmly at Lyric's tender thanks. He was happy to help the woman though he wished that it wasn't by riding on The Widow-Maker. The man stepped toward the car that would take him high above the ground on narrow tracks. His heart raced with fear though he tried to choke it down as he climbed into the seat next to Lyric. *Why am I doing this? I decided that there was no way to get me on this thing. Now I'm here. What happened?*

Aiden snapped his attention over to Lyric who was clinging to the bar in front of her tightly. He smiled at her beauty thinking about the pleasant attitude that she seemed to share with him at times. The man knew that he was falling in love with the woman though he was sure that she didn't feel the same way. *How could she? It's like a peacock loving a pigeon.*

Aiden placed his hands on the bar trying to forget about his feelings for Lyric. He swallowed hard as the rollercoaster car lurched forward starting its journey up the mountain of track. *Lord, please don't let me die.*

The man smiled weakly at the faith in God that he had lived with most of his life. He was thankful for the hope that he felt in scary situations. However, Aiden was certain that The Widow-Maker was going to take more than a short prayer.

The rollercoaster car began to increase in speed. The man closed his eyes knowing that they were now far off the ground. He held his breath afraid of the deep drop that would be coming soon.

Suddenly, pain came to Aiden's arm. His eyes snapped open as he stared down. Lyric's hand was attached to his arm tightly. The man glanced over at the woman who was gritting her teeth with her eyes shut. He smiled warmly before jerking his arm out of her grasp.

Lyric's eyes flew open in surprise. Aiden placed the arm around her shoulders bringing her closer as if in a protective shield. He was pleased by the relieved smile that came to her face.

The peaceful moment was interrupted immediately when the rollercoaster car dropped treacherously. Aiden squeezed his eyes shut as a scream escaped his lips. He held onto Lyric tighter using her to keep him in the car as it went upside down. His stomach lurched. *I'm going to die!*

Lyric Sinclair's heart fluttered at the falling sensation that came as the rollercoaster car zoomed down a steep slope. She squealed in excitement. The woman blushed lightly as Aiden's arm pulled her closer. She looked at the man whose tan skin was paler than normal. Lyric suppressed a giggle at the discomfort of her tough bodyguard.

As the rollercoaster ride ended, Lyric was full of disappointment which increased as Aiden slowly removed his arm from her shoulder. She stood up to follow him off the ride. Her legs ached which surprised her. *I'm fine. It was just a fast ride.*

The woman watched the shaky stagger of the man amazed that the ride had affected him so much. *He looks like he is sick.*

In the next moment, Aiden rushed to an open trashcan vomiting into it. Lyric spun around looking at the crowd of people. She swallowed hard hoping to not become ill as well. The woman turned back relieved to see the man sitting on a bench resting.

"So, want to go on it again?"

Aiden Wilder groaned as he plopped down on a bright yellow bench. He closed his eyes breathing deeply hoping to settle his stomach. The sickly man couldn't believe that the rollercoaster had affected him so greatly. *I'm such a wimp.*

"So, want to go on it again?"

Aiden opened his eyes before glaring at Lyric. The amused woman was standing before him with her arms crossed. She looked completely unaffected by the horrendous ride that they had just survived.

"Not a chance."

Lyric giggled causing Aiden to scowl at her more fiercely.

"It's not funny."

The woman held her hands up in a defensive pose.

"You're right. I'm sorry. You were nice to go on The Widow-Maker with me. Thank you."

The man's annoyance dissipated at the apology. His scowl softened at the humble and grateful tone of the usually snotty woman. *She sounds sincere.*

"We can go back to the inn now if you are ready."

Aiden nodded, "Works for me. I mean if you are ready to rest."

Lyric smiled warmly, "Yes. I think we have done enough for one day."

The two adults moved toward the exit of the amusement park. Aiden had to admit that the day had been fun except riding on the rollercoaster of death. He wondered why Lyric was going to all these odd places when she was a fashion designer. *She must have other things to do with her time. Why the road trip?*

"So, what's the plan for tomorrow?"

"I thought we could go to a circus."

Aiden frowned, "Why are we going to all of these weird places?"

Lyric shrugged, "Why not?"

Lyric Sinclair climbed under the covers in her room at the Green Lion Inn. She was pleased with how successful the day had been. The woman thought about the fun that she had had with Aiden. Her lips formed a warm smile as she recalled the tender moments that she had shared with the man. *This has been a wonderful day.*

Lyric turned her cell phone on wincing at the number of missed calls that she had received while she was having fun at the amusement park. Several of them were from Dr. Nash, but the woman was surprised to see that most of the calls were from Harper. *Something has happened.*

Lyric listened to the voice messages from both callers who urged her to call them immediately. She sighed considering her options. The exhausted woman knew that the doctor must have contacted Harper who was now desperate for her to come home. *I can't. There is more to do first.*

Lyric tapped on her bucket list smiling weakly at the two tasks that she hoped to accomplish the next day. *I hope they will let me do it.*

CHAPTER 9

MAGICAL ATTRACTION

Desmond Wilder scrubbed his limousine with a soapy sponge as he listened to his contemporary Christian CD. He was glad to have a day of no customers, so he could catch up on all the tedious tasks that there never seemed to be enough time to complete. The man hummed along with the music before he made a face at the bug guts on his windshield.

"Excuse me?"

Desmond spun around in surprise. He stared at a young dark-skinned woman approaching him from a taxi cab. The man had never seen her before. *New customer.*

"Yes, ma'am. How can I help you?"

Desmond was confused as the woman stared at him with her mouth open.

"Aiden?"

The man shook his head with a smile understanding why the woman had looked surprised.

"No, ma'am. Aiden's my twin brother. I'm Desmond."

"Oh. That explains the close resemblance. My name is Harper. I need your help getting ahold of your brother."

Desmond frowned unsure of helping a stranger locate Aiden.

"Why? Is something wrong?"

Harper nodded, "Yes. My friend Lyric is with him. She isn't answering my calls. It is important that I talk to her. It's about her health."

Desmond thought about the fashionista who had hired Aiden for an unknown job. He remembered how she had collapsed at the fashion show where his brother had helped get her to the hospital. *Her health? Maybe she is in worse shape than we thought.*

Concerned, the man dropped his sponge in the bucket of water with a splash. He dried his hands on his shirt before reaching into his back pants pocket for his cell phone.

"I'll call him."

Desmond tapped on his brother's number waiting for an answer. After one ring, it went straight to voicemail. The man rolled his eyes as he waited for the beep.

"Aid, call me back as soon as you can. Lyric's friend Harper can't get her to return her calls. It's important."

Desmond ended the call with a sigh. He returned his attention to Harper who had an anxious expression on her face.

"Don't worry, Harper. Aiden always calls me back."

Aiden Wilder sat down on the red plastic seat enjoying the circus atmosphere. He stared at the inside of the towering red and yellow circus tent. Strings of lights were draped from the poles that kept the tent from falling in on the crowd. The sawdust floor was set up for the show. *This is going to be amazing.*

Aiden pulled out his cell phone to take a picture of the magnificent arena. He frowned as he noticed that his battery was almost dead. *I guess I better charge it when we get back to the new motel.*

The two travelers had driven to a small town in West Virginia. They had dropped their luggage at the Blue Owl Motel before heading to Lady Beatrix's Show of Magical Wonder.

"It's starting."

Aiden glanced over at Lyric who was leaning forward in excitement. He smiled at the beauty of the light shining on the woman's face. The man didn't understand why they were going to all the odd places, but he was loving the fun that they had experienced at each stop.

Movement from the center of the arena drew Aiden's attention to a plump woman with shiny black hair and olive skin. She wore a leathery red dress with black leggings and boots underneath. A black top hat sat on her head.

"Ladies and gentlemen, I velcome you to the Greatest Show of Magical Vonders."

Aiden raised an eyebrow at the exotic accent of the female ringmaster.

"I am your humble servant Lady Beatrix. Please sit back and relax as ve entertain you."

Suddenly, circus music floated up from the band. Aiden leaned back ready to watch the performance.

Lyric Sinclair beamed at the amazing acts of the tightrope walkers and acrobats. She loved the elegant costumes of the performers. The woman wished for the show to never end. *It is all so magical.*

Lyric moved her gaze to Aiden wondering if the man was enjoying the circus as much as she was. Her heart raced as she found the handsome man watching her.

Aiden blushed slightly no doubt at being caught staring at her. He shrugged with a sheepish grin. Lyric smiled warmly at him before turning her attention back to the show. She wished that they could hold hands like a couple. The woman knew that she was falling in love with the man though she still believed that it could never be. *I can't follow my heart right now. It can deceive me and get me off-task. I need to just focus on my bucket list. That's enough for me.*

As the circus show ended, Lyric clapped loudly standing up like the rest of the crowd. She followed Aiden as he led the way out of the tent.

"Ready to head back to the motel?"

Lyric frowned at the question. She knew that there were two tasks on her bucket list that she had hoped to accomplish at the circus.

"No. I need to talk to Lady Beatrix."

A snort caused the woman to stop. She crossed her arms ready for a smart remark or protest.

"Why am I not surprised? Okay. Let's find her."

Lyric smiled warmly, "Thanks, Aiden."

After speaking to a couple of circus workers, the two adults were escorted to a trailer by a man dressed as a clown.

"Let me ask if she will see you."

The clown knocked on the trailer door.

"Enter."

Lyric held her breath as the clown went inside the trailer. She hoped that the busy owner would give her a chance to explain what she wanted.

Suddenly, the clown scurried out without a word. Lyric and Aiden exchanged an uncertain glance. Movement drew them back to the trailer doorway where Lady Beatrix was standing in a white buttoned-down shirt and tan pants.

"Vell, Bobo tells me that you vould like to talk to me. Velcome to my castle. I am Lady Beatrix. Please come inside."

Lyric stepped carefully up the stairs of the trailer shaking Lady Beatrix's offered hand.

"Thank you for seeing us, Lady Beatrix. I'm Lyric and this is Aiden."

The circus owner shook hands with Aiden as he entered the trailer.

"Please have a seat."

Lyric sat down on a red velvet loveseat. She smiled weakly as Aiden sat down beside her. Lady Beatrix plopped down in a red velvet armchair with a sigh.

"Tell me vhat I can do for you."

Lyric replied, "First of all, your show was amazing. We really enjoyed it."

The circus owner beamed as she nodded her head in thanks.

"I know that what I am about to ask you may seem unusual, but please hear me out."

Lady Beatrix cocked her head.

"I see. Please continue."

Lyric took a deep breath.

"With your permission, I would like to bathe an elephant and hold a monkey."

The female owner's eyes widened in surprise.

"Those are unusual requests. May I ask vhy?"

Lyric sighed, "I may never have the chance to do it again."

Silence followed the redheaded woman's explanation. She waited as patiently as she could while Lady Beatrix stared at the floor. *She's not going to let me do it.*

"Mister Aiden, vill you please go back outside and get Bobo?"

Lyric frowned in confusion as the man nodded before leaving the trailer.

"Vhat is vrong vith you, Lady Lyric?"

The redheaded woman stammered, "I don't know what you mean."

Lady Beatrix sighed, "It is obvious that you are ill, dear. If this is your last chance, then you must be dying. Are you?"

Tears came to Lyric's eyes. She blinked them away wanting to deny her illness. However, the truth was that the woman was exhausted after only sitting through a circus show. Her head ached with fatigue. She had experienced blurry vision once during the performance.

Lyric whispered, "Yes. I am dying."

The silence became deafening as the ill woman stared down at her hands trying to compose herself. Two smooth hands grasped her own. She looked up at Lady Beatrix who had a warm smile on her face.

"Then you must bathe an elephant, hold a monkey, and anything else that you vant to do."

Lyric swallowed hard.

"Thank you, Lady Beatrix."

Aiden Wilder followed Bobo the clown back to Lady Beatrix's trailer. He was surprised to see that both women were waiting outside. *That's weird. I wonder what they talked about while I was gone.*

"Ah, Bobo and Mister Aiden. Lady Lyric vould like to interact vith the animals. I have given my permission. Bobo, go fetch Misha vhile I take them to Kavi."

Aiden moved to stand next to Lyric as Lady Beatrix led them into the heart of the circus grounds. He leaned closer to the redheaded woman lowering his voice.

"So how did you get her to agree?"

Lyric shrugged, "I paid her. Money can do anything."

Aiden cringed at the shallowness of the woman's words. He didn't like the haughty tone that she was using with him either. The man opened his mouth to reply. However, the trumpeting of an elephant changed his focus.

The trio had entered an area where an elephant was being led to an open spot.

"This is Kavi. He is only six years old. Kavi is a gentle soul. You may bathe him. It is safe."

As Lyric glanced over at him, Aiden gestured for the woman to go ahead and do what she came here to do. He crossed his arms leaning on a pole with a smile. The man watched as a worker show Lyric how to bathe Kavi. The young woman used a water hose to splash water all over the young elephant who trumpeted in delight.

Aiden chuckled as Kavi shot water out of his trunk at Lyric who squealed in surprise. He scanned the area noticing that several of the workers were watching the scene.

Suddenly, the bodyguard frowned as he saw a giant man covered in muscles. He didn't like the way that the strong man was leering at Lyric. Alerts went off in Aiden's mind as he watched the stranger. He decided to keep an eye on him in case he meant harm for Lyric. *I don't care how big he is. If he tries something, he's toast.*

Lyric Sinclair patted Kavi the elephant before accepting a towel from Lady Beatrix. She wiped at the water that that creature had spurted on her during the bath.

"That was wonderful. Thank you, Lady Beatrix."

The circus owner laughed, "You are velcome, Lady Lyric. You looked like you vere having fun."

"I was. It was a once in a lifetime experience."

Lady Beatrix motioned toward the side of the area. Lyric followed with her eyes smiling as she beheld Bobo the clown approaching with a monkey on his shoulder.

"This is Misha. She is a capuchin monkey. Be careful because she is very mischievous."

Bobo picked up Misha handing her to Lyric. The woman took the monkey gently into her hands marveling at the lack of weight in the creature. Misha chattered at her before reaching for Lyric's face with her furry paws. *She is so cute.*

"Lady Lyric, I need to go take care of some business. Vill you be fine here with Misha?"

Lyric nodded without looking at Lady Beatrix. She focused on the adorable monkey. The woman laughed as Misha hopped out of her hands landing on her shoulder.

"Misha likes you."

Lyric spun around at the unfamiliar deep voice. Her eyes widened at a muscular man who towered over her. She guessed that the man must be over six feet tall. The woman was uncomfortable by the leering stare that the man directed at her.

"My name is Lynx."

The uncertain woman glanced around searching for someone to help her in case Lynx meant her harm. She was surprised to see that no one was around. *Where are the workers? Where is Aiden?*

"It's nice to meet you, Lynx, but I need to be going."

Lyric backed up ready to bolt. She frowned feeling panic rise inside her as Lynx grabbed her arm.

"What's the hurry? Misha isn't the only one who likes to play."

CHAPTER 10

GIANT BRAWL

Aiden Wilder stared at the rented hunter green SUV with a frown. He couldn't believe that the band van had backed into it. The man knew that the damage could have been worse. However, he was relieved that no one had been in it when the crash happened.

"I am so sorry, Mister Aiden. I vill pay for the repairs of course."

Aiden smiled weakly at Lady Beatrix.

"It's fine. Accidents happen. There shouldn't be much to repair. Besides, Lyric paid for great damage protection for the rental. I think we're covered."

The circus owner nodded, "So she paid for the rental? You are not her man?"

Aiden shook his head.

"I work for her."

"I understand. Shall ve ask the boss vhat she vants us to do?"

The hired man nodded as the two adults headed toward the center of the circus grounds where they had left Lyric with Misha the monkey. He froze with a frown as they came to the spot though it was empty.

Panic filled Aiden at the idea that something had happened to Lyric. He remembered the man who had been leering at the woman. The bodyguard had left with Lady Beatrix when news about the damaged car had come, but he had noticed that the strong man was no longer in the area. *I wouldn't have left her if that creep was still stalking her.*

"Vhere is she?"

Desmond Wilder gritted his teeth as he dialed Aiden for what seemed like the hundredth time. He didn't understand why his brother wasn't responding to his calls. The man was beginning to worry though he tried not to show it to Lyric's friend Harper.

As the phone went straight to voicemail, Desmond ended the call setting his cell phone down on the table. He took a deep breath.

"Still no answer?"

The man shook his head. He met gazes with Harper who looked equally worried.

"It keeps going straight to voicemail. He must have it turned off or it's dead."

The young woman sighed, "Do you have any idea where they are?"

Desmond grunted, "No. Apparently, Lyric is only telling Aiden as they get there. Very mysterious."

"Yes. That sounds like Lyric."

The two adults sat quietly no doubt thinking of what their next step could be.

Harper groaned, "I don't know what to do. I just hope that Lyric is okay."

Desmond nodded, "I'm sure that she is fine. Aiden will take care of her." *He can handle anything.*

Lyric Sinclair pulled against the strong man as he dragged her toward his tent. She wished that she could scream for help. However, Lynx had placed his other hand over her mouth keeping her from attracting attention to them. *Where's Aiden? He would help me.*

"Don't worry, precious. I will be swift."

Lyric cringed at what she was certain that the brute intended to do to her. She kicked at Lynx hoping to hurt or distract him. However, the man continued to drag her toward the tent. *I'm running out of time. I need help now.*

Suddenly, Lynx's hand shifted. Lyric bit down on a finger as hard as she could. The strong man growled releasing her mouth.

Lyric didn't waste any time. She shrieked as loud as she could hoping that help would come.

"Aiden!"

Pain came to the frightened woman as Lynx punched her in the face.

"Stupid wench!"

Lyric cringed as the giant man raised his fist into the air. She held her breath knowing that she couldn't stop him from hurting her. *It's hopeless!*

In the next instant, the attacked woman fell to the dirt ground shocked. She stared at Lynx who was holding his face. Lyric snapped her attention to the direction that the giant was snarling.

Hope filled the woman at her rescuer. *Aiden.*

"Vhere is she?"

Aiden Wilder scanned the area hoping to see some clue of where Lyric had gone. His eyes widened as Misha raced from the shadows of one of the tents. The monkey climbed up Lady Beatrix's body before stopping to cling to the woman's neck.

"Vhat in the vorld?"

Aiden shook his head starting to run in the direction that Misha had come. His heart pounded in fear for Lyric. He didn't know what the strong man intended though he could guess.

"Aiden!"

The shrieking sound of his name caused the man to run even faster. He came into a clearing in time to see the giant strike Lyric in the face. The muscular man was holding on to her arm so that she couldn't escape.

Fury filled Aiden as the attacker raised his fist into the air no doubt to hit the woman again. He picked up a rock from the ground before hurling it at the strong man's head.

The giant roared as he let go of Lyric. He held his face while snarling toward Aiden.

The bodyguard snapped his eyes to the wounded woman who was lying on the ground. Her hopeful gaze gave Aiden an even fiercer overprotectiveness of her. *Don't worry, Lyric. I'll protect you from him.*

Aiden motioned for the giant to attack him.

"Come on, Big Boy. Try me on for size."

The muscular man stomped swiftly toward the former soldier who instantly took a combat stance. All his training came back to mind as the beast reached him.

The giant swung a meaty fist at his face. Aiden expertly ducked moving his body slightly to the side of his opponent. He swung a clenched fist into the strong man's face hitting him where the rock had hit moments before.

With another roar, the giant staggered back shaking his head. Aiden knew that he was probably experiencing dizziness from the impact. *Good. Maybe he will learn to keep his hands to himself.*

Suddenly, the muscular man brought a fist toward Aiden who dodged it skillfully. However, the other fist came out of nowhere knocking the soldier hard in the face. Aiden's vision swam at the force of the blow. He blinked his eyes determined to gain control, so he could continue to protect Lyric.

As his vision returned, Aiden gasped. The giant's fist slammed into his chest knocking the air out of him. He stumbled to the dirt ground gasping for oxygen. His mind raced in panic at the thought of not being able to breathe. Yet, his concern was not for himself. *Run, Lyric!*

Lyric Sinclair bit her lip in dread as she watched Lynx slam a fist into Aiden's chest. She could tell by the man's reaction that he couldn't breathe. The woman's heart thumped fearfully as the giant grabbed Aiden around the neck with one hand before beginning to punch him in the face repetitively with the other.

Lyric's eyes swept the area seeking anything that she could use as a weapon to help Aiden. Frustration filled her at the lack of options. The woman held her breath as Lynx clutched Aiden's neck with both hands choking him. *He's going to kill him.*

Lyric's heart wrenched the thought of the man she loved being killed while protecting her. She closed her eyes as tears came to her eyes. *Please don't let him die.*

"Lynx! You vill stop immediately!"

Lyric's eyes snapped open at Lady Beatrix's shriek. She was surprised to see the circus owner rushing toward the giant. Four large men were following her.

Relief filled Lyric as the circus workers pulled Lynx off Aiden. The bodyguard crumpled to the ground. He stayed motionless which scared the woman more than anything else she had ever experienced.

Lyric stood up surprised at the dizziness that she felt. She blinked her eyes certain that it was from the earlier punch in the face. The woman staggered over to Aiden's body kneeling beside him. She shook the man harshly willing him to prove that he was alive.

After a moment of no response, Lyric pulled hard on the man rolling him over onto his back so that she could see his face clearly. She cringed at the blood oozing from several cuts and bruises forming on his face and neck.

"Aiden?"

Lyric placed her right index and middle finger together on his neck seeking a pulse. She sighed as she felt thumping under her fingers. The woman closed her eyes relieved that the man was alive. *Now if he will just wake up.*

Suddenly, a warm hand touched her arm. Lyric's eyes popped open in surprise. She stared into Aiden's green eyes which were meeting her gaze. The relieved woman smiled warmly at the man who returned the smile.

"Are you okay, Lyric?"

Lyric snorted at the injured bodyguard's question.

"I'm fine. You're the one who looks like a gorilla sat on him."

Aiden chuckled before groaning in pain.

"I feel like a gorilla sat on me."

Aiden Wilder held his breath as the circus workers helped him to stand. He winced in pain hoping that nothing was broken. The man was glad that Lady Beatrix and her helpers had arrived in time to rescue him from the giant. *Another minute and I would have been dead.*

"I'm so sorry, Mister Aiden. I assure you that Lynx vill be dealt vith. Attacking you is bad enough, but Lady Lyric. That is shameful. I sent Bobo to phone the police. Please go to my trailer and use my first aid kit to clean yourself up."

Aiden nodded as he stepped carefully toward the direction of the trailer. He smiled weakly at Lyric who had her arm around his waist no doubt to help the wounded man reach their destination. Not that Aiden was complaining. In fact, he was enjoying the attention.

Once inside the trailer, the hurt man sat down on a chair while Lyric fetched the first aid kit. He leaned back in his seat closing his eyes. His body ached with pain and exhaustion. Aiden was ready to go back to the motel and sleep his troubles away.

Suddenly, a moist cloth touched the man's bruised face. He opened his eyes seeing that Lyric was using a washcloth to clean the blood from his wounds. The focused woman's mouth was set in a serious line. She didn't look into his eyes though it was obvious by the slight pink on her cheeks that she was aware of his scrutiny.

Guilt filled Aiden as the woman tended to his wounds. He sighed loudly drawing Lyric's gaze to his own.

"I'm sorry, Lyric."

Lyric Sinclair winced at the bruises that were forming on Aiden's face. She gently touched the wet washcloth to the cuts attempting to wash the blood away. The woman hated that the man had faced such pain and almost death protecting her from Lynx.

"I'm sorry, Lyric."

Lyric snapped her eyes up to meet Aiden's green ones. She was confused by the apology.

"For what?"

The man sighed, "I left you alone even though I knew that ape had been watching you. I didn't see him and thought that he went on with his business. I should have stayed close to you."

Lyric smiled warmly, "Well, I should have been more aware of my surroundings. Misha and I could have gone with you if I had been paying attention. I didn't even know everyone was gone until Lynx came up to me. It's my fault too."

Aiden moved his hand up to the woman's face. Lyric held her breath as he swiped the back of his fingers on the bruise that she had received from Lynx. She could feel her face growing warm as she blushed.

"I'm glad you're safe, Lyric."

The delighted woman placed a hand over his own.

"I'm glad you are safe too, Aiden." *I love you.*

Dropping her hand off his, Lyric cleared her throat returning the cloth to the wounded man's face.

"By the way, why did you fight that giant on your own?"

Assuming she knew the answer, the hopeful woman longed to hear the truth from her hero. *He did it because he loves me.*

"Because you're paying me to protect you."

Disappointment swamped over Lyric as she continued cleaning his wounds. Her heart was broken that Aiden didn't feel the same way as she did. She tried to keep the hurt out of her voice telling herself that it didn't matter. *He won't be heartbroken when I die.*

"Well, it looks like you are earning every cent of it."

Aiden Wilder found it hard to breathe as he stared into Lyric's eyes. He was thrilled that she placed her hand over his own. The man wanted to profess his love for the woman. *It's the perfect time.*

Suddenly, Lyric dropped her hand from his. She started to clean his face again. Aiden wondered if she had changed her mind about him. *Maybe I saw something that wasn't there.*

"By the way, why did you fight that giant on your own?" *Because I love you.*

The uncertain man shook the words away not wanting to be rejected. He had to be sure that she loved him before he told her how he felt. Aiden decided to answer in a serious manner.

"Because you're paying me to protect you."

Lyric continued wiping the wounds on the man's face not showing any emotion.

"Well, it looks like you are earning every cent of it."

Disappointment flooded over Aiden as he realized that his love was not returned. He kept his face solemn hoping that his expression of indifference would be convincing. *I don't want her to know what a loser I am.*

"Where did everyone go when I was playing with Misha?"

Aiden explained, "One of the workers backed their van into our SUV. There's not much damage, but Lady Beatrix wanted me to see it."

Lyric nodded, "So it should be covered by the damage protection plan, right?"

"Yes." *She's more concerned about a rental car than me. I wish I could still see her as a spoiled brat. Then it wouldn't hurt as much.*

Lyric Sinclair stepped toward her side of the rented SUV. Her heart was shattered from Aiden not loving her. She tried to focus on other things, but it was difficult. *I will just focus on my bucket list.*

"Lady Lyric, you dropped your phone in the struggle."

The redheaded woman accepted the cell phone that Lady Beatrix was holding out to her.

"Thank you, Lady Beatrix."

The circus owner's eyes looked sorrowful as she lowered her voice.

"Someone has been trying to get ahold of you, dear. It has buzzed much."

Lyric glanced over to where Aiden was already sitting in the driver's seat. She kept her door closed so the man couldn't hear her.

"I know."

Lady Beatrix took Lyric's hands into her own.

"You cannot run from the truth, child."

The ill woman sighed at what the truth was. She looked straight into the other woman's eyes.

"I'm not running. I'm flying."

Lady Beatrix squeezed her hands with a smile.

"Then fly, child, before it is too late."

75

Desmond Wilder stared at his digital clock irritated that Aiden still hadn't called him back. He had stopped dialing his twin brother's phone in frustration since it was still going straight to voicemail.

"Turn your phone on and call your brother, Aid."

Suddenly, Desmond's cell phone rang. He grabbed it eager to talk to his brother. The man sighed as he recognized the number as a repeat customer. He let the call go to voicemail unconcerned by the possibility of losing work. *All that matters right now is my brother.*

"Why aren't you calling me back, bro?"

Aiden Wilder lay on his motel bed resting his aching body and his broken heart. He couldn't believe that the woman that he loved didn't feel the same way as him. The man didn't know how he could continue to travel with Lyric now.

Aiden reached for his cell phone before remembering that the battery was dead. He reached for his suitcase to find his phone charger.

Suddenly, the man groaned. He clearly remembered leaving the Green Lion Inn without unplugging his charger from the wall. *Great! Oh, well. What do I need my phone for? Just so Des can say that he told me so.*

Aiden placed his cell phone in his suitcase to keep it safe. He turned the lamp off pulling the covers over him. The man closed his eyes hoping that he would have peaceful dreams though he doubted that would be the case.

CHAPTER 11

SENTIMENTAL SWIM

Lyric Sinclair stared out the SUV window as Aiden drove them along the beach. She couldn't believe that they had made it to Florida. The two adults had driven thirteen hours the day before to get to their next destination. After a night of sleep in the Palm Tree Hotel, they were heading to the next item on the list.

Lyric glanced over at Aiden who had his eyes focused on the road ahead. She frowned slightly before returning her attention to the ocean. The drive had been quiet which didn't really bother the woman since her mind was racing with the next item on her bucket list. *This will be a special one.*

Aiden cleared his throat drawing her attention back to him.

"So, what do you want to do here?"

Lyric smiled at the ocean loving the turquoise color of the water. "Become a mermaid."

Aiden Wilder climbed out of his side of the green SUV as the duo had reached their next stop. He stretched pleased that his body was healing nicely. The man looked at his reflection in the window noticing that the bruises and cuts were almost gone. *It's almost like it never happened.*

Aiden followed Lyric into an aquarium building. He waited as she checked in. A worker led them into an outside area where a small group of people were talking quietly.

Aiden's eyes widened at the beauty of the lagoon with its towering palm trees and rocky walls that surrounded the turquoise water that shone with sunlight. Movement in the water revealed why they were at the lagoon. Several bottlenose dolphins swam in the water occasionally peeking out at their guests.

Suddenly, a dark-skinned man dressed in a black and yellow wetsuit moved to address the crowd.

"Welcome to the Dolphin Discovery Extravaganza! My name is Declan Teel. I will be your guide today on your ultimate dolphin experience. Before we get started, you will need to go into our dressing rooms. There are wetsuits for you to change into. Then we will go over the rules to make your experience memorable."

Aiden turned to look at Lyric. He frowned as the woman had already started heading toward the women's dressing room. The man thought that she would at least say something to him. He was tempted to not participate. However, Aiden had never swam with dolphins before. *I might as well enjoy myself.*

Lyric Sinclair stood in the shallow water of the lagoon. She watched the graceful dolphins that were swimming nearby keeping an eye on their visitors. The woman's heart raced with excitement as their guide Declan Teel finished reciting the rules.

"You may begin your experience whenever you are ready."

Lyric took a deep breath before walking into the deeper water. She began to wade in the lagoon marveling at the beauty of the sun shining on the turquoise water. The woman suppressed a squeal as a dolphin came up to her. She reached out a hand tenderly touching the rubbery wet nose remembering that Declan had called it a beak.

"You are so beautiful."

The dolphin squeaked in reply as it moved its head under her hand.

"They're pretty amazing, aren't they?"

Lyric snapped her eyes over to Aiden who was treading water next to her. She smiled warmly at him pleased that he was having a good time too.

"Yes. They are."

"Do you want to ride on one?"

Lyric recalled how Declan had instructed them on the proper way to ride a dolphin. She knew that they only needed to hold onto the dorsal fin on the back of the creature allowing it to do the rest.

"Yes. I'll try it."

The woman rubbed the dolphin's head before moving her hand to its dorsal fin. She held on hoping that the creature would take her for a ride. Lyric giggled as the dolphin bolted into movement swimming around the lagoon with its passenger holding on. She glanced over to Aiden thrilled to see that his dolphin was also taking him for a swim. The delighted expression on the man's face pleased her. *I love when he is happy.*

Suddenly, Lyric's head ached deeply in pain. She gasped in surprise releasing her grip on the dolphin's dorsal fin. The woman sank under the water before forcing herself to resurface. She began to tread water relieved that the pain had faded.

"Lyric, are you okay?"

Lyric smiled weakly at Aiden who had swam to her side with a concerned expression on his face.

"I'm fine. I just got distracted."

"Are you sure?"

The woman liked that the man cared about her enough to question her. She tried to tell herself that it was just part of his job, but then she saw the love in his eyes. *It's more than his job.*

"Yes. I'm sure. Thanks."

Aiden tenderly swiped wet hair that was in her face moving it behind her ear.

"Of course."

Lyric blushed though she was glad about the attention. She held her breath as the man leaned forward. *He's going to kiss me!*

The woman's heart swooned at the idea. She stayed completely still as Aiden moved closer.

Suddenly, a dolphin moved in between the couple causing Lyric to back up with a squeal. She laughed at the fear that she had felt when the creature came up quickly. The woman beamed at Aiden who was also laughing.

The two adults returned to their dolphin experience. Lyric licked her lips wishing that the kiss had been completed. Yet, in her heart she wasn't sure that she could handle it. *Get a grip. You don't want to break his heart.*

Aiden Wilder chuckled at the playful dolphin that had interrupted the romantic moment. He was glad that the animal had chosen that moment to resurface between them. The man knew that the magical setting was the only reason that Lyric had allowed him to come so close. *She would have stopped me before the kiss.*

Aiden swam over to another dolphin trying to distract himself from the rejection that he kept facing when spending time with the woman. *Why do I love her? She is haughty and spoiled. She is a complete snob.*

The man moved his gaze back to Lyric who was petting her dolphin with a bright smile on her face. He shook his head. *No. She isn't. Her true self is different than what she showed those first few days when I met her. There is more to Lyric than her money.*

Aiden averted his eyes away from the woman remembering how Desmond had lectured him about being careful so that he didn't get hurt. *Too late for that, Des.*

Harper Raines glared at the television while clutching her phone in her hand. Her heart wrenched in a mixture of fury and sorrow at the lack of response from Lyric. She had hoped that her friend would come to her senses and call her. Yet, it had been several days and there was still no contact.

Harper's bad mood deepened as she thought about how useless Desmond Wilder's help had been. She knew that it wasn't the man's fault since he had as much control over his brother as she had over her friend, but the woman was still annoyed.

Suddenly, Harper's phone vibrated in her hand. Slowly, she raised it into view so that she could see who was calling. The woman sat up quickly as she recognized the caller. She tapped the accept button putting the phone up to her ear.

"Lyric, it's about time."

"Hi, Harper."

Harper frowned, "Hi, Harper? I have been calling and leaving you frantic messages for days and that's all you have to say to me?"

Silence followed the harsh retort. The woman bit her lip trying to stop even harsher words from escaping her.

"I'm sorry, Harper. I know that you have been worried about me."

"Yes, I have. You need to come home, Lyric. Right now."

Lyric sighed, "I can't."

Harper stood up with a huff.

"Yes, you can. You just tell that driver to turn the car around and take you home."

"Harper, I'm not finished with my list yet."

The frustrated woman began pacing back and forth across her living room. She took several deep breaths trying to cool her anger which was rising at her friend's stubbornness.

"Lyric, Dr. Nash said that it was crucial to your health that you call him. This is serious. You can't keep checking things off your bucket list while there is time for possible surgery or treatment. The longer you wait, the more likely that your health will suffer. Come home."

Another moment of silence aggravated the woman. She stopped walking and closed her eyes forcing the tears that were threatening to fall to stay trapped. Harper held her breath trying to remain patient.

"I'll call Dr. Nash, Harper."

Dread filled the woman.

"And?"

"And I will let you know what he says, but I am not coming home until I have finished my bucket list."

Harper gritted her teeth angrily. She opened her mouth to protest.

"I'm sorry, Harper, but that is the best that I can do. Bye."

"Lyric…"

As the call ended, the distraught woman sank back down on her couch. She set the cell phone beside her before allowing the tears to fall. Her sobs echoed through the apartment. *Lord, please help me deal with this.*

Lyric Sinclair sat staring at her cell phone. She knew that Harper was angry and scared at her decision, but she was certain that it was the only one for her. The exhausted woman sighed before dialing Dr. Nash's phone number. She waited as it rang bracing herself for the news that the man had for her.

"Hello?"

"Dr. Nash, this is Lyric Sinclair."

The doctor's voice blurted out excitedly, "Miss Sinclair, thank goodness. I have been trying to get ahold of you. I have your MRI results and I need to see you immediately."

Lyric cleared her throat nervously.

"I'm out of town, Dr. Nash. Just tell me over the phone."

Silence came. The woman waited as patiently as she could.

"You shouldn't be traveling, Miss Sinclair. That's dangerous with a brain tumor."

Lyric released the breath that she had been holding.

"So, it is definitely a brain tumor?"

"Yes, Miss Sinclair. The MRI shows that it is definitely a brain tumor. It is a bigger mass than we originally thought. The next step is to do a biopsy, so we can determine if it is benign or malignant."

The devastated woman let silent tears stream down her face.

"Miss Sinclair, you need to get back here as quickly as you can. If it is malignant, then it will be aggressive meaning that surgery and treatment must be started immediately if there is any chance of survival."

Lyric took a deep breath hoping that she would sound strong on the phone.

"I won't be able to return yet, Dr. Nash."

"Miss Sinclair, please…"

"I'm sorry, Dr. Nash, but I have to finish what I started. I will visit you when I get back in town. Thank you for the update. You have my permission to share this information with my sister Harper. Good night."

Lyric ended the call before the doctor could continue his pleading. She lowered her head closing her eyes believing that she was making the right decision. The sick woman placed her face in her hands as she wept at the horrible news. *It doesn't matter. I must finish my list while I am strong enough to do it.*

Aiden Wilder sighed in satisfaction as he unplugged his fully charged cell phone from the new charger that he had picked up. He turned the phone on marveling at the number of missed calls and messages that he had received from his brother. The man dialed Desmond wondering what could be so urgent.

"Aiden, why in the blazes haven't you called me?"

Aiden smiled at the anger and concern in his twin brother's voice.

"Take it easy, Des. My phone was dead, and I forgot my charger in Pennsylvania."

Silence came on the other end of the line.

"Desmond?"

"You're in Pennsylvania?"

Aiden smirked, "No. I'm in Florida."

Another bout of silence came. The man waited for his twin to respond to the news.

"Florida? Why? What is going on, Aiden?"

"Don't freak out, bro. Lyric has a list of places that she wants to go. Apparently, they are in different states."

Desmond grumbled, "But why? What is going on? Is she feeling okay?"

Aiden frowned, "Why do you ask that? Of course, she is feeling okay."

"Look, Aid. I don't know what is going on, but her friend Harper came by work and said that she needed me to call you so that you would have Lyric call her. She said it was something about her health."

The man stared at the wall trying to figure out what his brother was saying.

"Okay, Des. I'll tell Lyric to call Harper. Anything else?"

"Just try to get her to come back to New York. I don't care what she is paying, there is something fishy about this whole road trip."

Aiden smiled at the use of "fishy" remembering the fun that the duo had had at the dolphin lagoon.

"Don't worry, Des. I'll see what I can do." *She's so strong-willed though. It probably won't work.*

CHAPTER 12

HOVERING HEIGHTS

Lyric closed her hotel room door with a slam. She marched down the hallway eager to start the day. The woman saw Aiden leaning on the hunter green SUV waiting for her. She smiled weakly at the man as he opened her car door for her.

Lyric climbed into her passenger seat with mumbled thanks. Her mind raced with the burden of what Dr. Nash had told her the night before. She wished that she could talk to someone about the rollercoaster of emotions that were swarming through her. However, the woman didn't want to talk to Harper who would demand that she end the bucket list adventures to come back home. She wanted to tell Aiden, but then she was afraid that he would be kind to her out of pity. *I couldn't stand that.*

"I talked to my brother last night. He said that Harper wanted you to call her."

Lyric nodded, "I called her last night."

The man glanced over at her before returning his attention to the road.

"Is everything okay?"

"Yes. She's annoyed that I left without telling her. I think that she wanted to go with us. Anyway, I calmed her down and everything is fine."

Aiden cleared his throat.

"And your health?"

Lyric's eyes widened in surprise at the question. She glared at the driver who was still staring ahead.

"What do you mean?"

Aiden shrugged, "Desmond said that Harper was concerned about your health. That's why she wanted his help contacting us."

The furious woman's anger faded at the explanation. She took a deep breath to calm herself further.

"I'm fine. Harper is just worried because I collapsed at the fashion show."

The man nodded, "What did the doctor say?"

Lyric wanted to snap at Aiden about minding his own business. However, she was touched by his concern. *He cares about me.*

The woman shook her head. She needed to believe that the man didn't love her. *He just doesn't want the responsibility of taking care of me.*

"He said that it was stress and working too hard. That's why I thought that this vacation was in order." *Liar.*

Lyric stared out the car window wishing that she could tell Aiden the truth. However, she knew that it wasn't possible. *He'll try to get me to go home too. I need to finish this.*

Aiden Wilder stared up at the massive hot air balloon that was stationed on the beach. He was surprised at the next part of Lyric's vacation. The man suspected that there was something that the woman wasn't telling him. However, he decided to pretend like he believed her story. *She'll tell me if she wants to.*

"Isn't it beautiful?"

Aiden cringed at the heights that he knew the hot air balloon would take them.

"Do we have to do something that involves death-defying heights?"

Lyric giggled, "Oh, come on. It's better than The Widow-Maker, isn't it?"

The man shrugged, "I guess. At least, the balloon won't go upside down."

"Not unless something bad happens."

Aiden shot a disapproving glare at the woman who shook with laughter.

"Very funny. Let's get this over with."

The two adults walked toward the yellow and blue striped hot air balloon. Aiden noticed a tall woman dressed in a black tank top and white pants sitting on a chair beside the balloon. He smirked at the choppy blue hair of the woman.

Lyric stepped forward addressing the woman.

"Are you Miss Azul?"

The blue haired woman snapped her attention to the duo before snorting.

"It's Carissa. No one calls me Miss Azul. Are you Lyric and Aiden?"

The other woman nodded, "Yes. We are ready for our hot air balloon adventure."

Carissa Azul stood up stretching her arms above her head.

"Great! Let's go."

Harper Raines tapped her foot nervously as she waited in Dr. Nash's office. She had received a call that Lyric had given the doctor permission to share her medical information with her "sister". The woman dreaded the news that Lyric couldn't even share with her herself. *It must be bad.*

The door opened with a swish as Dr. Nash came into the office. Harper held her breath trying to stay calm.

"Ms. Raines, thank you for coming in."

The woman nodded, "Of course. Lyric was supposed to call me with an update, but I guess she decided that you should tell me what is going on."

Dr. Nash sat down in his chair before folding his hands on the desk. He leaned forward.

"Forgive me for saying so, Ms. Raines, but your sister is a very stubborn woman."

Harper snorted, "Don't I know it. What happened?"

"I told her that the mass on the MRI was bigger than we originally thought. I informed her that it was important for her to return to the hospital to do a biopsy, so we can determine if the tumor is benign or malignant. However, she refused to cut her vacation short and said that she would come by when she was finished."

The concerned woman was shocked by the news of a bigger brain tumor. She took several deep breaths as her mind raced with their options. Frustration filled her at the information of Lyric refusing to come home to deal with her illness.

"I'm sorry, Dr. Nash, but there is nothing I can do to force Lyric to come back. She has always done what she wanted to do. I will try to convince her to shorten her trip, but I don't know if it will work."

The doctor nodded, "Thank you, Ms. Raines. Please let me know when she returns. I will be ready to do the biopsy. Then we can see if surgery and treatment are needed."

Harper agreed with the man as she stood up to leave. *No wonder Lyric didn't call me back.*

Lyric Sinclair's heart soared in excitement as Carissa's hot air balloon floated above the beach. She stared down at the people enjoying their vacations. Children pointed happily at the balloon waving at the passengers.

Lyric waved back. She glanced over at Aiden to see if he was doing the same. The woman suppressed a giggle at the anxious man who was staring inside the basket. She touched his arm causing Aiden to jump startled.

"You're missing it, Aiden."

The man shook his head.

"I'm fine."

A chuckle drew both adults' attention to Carissa.

"What's the matter, man? You aren't afraid of heights, are you? A big tough guy like you?"

Lyric smirked at Aiden who was trying to keep a scowl off his face. She shrugged at him when he turned to see if she would help him out of the embarrassing situation.

The man moved closer to the side of the basket. He leaned slightly over to look at the depths below. Lyric could tell by his tight jaw and tense body that he was forcing himself to stay frozen looking at the beach.

"Maybe you will like riding over the ocean better."

Carissa's suggestion was followed by the balloon changing directions. Aiden's hands clutched the wicker basket tightly. With a sigh, Lyric placed a hand onto the man's arm. She smiled warmly at the surprised look that he shot her.

"Don't worry, Aiden. I will protect you."

Lyric giggled as the man rolled his eyes. She was pleased to see that he didn't seem as tense. The woman moved her hand down his arm toward the basket. When she reached his hand, Aiden released the basket taking her hand into his own.

Lyric stared out at the ocean with its peaceful waves and colorful boats. Her heart wrenched as she watched the swimmers. She remembered how her father had always taken her and Harper to the city pool where they would swim for hours. The woman blinked away the tears that were threatening to fall.

"What's wrong, Lyric?"

Lyric smiled weakly, "I was thinking about my dad. He was a sweet man and a loving father. Every summer he would take a couple of weeks off work, so we could spend time at the pool. Harper and I would pretend that we were mermaids."

The woman pictured herself as a child splashing around in the water with her best friend. *Good times.*

"One day, Harper jumped off the high dive. She wanted me to do it, but I was scared. I climbed up to the diving board, but then I started to chicken out. Dad yelled for me to jump and said that he would catch me. I knew that I could trust him. I jumped, and he saved me. Then he told me something that I just recently thought about. It was actually what made me take this trip."

Lyric closed her eyes cherishing the warm breeze that caressed her face.

"What did he say?"

The woman recited, "You'll never live if you don't take a leap of faith."

Silence followed the statement. Lyric opened her eyes moving them to regard Aiden. The man was staring out at the ocean.

"Sounds like good advice. Your father would have been good on this trip."

Sorrow filled the woman. She knew that her father would have loved to have traveled through her bucket list with her though he would probably have dragged her back to Dr. Nash by now.

"He died from cancer."

Aiden's hand released her own causing the woman to feel abandoned. However, in the next moment, his arm was around her shoulder. Lyric leaned against him cherishing the comfort that seemed to come.

"I'm sorry, Lyric. My folks are gone too. They were both killed in a car accident a couple of years ago."

The sympathetic woman sighed, "I'm sorry too, Aiden. I guess we both know what it feels like to lose someone close to us."

Standing in silence, the adults continued their hot air balloon ride. *I'm glad that Aiden is here with me. Dad would like him.*

"Time's up. I'm heading back to shore."

Carissa's voice interrupted the pleasant moment. Lyric stood up straighter as Aiden took his arm off her shoulder. *It's over too soon.*

Aiden Wilder's heart raced as he escorted Lyric to her hotel room. He had enjoyed the time that he had spent with the woman in the hot air balloon. The man treasured how Lyric had held his hand when he was nervous about the heights. He also was grateful that she thought enough of him to share her feelings with him. *Things have changed.*

Aiden waited as Lyric pulled out her key card sliding it into the lock. With a click, the door opened.

"Thanks for walking me to my room, Aiden."

"Anytime. Sleep well. I'm sure you have another busy day planned for tomorrow."

The woman smiled with a nod, "Yes, I do. Good night."

As Lyric closed her door, Aiden turned toward his own door. He was exhausted, but it was a good exhaustion. *Such a special day. I wish it didn't have to end.*

CHAPTER 13

DROWNING SORROWS

Aiden Wilder drove down the wooded path enjoying the pine-scented breeze that splashed on his face through the open window. He was tired by the long drive, but it was his kind of landscape. The man had always loved the outdoors Yet, the forest trips camping as a kid were the most memorable. *We always had so much fun.*

"There's our cabin."

Aiden nodded with a smile as he turned down a side path. His good mood increased as he saw the wooden log cabin that was waiting for its guests. It was a two-story house with a lengthy front porch. *Perfect.*

"It's beautiful."

The man nodded in agreement with the woman. He had to admit that she had booked a fancy cabin in the woods. Aiden turned the SUV off before glancing over at Lyric. A peaceful smile was stationed on her face. He smiled thinking about the pleasant trip that the two adults had taken from Florida to Tennessee. They had found many things to talk about as well as songs to sing on the radio. *This trip keeps getting better and better.*

"They must be our hosts."

Aiden followed Lyric's finger as she pointed out her passenger window. His eyes widened at a couple walking around the side of the cabin toward the car.

The rugged man, towering over six feet tall, was dressed in a variety of animal skins. On his head, he had a cap that was made from a furry beast that Aiden wasn't sure of its origin. The wilderness man's gray beard covered most of his face leaving only beady eyes peering out. *This is not a man to mess with.*

Aiden stared at the woman who stood beside the man. She was short and stocky with long gray hair tied in a single braid. Her clothes were also made from animal skins though hers were smooth instead of furry. Aiden marveled over her lovely bronze skin and almond-shaped eyes.

"Let's go."

The man climbed out of the SUV as Lyric hopped out of her own side. He walked closely by her as they approached the rustic couple. Aiden swallowed hard as he stood facing the other man. *I feel like David standing in front of Goliath.*

"Hello. I'm Lyric and this is Aiden. Are you the Wests?"

The giant man stared down that the two young adults with a scowl. However, his wife stepped forward with a smile.

"Yes. Welcome. My name is Chenoa. My husband is Bartholomew, but we all call him Bear." *Seems to fit him.*

Aiden glanced at Lyric who was staring up at Bear West. He inched closer to her protectively. The man didn't like the silence of their male host. *He doesn't seem to like having us here.*

"Bear has some work to do in the woods, but I will show you your cabin. You will want to rest tonight so that you will be ready for the adventures tomorrow."

Lyric nodded, "Yes, Chenoa. We have been driving all day. Rest sounds great."

Chenoa put a tender arm around the redheaded woman as she led her toward the cabin. Aiden returned his gaze to Bear who was still standing frozen in place scowling at him.

Suddenly, the gigantic man stomped toward the SUV.

"You have bags?"

Aiden gawked at Bear before following him to the vehicle. He clicked the button on the keys to unlock the trunk. The military man opened the hatch watching the host carefully.

"I can handle these by myself, Mr. West. Thank you."

The large man glared deeply at him. Aiden gulped expecting a fight. He inwardly winced remembering the fight against Lynx days ago.

"Bear."

"What?"

"Not Mr. West. Bear."

Without waiting for a response, the giant man stomped off toward the tree line. Aiden released the breath that he didn't realize he was holding.

"Aiden?"

The man snapped his attention toward the cabin. Lyric was standing on the porch with Chenoa. The two women were waiting for him to join them.

"Coming."

Aiden grabbed their luggage before hurrying toward the beautiful cabin that he hoped they would stay in for a few days. *I could use something more relaxing like the forest.*

Lyric Sinclair's eyes widened in awe as she saw the massive inside of the cabin. The beauty of the stone fireplace with a crackling fire waiting amazed her. She scanned the living room area which had brown leather furniture and an ornate coffee table. On the far side of the room was a kitchen complete with a stone island and all the appliances that visitors would need. *So beautiful.*

"It's not like any cabin I have ever been in."

Lyric smiled at Aiden's statement.

"Me neither."

Movement drew the woman's attention to Chenoa who was gesturing toward the wooden stairs which had a lovely carved bannister.

"There are two bedrooms upstairs."

Lyric frowned, "Chenoa, Aiden and I are not married so we will need separate rooms."

The older woman smiled brightly in understanding, "Yes. The rooms are for you two. Bear and I sleep in the forest. We will return at dawn to begin your first requested adventure."

"Thank you. That will be fine."

Chenoa waved goodbye to the two guests before taking her leave. As the door closed, Lyric sighed turning to look at Aiden. The man was staring at the intricate designs that were carved on the walls.

"This place is amazing."

Lyric smiled warmly, "Yes. It is."

The duo stared at each other silently. After a moment, the young woman cleared her throat and looked away. She reached for her suitcase which held all her essentials.

"I think I will go check out my room and maybe unpack a bit."

Aiden surrendered the bag with a nod.

"Good idea."

Lyric climbed the stairs marveling at the height of the second floor. She stopped at the top feeling dizzy and disoriented. Her heart pounded as she tried to breathe. *I'm just tired.*

"Are you okay?"

The woman looked over the railing at Aiden who was standing in the kitchen. She blinked away the blurriness.

"Yes. Just admiring the handiwork."

The man nodded as Lyric turned to continue to her bedroom. She opened the first door gasping at the place where she would spend the night. The spacious room was true to the rustic atmosphere. There was a twin bed with a wooden frame. A blue and white quilt covered it giving Lyric a feeling of comfort. In the corner, she saw a wooden dresser with multiple drawers. The woman set her bag on the wooden floor with a sigh. *It feels like home.*

Lyric knew that the idea was silly because she had never lived in a cabin or even been in a forest before. She was a city girl from birth. However, the peacefulness of the bedroom made her feel safe. *Especially with Aiden here with me.*

The woman shook the thought away as she began to unpack a few of her items. She wanted to forget her feelings for the handsome man who had been so kind to her. However, it seemed like her fondness of him continued to pop up in her mind. *I must stay unattached. It's not right to love him when I may not be here long.*

Harper Raines took a deep breath before touching her manicured finger to the doorbell. She jumped slightly at the loud ring that filled the house. The woman's heart thumped nervously as she waited for an answer. *Lord, I hope I'm doing the right thing.*

Suddenly, the door swung open. Harper held her breath as an older woman came into view. Tears filled the younger lady's eyes at the sight of her hunched back and withered face. She blinked trying to calm herself, but the pain and sorrow that she felt about Lyric overwhelmed her.

"Hi, Grammy."

The rotund woman pushed her bifocal glasses up her nose squinting at Harper. Her chocolate brown face transformed from confusion to excitement. She stepped out on the porch opening her arms with a toothless grin.

"Welcome home, Baby."

Grammy Raines wrapped her fleshy arms around her granddaughter tightly. She rocked back and forth while planting a kiss on the side of Harper's head. The young woman wanted to pretend that she was embarrassed by being treated like a child. However, the truth was that she was pleased that her grandmother didn't close the door in her face. *It has been so long. I have treated her like a stranger. No. Worse. I have treated her like a ghost.*

"Come inside, Baby. We've got some catching up to do."

Harper frowned, "Okay, Grammy. I could really use your advice."

The older woman raised an eyebrow in surprise before gesturing toward the house. She led the way bringing her granddaughter back into the life that had been full of disappointment and struggles. Harper winced at the living room that appeared to be frozen in time. The tan couch with a red and brown quilt draped over the back of it waited in front of the old box television. At the feet of the couch sat the coffee table with a large black Bible resting on top of it. *Nothing has changed.*

"Would you like something to drink?"

Harper shook her head as she recalled her mother lying on the couch passed out with a beer bottle in her hand. She had seen it too many times to count.

"Let's sit down, Harp."

The young woman smiled weakly at the nickname that her grandmother had always used when talking to her. She remembered how the older woman had explained that since she sang with the same beauty as a harp, then her name should be Harp.

"Now, what brings you here? It has been a long time since you last visited. I believe it was before Mr. Sinclair passed away. You came because he wanted me to have some pictures of you."

Harper remembered the dark time. She nodded without a word. The young woman hated that she had lost the man she considered her father. *He was the only one who wanted me.*

"You remember Lyric?"

Grammy Raines beamed, "Sure, I do. That precious child was like a sister to you."

The other woman nodded, "She still is. We have stayed close even after Mr. Sinclair died."

"That's good. You two were always like peanut butter and jelly. You belong together. How is Lyric?"

Harper frowned, "She has a brain tumor."

Suddenly, the distraught woman found herself spilling out the whole story to her grandmother who listened silently with sorrowful eyes. Her heart ached as she sought comfort and understanding in a time where there wasn't any to be found. *I need this all to make sense.*

Odessa "Birdie" Raines listened to her granddaughter's story feeling her heart wrench at the struggles that she was facing. She had always been thankful that the Lord gave Connor and Lyric Sinclair to take the place of the family that had not loved Harper. The older woman had spent many years working hard to pay the bills while her daughter drank herself to death. *If only Harper's mama could have seen how much she needed her.*

Birdie shook the past away as she focused on the present. She could tell that Harper was in pain over her friend's decision. The woman found it disturbing as well. However, she understood why Lyric was trying to fulfill all her dreams before she ran out of time. *If only we could all do that.*

"I'm so sorry, Harp. I know that you are heartbroken over Lyric's decision. Just remember that God is in control."

Harper snorted averting her gaze to the Bible on the coffee table. Birdie bristled at her unbelief. However, she knew that a sermon would only drive the girl farther away from the truth.

"I actually prayed the other night, Grammy. Do you know the result? Lyric has a brain tumor."

The older woman folded her hands with a sigh. She waited for Harper to let out all her feelings. Birdie didn't have to wait long.

"Why is He doing this? Why is God taking away the only family that I have?"

The grandmother swallowed hard at how her grandchild had forgotten that she still had her. *Harp has always blamed me for her mother's death, but I couldn't stop her drinking.*

"It was bad enough that He gave me a mother who didn't want me. It was even cruel for him to give me Mr. Sinclair and then take him away. But why Lyric? She doesn't deserve this. I don't deserve this!"

Birdie held her breath as Harper's voice became desperate. Tears streamed down her granddaughter's face. The older woman inched closer on the couch. She debated with herself about hugging the girl to give her comfort. The thought of Harper rejecting her kept her motionless. *What do I do? What do I say to a broken heart?*

"I lift up my eyes to the mountains. Where does my help come from? My help comes from the Lord, the Maker of heaven and earth."

Birdie was surprised by the shakiness in her voice as she recited the verses from Psalms that had always brought her peace.

"He will not let your foot slip. He who watches over you will not slumber."

Suddenly, the older woman was surprised as Harper leaned against her. She wrapped her arms around the girl drawing her closer. Birdie placed her cheek on the top of her grandchild's head.

"Indeed, He who watches over Israel will neither slumber nor sleep. The Lord watches over you. The Lord is your shade at your right hand. The sun will not harm you by day, nor the moon by night."

Slight shaking from her grieving granddaughter broke her heart. Birdie held her closer hoping that at least a little comfort was reaching Harper. She rocked gently back and forth on the couch.

"The Lord will keep you from all harm. He will watch over your life."

Birdie paused before whispering, "And Lyric's life."

A slight nod came from Harper proving that the truth was getting through the thick wall that the girl had always kept surrounding her heart.

"The Lord will watch over your coming and going both now and forevermore." *Thank You, Lord.*

Lyric Sinclair held the wooden bannister as she walked back to the downstairs of the cabin. She had thought about resting for the night. However, her growling stomach demanded that she eat something before going to bed. *Hope there is something simple to make. I'm too tired to cook.*

Suddenly, Lyric froze on one of the lower steps. Her eyes widened at the sight of Aiden standing in front of the oven door checking something hidden inside. Steam rose into the air bringing a delicious aroma to the woman.

"What are you making?"

The man snapped his eyes over at her.

"Dinner."

Lyric rolled her eyes.

"I figured, but what are you making for dinner?"

Aiden smiled wickedly, "You will just have to be patient and wait. Now, go enjoy the fireplace while I finish."

The woman opened her mouth to protest. However, she closed it as the cook raised a wooden spoon in the air with a serious expression on his face.

"Go or I won't share."

Lyric threw her hands up in mock-surrender as she finished coming down the stairs before walking over to a brown leather armchair. She plopped down onto the soft chair. The woman stared at the crackling fire before she pulled out her cell phone.

Lyric tapped on her bucket list crossing off their adventures in Florida. She smiled at the next item on the list. The woman couldn't wait though she was slightly nervous. *This could be dangerous.*

"Ready to eat?"

Lyric glanced up from her cell phone. She smiled warmly at Aiden who was holding two white plates in his hands. The woman nodded before following the man over to the island which served as a table.

Lyric sat on one of the stools. Aiden placed a hot plate in front of her. Her eyes widened impressed by the elegant dinner that the man had cooked.

"Tonight, our chef has prepared roasted salmon, golden potatoes, and buttered green beans."

"Wow! I'm impressed. Where did you learn to cook like this?"

Aiden looked around secretly before lowering his voice.

"I cannot divulge my secrets. Iced tea?"

Lyric nodded, "Sure. Fine. Keep your secrets and I will keep my feedback to myself."

The man chuckled as he poured two glasses of iced tea from a clear pitcher. He placed it at the top of Lyric's plate. Aiden sat down on his stool before bowing his head. His eyes closed surprising the woman.

"Amen."

Lyric picked up her fork awkwardly. She felt uncomfortable as she remembered how her father used to pray before every meal. The woman had never really prayed on her own. She didn't see any reason. *Why should I pray to Someone who took my father away? And now He has given me a brain tumor.*

Lyric took a bite of salmon swooning at the savory yet sweet taste that exploded in her mouth.

"What do you think?"

The woman grinned evilly, "I cannot divulge my secrets."

Aiden rolled his eyes causing Lyric to laugh.

"Fine. Keep your secrets. You're good at it. Each day I have no idea what we are doing."

Lyric nodded, "True. Would you like to know what we are doing tomorrow?"

The man sighed, "Yes. What is our next adventure?"

Lyric continued to eat in silence. She tried not to laugh at the exasperated expression on Aiden's face.

"You're not going to tell me, are you?"

"Not a chance."

Aiden Wilder stared at the rushing river that swept past him. His heart pounded as he glanced over at Lyric who was strapping on her lifejacket.

"You're kidding, right?"

The woman giggled, "At least river rafting has nothing to do with heights."

"True, but drowning is about as scary."

A grunt caused Aiden to turn his attention to their guides. Bear West was dragging the rubber raft toward the river.

"No drown."

His wife came to their side with a nod.

"Bear is right. It is safe."

Aiden snorted as he returned his gaze to the river. *Oh, sure. Completely safe.*

"Come on, Aiden. Let's do it."

Lyric's excitement brought a smile to the concerned man's face.

"Okay. Let's get this one marked off your list."

As Bear tied the raft to a tree and placed it on the water, the four adults took turns climbing into the boat. Each person had an oar to paddle with as they travelled. Aiden tried to stay brave, but fear was rising by the second.

Suddenly, Bear cut the rope releasing the raft to the mercy of the river. The group was tossed about as they began to move downstream.

"Paddle!"

Aiden obeyed by placing his honey-colored oar into the fast-paced water. He glanced over at Lyric who was laughing as she slammed her own oar into the river. The joy on her face calmed the man's fears. He wanted the expression on her face to never fade. *She is so beautiful.*

"Hold on!"

A huge wave followed Chenoa's shout. Aiden gasped as cold water slammed into his body. He grabbed a rope rung that was on his side of the raft. The group bounced up and down several times before the water decreased in ferocity. *Thank You, Lord!*

The relieved man turned to check on Lyric. His eyes bulged in shock as his heart wrenched violently.

"Lyric!"

Lyric Sinclair screamed in panic as the wave knocked her out of the raft. Her oar fell from her fingers. The woman went under the cold rushing water which seemed to be hungry for her life. She kicked her legs and flailed her arms desperate to return to the surface. However, the force and strength of the water was too much for her.

Lyric held her breath as long as she could. Her mind raced with what she could do. She felt weak as she recalled how her father had helped her at the swimming pool when she was a girl. *Trust me, Lyric.*

Her heart ached as she closed her eyes feeling the life drain from her body. She thought about her father's faith in God. As she prayed, the woman hoped that she would not be disappointed by the results. *I trust You, Lord. Save me!*

Aiden Wilder fumbled with the buckle on the straps of his lifejacket. His mind raced desperately at the idea of losing Lyric. The man refused to let the woman that he loved die even if she didn't feel the same way about him.

"No. You stay."

Bear West's deep voice growled at the man. Aiden opened his mouth to protest. However, the huge wilderness man had already hopped into the fast water.

Aiden's eyes widened as the deep river came only up to the tall man's shoulders.

"We are in shallow waters now. Paddle toward the shore. Bear will get the girl."

The man wanted to argue. However, he knew that it was useless. Aiden obeyed Chenoa helping her to paddle toward the nearby shore. He saw a side channel that led to calm waters. The duo paddled hard until the rubber raft went the way that they wanted.

In the next moment, the raft slowed and stopped. Chenoa climbed out of the boat into the calm water.

"We must put the raft on the shore. Please help me."

Aiden nodded before climbing into the water. He helped the woman dragged the raft out of the river. Once it was safely on the grass, the man turned toward the roaring water that rushed nearby. His eyes bulged in horror as he saw Bear stomping down the shoreline with Lyric in his arms. *She looks dead.*

"No life."

Bear set the drowned woman on the ground before stepping back toward his wife. Feeling like he was moving in slow motion, Aiden came to Lyric's side. He checked for a pulse finding none. The man remembered his training as a swimming pool lifeguard. He didn't know if it would work or if there was still time. However, Aiden knew that he had to try. *Please don't take her from me, Lord.*

The desperate man tilted Lyric's head back slightly lifting her chin. He opened her mouth listening for any sounds of breathing. His heart wrenched as no breaths came. Aiden pinched her nose shut before placing his mouth completely over hers. He blew into her mouth twice. The man leaned back placing his hands on top of each other on her chest. He pushed hard and fast praying that it wasn't too late.

The former lifeguard continued the compressions and rescues breaths for several minutes. Tears came to his eyes as he began to accept that he had lost her.

Suddenly, Lyric spat out water gasping. Her eyes flickered open as she took more breaths on her own. Aiden smiled weakly as he helped her to sit up.

Emerald green eyes surrounded by wet red hair stared back at him. Lyric smiled weakly at the man. She hugged him with whispered thanks. Aiden held her with relief flooding over him. *Thank You, Lord!*

CHAPTER 14

UNLIMITED LOVE

Lyric Sinclair shivered in the cool night air as she sat on a log. The group had decided that they should make camp to give the woman a chance to rest from her frightening ordeal. She had wanted to protest that she was fine. However, the look on Aiden's face told her that he would not let her go on without rest. *He's so stubborn.*

A light smile crossed Lyric's face at the thought. She winced as the chilly breeze knocked against her damp clothes. The woman stared at Bear who was crouching down on the ground making a campfire. *Hope he gets it going soon.*

Suddenly, a heavy object fell on Lyric's shoulders. She glanced down seeing a red and blue blanket with designs on it. The woman looked up to thank Chenoa but stopped in surprise as she saw Aiden adjusting the blanket around her. She smiled warmly at the man as he sat down beside her on the log.

"How are you feeling?"

Lyric wanted to shout out that she was fine and could take care of herself. However, she let the natural words fade at the concerned look in the man's eyes.

"I'm cold and tired, but thankful to be alive."

Aiden nodded, "I'm thankful you're alive too."

A clap captured the attention of the two young adults. Bear was celebrating the spark that was growing into a fire. He glanced over at them with a slight sparkle in his eye. The large man regained his composure quickly returning to his solemn demeanor.

"A fine fire, Bear."

The husband snorted at his wife as Chenoa knelt beside the fire with a bag full of supplies. The couple began working on fixing dinner for their guests.

"I was scared."

The quiet whisper brought Lyric's gaze back to Aiden. She was surprised by the man's lowered head as he stared at his hands. The woman reached one of her cold hands out of the blanket. She grabbed one of Aiden's hands holding it tenderly.

"Me too."

"I was scared."

Aiden Wilder felt like a big wimp as he confessed that he had been scared during Lyric's near-death experience. He hated being vulnerable and weak, but he couldn't keep his feelings inside any longer. Embarrassed, the man stared at his hands.

Suddenly, a cold gentle hand touched his own. Aiden allowed the woman to take his hand longing for her comfort that everything was okay now.

"Me too."

Aiden squeezed her hand hoping that she would understand that he was there for her. He placed his other hand on top to help Lyric's hand to find warmth. The man's heart swooned in love for the woman. He wondered if she had changed her mind about him. However, Aiden refused to ask in case she rejected him again. *I'm still poor. I'm still beneath her. She deserves better. I'll just enjoy this moment.*

Lyric Sinclair finished eating the simple meal that Chenoa and Bear had cooked for them. She was glad that the guides had been with them when she had almost drowned. The woman was thankful for Bear's help. She was also grateful that Aiden knew CPR. *I would have died if it wasn't for them.*

Lyric's mind went to her desperate prayer that she had pleaded as the water kept her captive underneath. A weak smile came to her lips at the thought that God had answered her prayers. *You saved me. Thank You, Lord.*

"Seek the wonder of life and love, for it lasts but a short time."

Chenoa's soft voice drew Lyric's attention. The older woman was sitting on the ground beside Bear who was eating the last of his meal. Her almond eyes were focused on her husband though the words seemed to be for the young adults.

"Open your heart to the unknown, though it may bring fear or pain."

Tears sprang up in Lyric's green eyes at the words that seemed to fit her current situation. She wanted to love Aiden and spend time with the man, but she was afraid of leaving him in pain when she died.

"Believe that the Creator will guide you, for there are great rewards within mystery."

Lyric took a deep breath at the words. She was certain that her beliefs were different from the other woman. However, the advice struck her heart in a new way. She thought about how God had helped her in the river. The woman wondered if He would guide her in love.

"True."

Bear's single word was followed by the large man placing an arm around his wife. Chenoa smiled warmly as she leaned against her husband. Silence came to the campsite.

Lyric set her plate at her feet thinking about Chenoa's words. *They seem so different. Yet, it is obvious that Bear and Chenoa love each other. She probably had to take a big chance when getting to know him. He seems so scary.*

The young woman smiled weakly as she remembered what her father had told her at the pool when she was a child. *You'll never live unless you take a leap of faith.*

Lyric's heart twinged at the thought of her illness. She wanted to say that love wasn't possible since the tumor might take her life too soon. However, hope filled the woman as she stared at Bear and Chenoa. *I wonder if even a short time with someone you love is better than no time at all.*

Harper Raines groaned at the sweet nutty flavor of Grammy's pecan pie. She had to admit that she had missed her grandmother's cooking. The woman had always found comfort in her pies. *It was the only thing that was always constant in my childhood.*

"What are you going to do next, Harp?"

Harper shrugged, "I don't know. There's not much I can do. I will keep working on our fashion business and hope that Lyric gets homesick."

Grammy nodded, "Keep praying, Baby. God will be faithful to both of you."

The younger woman took another bite of pie wishing that she believed so strongly in God's faithfulness.

"Do you have a young man in your life yet?"

Harper snorted, "I've dated, but there hasn't been anyone serious yet."

Grammy sighed, "That's okay, Harp. You don't want to rush into something and end up with someone who doesn't really love you."

"Yeah. Like my real father."

Silence followed the statement. Harper waited for the lecture that she assumed was coming.

"True. That man did not love your mother. He got what he wanted and then moved on to get it somewhere else. Don't fall for a man like that, Baby. You deserve better."

The young woman was shocked by the bluntness of her grandmother. She had never heard her speak that way about anyone.

"I think Lyric is in love. Of course, she won't admit it. I think she doesn't want him to be hurt if she dies."

Grammy grunted, "Well, she can't stop that."

"What do you mean, Grammy?"

The older woman pushed her bifocal glasses up her nose before speaking.

"If that man, what's his name?"

"Aiden."

"Well, if Aiden loves Lyric, then he will be hurt if she dies whether they have become a couple or not. His greatest sorrow will be that he didn't get to show his love to her before she's gone. That will eat at him. Those two need to hold onto each other tightly and enjoy the time that God has given them."

Harper reflected on the words. She believed that her grandmother was right. *Lyric needs to show her love before it is too late.*

Suddenly, a strong feeling came over the granddaughter. Her eyes widened as Grammy's advice twisted to apply to her own life. *Oh, my.*

Odessa "Birdie" Raines stared down at her empty plate. She prayed that Lyric would come to her senses and live a life of love before she ran out of time.

"Grammy?"

Birdie glanced up at Harper who was staring at her with a serious expression on her face.

"Yes, Harp."

"I want to show my love before it is too late."

The older woman cocked her head in confusion.

"To who? I thought there wasn't anyone serious in your life."

Harper reached a hand across the kitchen table.

"To you, Grammy."

Tears came to Birdie's eyes. She had wanted a better relationship with her granddaughter for years. Now, there might be a chance of one. The woman bit her lip afraid that she was misunderstanding what Harper was saying.

"What do you mean, Harp?"

"I mean that I want to spend some time with you. Is that okay with you?"

Birdie blinked the tears away as joy filled her heart.

"Yes. That is more than okay with me." *Thank You, Lord my God. You overwhelm me with blessings.*

Harper Raines' heart filled with relief as her grandmother agreed that she wanted to spend time together. She could see the tears that were brimming in the older woman's eyes. The young woman averted her gaze to keep her own emotions in check. Her eyes fell on the yellow kitchen clock on the wall. *I didn't know that it was that late.*

"I need to go, Grammy."

The words hurt Harper's heart. She realized that she didn't want the conversation to end. The woman wished that she could spend more time with her grandmother.

Suddenly, a thought came to Harper's mind. She tried to shake it away knowing that it was impossible. However, the idea would not leave her.

"Grammy, would you want to live with me in my apartment?"

The older woman's eyes widened at the question. Harper braced herself for the rejection.

"You know, don't you?"

"Know what?"

Grammy frowned, "You know that they are evicting me from my house."

Harper gasped, "What? No. I didn't know that. When, Grammy?"

The older woman placed a hand on her heart with shock clear on her face.

"I have until the end of the week. I've been so worried. In fact, I was just praying before you came because I don't have anywhere to go."

Harper stared at her grandmother in awe.

"Oh, Harper Neveah Raines. God has sent you here for both our sakes." *Yes. I think that He has a plan for us yet.*

"Don't worry, Grammy. I'll help you pack. We can have a fresh start in my apartment." *This is amazing.*

Lyric Sinclair stared up at the great white moon as she tried to settle down for the night. She had to admit that the day had been difficult and scary. However, the woman knew that she had made it through another item on her bucket list. She smiled weakly at the image of waking up to Aiden leaning over her. Lyric knew that he had used CPR to save her life. Her heart swooned with love for the man who was willing to go to all these places without needing to know the full details. *I couldn't do this without him.*

Lyric closed her eyes feeling exhaustion cover her. Her head had been aching off and on since her near death experience. She wished that she could just forget about her illness. Yet, the uncertainty and fear continued to pop up even in the most wonderful moments.

The redheaded woman sighed deeply thinking about how she had been desperate enough to pray to God while she was drowning in the river. She wondered if He really was the reason that she was alive. Lyric rolled over on her side as tears began to fall. She pleaded with the Lord hoping that He could really hear her. *I don't know if You are there. Dad always said that You were. Even if You can hear me, I don't know if You care enough to answer my prayer, but I guess it doesn't hurt to ask. Please keep me healthy long enough to finish my bucket list. I don't want to die until all my dreams come true.*

Aiden Wilder groaned as a firm push came to his side waking him up. He opened his eyes glaring at Bear who had used his boot to awaken the man.

"Up now."

Aiden nodded with a yawn. He stretched his arms before sitting up. The grizzly guide stomped away.

"Good morning, Aiden. I have breakfast for you."

The hungry man stood up excitedly taking a plate of food from Chenoa with thanks. He scanned the camp searching for Lyric. A frown covered his face as he found her. The woman was wearing a red safety helmet on her head. She was buckling a harness on her upper body. Dread filled Aiden at the equipment.

"What are you doing?"

Lyric snapped her gaze to him before smiling.

"Good morning, Aiden. I was just getting ready for our next adventure."

Aiden recalled the fear that they had shared the day before when Lyric had almost drowned. He stared at the reckless woman feeling annoyed with her endless road trip.

"Haven't you had enough?"

The woman's green eyes widened in surprise before she cocked her head clearly confused.

"What do you mean?"

The man grumbled, "You almost died yesterday. How many more times must you put your life in danger? What do you have? A death wish?"

Lyric's confusion melted into rage as her face transformed into a scowl.

"That is not your business, Mr. Wilder. I am not paying you to lecture me. I'm the boss and I am going ziplining. You can stay here for all I care."

The woman turned away with a swish of her red hair. Aiden's face blushed hot with humiliation. He couldn't believe that after all that they had been through, they were now back to square one. The man cringed as he was brought back to reality. *She doesn't love me. I am just her employee.*

"Yes, ma'am. I'll be ready to go in a few minutes, Miss Sinclair." *Back to carpooling a snob.*

Lyric Sinclair winced at the solemn tone that Aiden used when he called her "Miss Sinclair". She was sorry for snapping at the man and treating him like only an employee. *He doesn't deserve that.*

Her heart ached to apologize to the man that she loved. However, the woman's stubbornness won out. *This is my bucket list. He can't be allowed to stop me from fulfilling my last dreams.*

A throat cleared behind Lyric.

"Are you ready to go?"

The determined woman spun on her heel to face the speaker.

"Yes, Chenoa. I'm ready."

The four adults gathered their packs before walking downriver. Lyric listened to the flowing river and chirping birds as they headed to where Bear West had set up the zipline wire.

Suddenly, the explorers came to a canyon that had to be over 500 feet wide. Lyric's eyes widened in fear as she glanced down at the opposite side which was several feet lower than the cliff she stood on now. She swallowed hard as she saw the thin gray cord that was attached to trees on both sides of the canyon. *That's a zipline? Couldn't they use a thicker rope?*

"Are you ready, Lyric?"

The frightened woman stood taller attempting to look brave. She nodded as she stepped forward.

"What do I do?"

Aiden Wilder bit his lip as he watched Bear attach his pulley strap to the zipline. The large guide approached the edge of the cliff before leaping forward. He swiftly fell down the gray rope toward the other side of the canyon.

Aiden averted his gaze feeling uneasy by the heights. He noticed that Lyric was watching Bear cross the canyon. The woman looked uncertain. The protective man wanted to try to persuade her from the dangerous stunt. However, he remembered how harsh her treatment had become the last time. *It's her business. I can't stop her anyway. She is going to do what she wants to do.*

"Let me help you strap on, Lyric."

Chenoa's voice made Aiden cringe. He stared at the two women as Bear's wife helped Lyric clip on to the zipline. The man held his breath as the redheaded woman stepped toward the canyon. *Please don't let her fall.*

As Lyric moved off the cliffside, Aiden stepped forward. He watched as she fell down the zipline toward the other side. The man clenched his fists tightly at the scream of the woman.

Suddenly, Bear West caught Lyric as she reached the end of the line. He began to unclip the woman who was smiling brightly. Aiden released the breath that he had been holding in relief. *She's safe.*

"Are you going to try it?"

The man snapped his gaze to Chenoa who was staring at him with a small smile. He swallowed hard at the idea.

"You don't have to, Aiden, but it is several miles around this canyon to catch up with Lyric."

Aiden glanced over at Lyric who was sitting in the grass on the other side with her eyes closed and a peaceful smile on her face.

"I don't like heights."

Chenoa chuckled drawing a scowl from the man. She held her hands up in protest.

"I'm sorry for laughing. It is just that you remind me of myself. I grew up well protected by my family. I never really faced any fear or danger until I met Bear. He showed me that the world is a beautiful place if I will face it with boldness. When I started to try new things, I truly began to live."

Aiden frowned as his mind recalled what Lyric had told him about her father.

The man mumbled, "You'll never live if you don't take a leap of faith."

"Ah, that is true too."

Aiden's heart raced at the thought of ziplining. However, he wanted to take a leap of faith. *Okay, Lord. I am trusting You with this crazy adventure. Please help me safely to the other side.*

"Okay, Chenoa. I'm going to take a leap of faith."

The woman moved forward with a harness and helmet. She held them out to the man who took them with a gulp.

"And you will never regret it, Aiden."

Lyric Sinclair cherished the warm breeze that caressed her face as she sat in the grass on the lower cliff. She couldn't believe how empowering and exhilarating the trip down the zipline had been. At first, she had been terrified. Then the woman had noticed that it was like going down a slide. Of course, she didn't have the safe plastic underneath her keeping her from hitting rock-bottom.

"Look."

Bear's quiet voice brought Lyric out of her thoughts. She opened her eyes to see what had captured the gruff man's attention. The woman's eyes widened in surprise as she saw Aiden standing on the edge of the upper cliff wearing a blue helmet and harness. *I can't believe he is going to try it. He hates heights.*

Lyric bit her lip as the man seemed to stare down toward her. She waited unsure that he was really going to step off the cliff. The woman gestured for him to come. She blushed as a warm smile came to Aiden's face before he leapt off his side of the canyon.

Lyric placed hands over her mouth as she gasped in surprise. She swallowed hard as the man she loved fell down the zipline rapidly coming towards her.

"Move."

The woman moved to the side as Bear approached the gray rope that held Aiden's life in its control. She held her breath as the young man reached the large guide who snatched him before he could hit the tree that held the zipline.

Lyric beamed at Aiden as the man was unclipped and set on his feet. She rushed forward hugging him before she could stop herself. The woman half-expected the man to push her away still angry at her earlier words. However, delight filled her as his arms went around her drawing them closer.

Aiden whispered in her ear, "You'll never live if you don't take a leap of faith."

Tears came to Lyric's eyes at her father's words that were clearly affecting the man she loved.

The touched woman whispered, "Thanks for taking that leap with me."

"What's the next leap?"

Lyric leaned back smirking at the man.

"Something cool."

CHAPTER 15

DARK HEARTS

Lyric Sinclair stared out the window amazed at the massive rock structure that they were approaching in their green SUV. Her heart pounded in excitement at the next adventure on her list. She had researched this one deeply eager to make the most of their time in Missouri.

"So how does this cave exploration thing work?"

Lyric snapped her eyes over to Aiden who was staring at the road ahead. She smiled warmly thrilled to be continuing the journey with him.

"I arranged a tour for us with some others. It is a small group, so we shouldn't be forced to endure annoying children or endless questions."

"Sounds good."

The slight pause in the man's voice caused the woman to frown. "But?"

Aiden shrugged, "Nothing. It's just that it seems like your adventures have been growing in intensity. I didn't expect a simple cave tour to be your next one."

Lyric nodded in understanding, "I thought you might like a slow-paced adventure this time. We have done some amazing things. Now let's see some amazing things."

The two adults parked and headed toward the cave entrance. Lyric smiled at a young woman with mocha colored skin and long black braids. She was dressed in a light brown tank top and khaki shorts.

"Welcome, everyone! My name is Toya McKinley. I will be your cave guide today. Before we can start our exploration, we need to go over some rules. We want this to be fun and safe."

Lyric rolled her eyes at the sing-song perky voice of Toya. She glanced at Aiden who looked equally annoyed. The man leaned toward her.

Aiden whispered, "You forgot to book a tour without an annoying guide."

The woman snorted before covering her mouth with her hand. She focused on Toya as their guide listed the rules and expectations for the day's adventure.

"Now that the boring part is over. Let's go cave exploring."

The small group of adults moved toward the cave entrance. Lyric held her breath trying to contain her excitement. *Here we go.*

Aiden Wilder's eyes bulged at the vast inside of the first cavern on the tour. He was amazed by the beige spikes that hung from the ceiling of the cave.

"Ladies and gentlemen, this cavern is an excellent example of the difference between stalagmites and stalactites. You see the points coming down from the ceiling. Those are stalactites. Water drips off them and form stalagmites. Columns form when stalactites and stalagmites join."

Aiden sighed at the droning guide as she spouted off several more facts about the cavern. He moved closer to the man-made silver railing that kept the tourists safe from falling into the dark pits below.

"Careful, Aiden. You don't want to fall down there."

The man chuckled, "That's true. Who knows if there is even a bottom to that pit?"

"Toya probably knows. Do you want me to ask her?"

Aiden snapped a scowl at Lyric who was leaning on the railing with a smirk on her face.

"Don't you dare."

The redheaded woman laughed as she moved to follow the rest of the group who were heading toward the next cavern. Aiden took a final look into the pitch-black hole before moving to rejoin the other tourists.

Lyric Sinclair winced as her head ached. She bit her lip in annoyance. Her health had seemed to improve since they had left Tennessee. She had hoped that she wouldn't be bothered with headaches for a while. *I'm not going to let it ruin my fun.*

"Lyric."

Lyric spun around finding Aiden standing off to the side. She cocked her head in confusion before walking over to stand in front of him. The woman glanced over to Toya and the others who were moving deeper into the caverns.

"What, Aiden? We're going to be left behind."

"Good. I can't take anymore of Perky Polly."

Lyric giggled, "Me neither. Do you want to leave?"

The man shook his head with a frown. He motioned toward the cave wall where there was an opening.

"No. I want to explore a little on our own."

The woman's eyes widened in surprise.

"I don't think we should, Aiden. What if something happens?"

Aiden stepped closer to her making Lyric hold her breath.

"Nothing is going to happen. We will take a short walk and then come right back."

"Okay, but we can't go too far."

Harper Raines sank onto her couch exhausted from the day of moving her grandmother into her apartment. She had to admit that it was going to be an adjustment since she was used to living alone. The woman glanced over at Grammy who was putting away some of the dishes that she had brought from her house.

"We can unpack more tomorrow, Grammy. Why don't we just relax?"

The older woman set the dish she was holding on the shelf before closing the cabinet door. She hobbled over to sit down in the rocking chair that Harper had agreed she could put in the living room.

"We sure got a lot done today, Harp."

"Yes, Grammy. There's still a lot to unpack, but there's no rush."

Grammy pointed toward a flat wrapped package that was leaning against the wall.

"Well, we have to hang my Jesus picture before we can call it a night. Where shall we put it?"

Harper shrugged not caring where her grandmother put the picture that she had always treasured.

"It doesn't matter."

"Of course, it matters. The Lord deserves a special place in our home."

The younger woman sighed, "Why?"

Odessa "Birdie" Raines frowned at her granddaughter's question. She snapped her eyes toward Harper.

"What do you mean?"

The younger woman explained, "I know you believe in all this religious stuff, Grammy, but I don't. Why don't you put the picture in your room?"

Birdie crossed her arms with a scowl.

"Jesus isn't religious stuff. He is my Lord. I thought that He was yours too."

"Grammy, I don't want to fight with you. You can put the picture wherever you want."

The older woman softened her harsh expression pleased that Harper didn't want to argue with her. Birdie didn't want to quarrel either. She knew that God had brought the two of them back together for a reason. *I can't let anything ruin our second chance.*

"Okay, Harp. We'll pick a place for my Jesus picture tomorrow." *We don't have to fix everything in one night.*

Aiden Wilder led the way through the side tunnel that was not included in the tour of the caverns. He used the flashlight app on his cell phone to provide light in the endless darkness. The man could tell that Lyric was enjoying the detour though her faster breathing proved that she was also nervous about exploring on their own.

Aiden reached his free hand over to the woman. He was pleased as she took his hand into her own. The man lowered his head as they came to another opening. His eyes sparkled in awe at the new cavern that they had discovered. The massive room had a bluish tinge which seemed to come from an unknown source of light. At the far end was a flowing waterfall which streamed down below them out of view.

Aiden stepped forward bringing Lyric with him. The duo walked along a rocky bridge toward the waterfall.

"This bridge is so narrow. Maybe we should stop, Aiden."

The man smiled at the woman's concern.

"You worry too much, Lyric. We are perfectly safe."

With a nod from Lyric, Aiden moved forward using his cell phone to light the way.

"This is so beautiful."

The man stared at Lyric's pale freckled face and emerald eyes.

"Yes. Beautiful."

Suddenly, a rumble echoed through the cavern. The rocky ground shook violently.

"Aiden, what is it?"

Before the man could answer, Aiden saw Lyric slipping toward the edge of the bridge. He squeezed her hand trying to keep a firm grip on her. However, in the next moment, their hands fell apart. The woman screamed as she fell off the edge.

"Lyric!"

Lyric Sinclair's heart thumped in fear as the narrow rock bridge jerked under her feet. She clenched her hand on Aiden's own pleased that the man did the same. However, gravity pulled her down toward the dark hole.

Suddenly, the two adults' hands broke their connection. Lyric stumbled backwards until her feet were no longer on the bridge. She screamed as her body fell into the deep darkness.

"Aiden!"

CHAPTER 16

FROZEN FEARS

Panic filled Aiden Wilder as the shaking stopped. He peered over the side holding his cell phone up so that the light shone into the darkness. The man darted his eyes around searching for Lyric. The fallen woman was nowhere in sight.

"Lyric!"

His own echo was the only response. Aiden thought about returning the way that he had come to get help. However, his heart wrenched at the idea of leaving the area without the woman he loved. *I must find her.*

Aiden used his flashlight app to scan the rocky bridge hoping to see a safe way to climb down to the area below. His heart pounded in excitement as he saw that the bridge sloped downward at the end. Carefully, the determined man approached the edge sitting down on the slope. He inched down it using his hands and feet to slow his descent. *Hang on, Lyric! I'm coming!*

Lyric Sinclair gasped as she fell into a pool of water at the bottom of the great hole. She scowled at the foul-tasting liquid that entered her mouth. The woman pushed her feet on the hard bottom of the pool forcing her body to resurface. She spat out the water as cavern air reached her face.

"Aiden!"

Silence was the only response. Lyric's heart thumped in fear. She was thankful that the pool of water was at the bottom of the hole to catch her safely. However, now she wondered how to get back up to Aiden. *Don't panic. There must be a way.*

Lyric swam toward the rocky shore eager to get out of the cold water. She was pleased at how shallow it was as she neared the shore.

The woman was able to stand up with the water only coming up to her knees. She looked upward before cupping her hands to her mouth.

"Aiden!"

The lack of response frustrated Lyric. Movement in the shadows caused the woman to shriek. She backed up slightly certain that it couldn't be Aiden. *He hasn't had time to come down here.*

The woman reached into her pocket for her cell phone which she knew was waterproof. A groan escaped her lips as she remembered that she had left it in the car so that no one could ruin her cave tour. *I guess I am stuck in this dim light until Aiden finds me. If he finds me.*

Suddenly, rumbling echoed through the lower cavern. Lyric jumped startled as large rocks splashed in the water around her. She screamed in fear as one hit her in the shoulder knocking her off-balance. The fearful woman fell into the pool with a splash. She scrambled to get to the shore. However, her body suddenly felt very heavy. *Lord, please save me! Don't let me drown!*

Aiden Wilder paused at the bottom of the slope as the cavern shook and rumbled. He bit his lip at the earthquake that was slowing him down from finding Lyric. The man took a deep breath as the rumbling ceased. He stood up on the rocky ground before using his flashlight app to provide light in the deep underground.

Aiden stepped carefully through the cavern seeking any movement or sound that could give him a clue as to where the missing woman had ended up. Disappointment filled him as he moved farther away from the bridge. The man swiped the cell phone light to the left and then the right. He sighed in relief at the pool of water that was on the right of him. *At least she didn't fall onto hard ground.*

"Lyric!"

Aiden paused listening for a response. His eyes widened as he heard his own name echo around him.

"Aiden!"

The man stomped forward following where the source of the sound had come from. He flashed the light on the shore hoping to see the woman waiting for him to rescue her. However, confusion covered him at the empty shore. *Where is she?*

Suddenly, a splash drew Aiden's attention to the pool of water. His eyes bulged in shock as his light revealed Lyric struggling to keep her head above water.

"Lyric!"

The man entered the pool of water with his heart racing. He was surprised to see that the water only went up to his knees as he reached the woman's side. Aiden knelt beside Lyric putting an arm under her neck to bring her head above the water safely. He flashed his light toward the rest of the woman's body feeling fear grip him tightly.

Large rocks were piled on the lower half of Lyric's body trapping her in the cold pool of water. Aiden's heart wrenched at the massive barrier to the woman's safety.

"Aiden."

The man snapped his gaze to Lyric. He could see the fear in the woman's green eyes.

Aiden smiled weakly, "Don't worry, Lyric. I've got you."

Lyric Sinclair tried to relax as Aiden held her in his arms. She was relieved that the man had found her. The woman did not want to die alone. She knew from the heavy weight on her legs that she was trapped. *If Aiden hadn't come, I would have drowned.*

"Don't worry, Lyric. I've got you."

Lyric's fear lessened at the man's comforting tone. She stared into his eyes pleased at the smile that he was throwing at her.

"I know."

Aiden's smile grew at her trust in him.

"Lyric, I have to remove the rocks from your legs. Can you use your hands to keep above the water?"

Lyric frowned at the question. She wanted to blurt out that she was too scared and weak to keep herself afloat. However, the woman knew that they didn't have a lot of options especially since no one was aware that they had strayed from the tour. She swallowed hard.

"Yes."

Lyric moved her wet cold hands to the rocky bottom of the pool of water. She stared up at the dark ceiling bracing herself.

Suddenly, Aiden released her before moving toward the rock pile that held her captive. The woman cringed at the pain that came to her arms as she attempted to keep her head above the water. She hoped that the man would be able to free her quickly. *I can't hold on for long.*

Aiden Wilder gripped a large boulder that had fallen on Lyric trapping her. He pulled with all his might begging the rock to move. The man moved his grasp to another boulder jerking it roughly. He growled in frustration as he moved from rock to rock only able to remove a couple of smaller ones.

"Aiden!"

Lyric's desperate shout caused Aiden to return his attention to her. He waded toward the woman who was sinking back below the water. The man scooped an arm under her bringing her back to the surface. He cringed as Lyric spat out the water with several gasping breaths.

"I'm sorry. My arms hurt so bad. I couldn't stay up."

Aiden held the woman closer wiping wet strands of red hair out of her eyes.

"It's okay. You're safe. You did great."

A small smile twitched at Lyric's mouth. She nodded slightly before raising her head to look toward the rock pile.

"Any luck?"

Aiden cringed at the question. He thought about lying to the woman to give her hope. However, the man knew that it would only be false hope. *I must tell her the truth.*

"No. The rocks are too heavy for one person to move. I need to find help."

Lyric Sinclair lowered her head back to Aiden's arm. She didn't like the news of remaining trapped longer. The woman frowned deeply at the idea of Aiden leaving her to find help.

Panic swamped over Lyric as tears came to her eyes.

"No, Aiden. You can't leave me here. I can't stay above water. I'll drown. Please don't leave me. We'll think of something. Please."

Sobs escaped the woman as all hope faded away. She couldn't endure the thought of dying down in the dark cavern.

Suddenly, Aiden wrapped his arms tighter around her pulling her closer to him. He placed a gentle kiss on her forehead surprising yet pleasing her.

"Shh, Lyric. I'm not leaving you. It's okay. I promise I won't leave you here alone."

Aiden Wilder placed his cheek on the top of Lyric's head attempting to comfort and reassure her. His heart wrenched at the desperation in the woman's voice. The man didn't know what they were going to do. His mind raced with possible solutions to their deadly problem. Guilt crept in though he shook it away for the present. *I can focus on this being my fault once Lyric is safe.*

"What are we going to do, Aiden?"

Aiden winced at the woman's weak tone. He planted another kiss on her forehead before responding.

"I don't know, but I'm not going anywhere." *Someone in the tour is going to miss us. They will send a search and rescue team. We'll be fine. I hope.*

Toya McKinley stacked the comment cards that the tourists had filled out at the end of the tour. She was pleased with the glowing reviews that she had received from her guests. The tour guide placed the cards into the comment box before standing up with a yawn. She was exhausted from the long day of work. All Toya could think about was taking a hot shower and climbing into bed for a good night's sleep.

"Good night, Toya."

Toya waved at a male tour guide.

"Night, Sam."

The two adults locked up the man-made cavern entrance before walking through the dark parking lot to their cars. *I wish they would replace those burned bulbs. It gets too dark out here at night.*

Toya climbed into her red jeep before turning the key in the ignition. She focused on driving home as the music on her radio blared out into the night. *Another day of no accidents. Our safety record rocks!*

Aiden Wilder shivered as he held Lyric's head out of the water. He gritted his teeth at the dimming screen of his cell phone. The man knew that the battery needed to be charged. He stared at the time amazed that it was nighttime. *Where is the search team? They must know that we are missing by now.*

"Aiden."

The soft whisper caused the man to cringe. He moved his gaze to Lyric who was staring up at him. Her lips appeared bluer than before in the light of the phone. Aiden hoped that it was an illusion. However, he knew that hypothermia was a true threat that they were facing in the cold water of the dark cavern.

"Why haven't they come for us?"

Aiden smiled warmly hoping to hide the fear on his face.

"Don't worry, Lyric. They'll be here any minute."

Harper Raines sat up in her bed with a gasp. She didn't know why she had awoken so frightened. The woman couldn't remember any details of a nightmare that could have brought her out of dreamland. She listened hard wondering if a noise in her apartment had awakened her. Silence was all that she heard.

Harper climbed out of bed pulling on her bathrobe. She tossed a hand through her mussed hair before heading out of her bedroom toward the kitchen. The woman froze as she entered the dining area where her grandmother sat reading her Bible. She wondered why the older woman was still up. *It must be after midnight. Grammy was always in bed early.*

"Grammy?"

The other woman snapped her gaze to her granddaughter.

"What are you doing up, Baby?"

Harper sighed as she headed to the refrigerator. She opened it peering inside for something to comfort her. However, nothing appealed to her. The woman closed it harshly as frustration filled her.

"I don't know why, but I have a bad feeling that something has happened."

"To Lyric?"

Harper spun around shocked at the question. She had not thought about her friend since waking up. However, now the woman had a sinking feeling in her stomach. She wondered if something had truly happened to Lyric.

"I don't know. Maybe I have a message from her or Aiden on my phone."

The frantic woman picked up her cell phone from the charger tapping the screen. She frowned at the lack of news from either of the adults.

"Nothing."

Harper plopped down on a chair placing her phone on the dining table. She stared at it wishing that Lyric would call or text with an update about her trip or her health. The young woman placed her arms on the table before laying her forehead down on them. *Oh, Lyric. Where are you?*

Odessa "Birdie" Raines watched her granddaughter lay her face on the table clearly distraught. Her heart ached at the fear and pain that she knew that Harper was feeling at the lack of news from her friend.

Birdie closed her eyes tightly praying for the Lord to give Harper peace. She pleaded for Lyric to be safe as well as her bodyguard Aiden. The older woman prayed for words that she could share with her granddaughter to bring her hope in the dark moment.

"When peace like a river, attendeth my way."

Birdie rocked gently as the old hymn floated in the air of the fearful room.

"When sorrows like sea billows roll; Whatever my lot, Thou hast taught me to say; It is well, it is well, with my soul."

The Christian woman didn't know if the message of the song was reaching her granddaughter. She continued singing the chorus hoping that the Lord would use the song to bring peace to Harper.

"It is well, with my soul. It is well, it is well with my soul."

Harper Raines snorted softly at the ancient church song that she remembered hearing when she was a child. She didn't know why Grammy insisted on invading her mood with the song during such a scary time. She wanted to shout at the old woman or leave the room to escape the message of the hymn. However, something kept her in her chair. She listened as Grammy began to sing the second verse.

Her heart swelled as memories of Mr. Sinclair and Lyric flooded over her.

"Though Satan should buffet, though trials should come; Let this blest assurance control; That Christ has regarded my helpless estate; And hath shed His own blood for my soul."

Harper's mind filled with truths that she had learned in church so many years ago. She recalled hearing about Jesus especially at Christmas and Easter. The woman wondered if all the stories that she had been told were true. *Will You really make it well with my soul?*

"It is well."

Harper sat up with her eyes closed. She opened her mouth to sing the repeat portion of the chorus.

"It is well."

A slight pause told the woman that Grammy was surprised by her participation. After a couple of seconds, the older woman began to sing once more.

"With my soul."

Harper added, "With my soul."

Together the two women from different generations finished the song.

"It is well, it is well with my soul."

CHAPTER 17

MELTING TRUTHS

Lyric Sinclair shuddered at the icy water that surrounded her body. She didn't know how long she had been stuck under the rock pile. The woman's body was exhausted though she refused to close her eyes. She knew from stories about hypothermia which claimed people when they fell asleep in the bitter cold.

Lyric slowly moved her eyes over to Aiden who was still holding her above the water. She could tell by his face that the man was equally cold and exhausted. The woman smiled weakly at him though his attention seemed to be on his phone. She noticed that the screen didn't seem as bright as before. *The battery is dying.*

A shiver ran up Lyric's spine at the thought of death. She hoped that the battery would be the only thing dying in the deep cavern. The woman stared up at Aiden's handsome face. Her heart swooned with love for the man. *He's in this mess because of me. I should have stayed home. None of this would have happened.*

Lyric clenched her teeth. She thought about her health which had led her to this bucket list journey. Her mind traveled through each place that she had experienced with Aiden by her side. She saw their horseback ride at the Calhoun's farm. The woman remembered the fun at the amusement park where she had first felt fond of the man. She recalled their circus adventure where Aiden had put his own life in danger to save her from Lynx. Lyric smiled weakly as she thought about swimming with dolphins and hovering over the ocean in a hot air balloon. Her heart swooned at the reminder of the dinner that Aiden cooked for her at the cabin in the woods. She thought about how the man used CPR to breathe life back into her after she nearly drowned in the river. His overprotectiveness of her during the ziplining touched her. *I would never have made it through such wonderful adventures without Aiden.*

Guilt covered Lyric as she thought about the lies that she had been telling about her health and the reason behind their journey.

The woman knew that the man that she loved deserved to know the truth. *I can't lie anymore even if the truth drives him away from me.*

"Aiden."

Lyric smiled weakly as the man shifted his focus to her. She took a deep breath hoping that she would be able to endure Aiden's reaction.

"I need to tell you something."

Aiden nodded with a smile.

Lyric continued, "I have a brain tumor. That's why I have been going on this journey. I am fulfilling my bucket list before it is too late. I'm sorry that I didn't tell you before. At first, I didn't think that you needed to know because you were my driver and bodyguard, but that has changed."

Aiden Wilder listened to Lyric's confession with disbelief and anger growing by the moment. He couldn't believe that the woman had lied to him about her health. The man wished that he could storm away to be by himself for a bit. However, he knew that he couldn't since she would drown.

Aiden bit his lip averting his gaze from the woman. He breathed deeply trying to comprehend the information. The man swallowed hard as he thought about the dangers of having a brain tumor. He knew that Lyric had been risking her life by keeping them so far from her doctor. *Why would she do that? She needs treatment.*

"Over this journey, you have become my friend, Aiden. I have enjoyed spending time with you. You have become an important part of my adventures."

Aiden tensed at the words. He stared off into the darkness unable to speak to the woman. The man wanted to believe her, but she had been lying to him from the beginning. *How can I trust her?*

Lyric Sinclair blinked away tears as she told Aiden the truth. She was disturbed by the man's reaction. His gaze stared away from her revealing how angry he was at her lies. The woman couldn't blame him though she wished to fix the ever-growing rift that was forming between them. She spoke of their friendship hoping that it would smooth things over. However, Lyric knew that she was still lying to him. *I need to tell the full truth.*

Taking a deep breath, the woman whispered, "I love you, Aiden."

"I love you, Aiden."

Aiden Wilder's eyes snapped back to Lyric who had closed her own. He swallowed hard wondering if he had heard right. The woman's voice had been so soft. He knew that it was possible that he had misheard her. She could also have meant that she loved him as a friend. The man also realized that she could be delirious from the cold and trauma from being trapped under the rocks for so long.

"Lyric?"

The woman's eyes remained closed. Her breathing seemed shallower than before. Aiden frowned as he shook her. The lack of response scared him. *Please don't let her die!*

"Lyric!"

Lyric Sinclair groaned as her body shook. She tried to open her eyes finding them heavy and uncooperative.

"Lyric!"

The scream blared in her ears causing her to frown. *Aiden?*

The woman's body was jerked back and forth again causing Lyric to force her eyes open. She blinked a couple of times before her vision focused on Aiden's face which was dim in the pale light.

"Lyric, good. Stay awake please. Don't go to sleep."

Lyric nodded stiffly with a gasp at the pain in her cold body. She could feel panic fill her. *I'm going to die down here.*

"Aiden, can you forgive me for lying to you? For treating you like you were beneath me?"

The man's face became solemn. He took a deep breath before answering.

"Yes. I forgive you, Lyric. Don't worry about the past now. We need to stay strong until a rescue comes."

Lyric snorted at Aiden's endless faith in a positive outcome. She was fully aware that not all stories had happy endings. Her heart told her that her life would not be a fairytale. *My journey ends here. But what about Aiden's?*

With a great deal of effort, Lyric raised a hand out of the water placing it on the man's cheek. She watched as Aiden winced at the coolness of the flesh.

"I need you to promise me something, Aiden."

The man cocked his head before nodding with uncertainty covering his face.

"I need you to promise me that you will get out of here even if I can't." *Please promise me so I can be at peace.*

Aiden Wilder held his breath as he waited to hear what Lyric wanted him to promise. He clenched his teeth dreading what the woman would say.

"I need you to promise me that you will get out of here even if I can't."

Aiden held the woman with one arm as he reached his other hand up to cover her own which was still stationed on his cheek. He stared down into her pale face which was illuminated by the dim cavern light.

"I don't need to promise that, Lyric, because we are both going to leave this place together. We are going to finish your bucket list before returning to New York where the doctors will heal you."

Aiden took a deep breath at the tears that glistened in the woman's eyes. He thought about how Lyric had said that she loved him. The man wondered if he had truly heard those words. He decided to take a risk. *Whether she loves me or not, I can't change how I feel about her.*

"I love you, Lyric."

Lyric Sinclair's heart swooned as the man professed his love for her. She stared up into his sparkling eyes wishing that the two of them could leave the cavern and finish the bucket list. The woman was thankful for the time that they had had together. She longed for more time with Aiden. Her mind went to the river where she had been drowning. She thought about how she had prayed that God would save her. *Then Bear and Aiden rescued me.*

Lyric's heart thrilled at the truth that God had used the two men to save her. She wondered if He would help them again. The woman paused for a moment unsure that God would really help her and the man that she loved. *What if He doesn't?*

The trapped woman sighed as weakness swamped over her. She knew that it didn't hurt to ask since they didn't have any other options. *Lord, we need Your help. Please get us out of here alive. I am trusting You with this leap of faith.*

CHAPTER 18

DETERMINED RESCUE

Toya McKinley drove her red jeep into the cavern parking lot. She hummed along with the radio as she twisted a long braid around a finger. The tour guide could feel that it was going to be another great day working in one of the coolest places in the world.

Suddenly, Toya hit the brakes too hard. She jerked forward as her eyes stared at a hunter green SUV parked in one of the visitor's parking space. The woman cocked her head confused by the vehicle. She pulled into her reserved parking spot.

Climbing out of her jeep, Toya squinted in the morning light toward the SUV. She frowned at the lack of driver or passengers. The tour guide hurried into the cavern lobby seeking out the visitors who must have come early for a tour.

"Good morning, Toya."

"Hey, Sam. Do we have guests already?"

The male tour guide set down his newspaper with a shake of his head.

"I haven't seen anyone. Why?"

Toya gestured toward the entrance door.

"There's a green SUV outside in the visitor's lot. No one's in it."

Sam frowned, "I wonder where they are."

The other tour guide entered the office picking up the review comment cards. She counted eleven cards that had been collected as the tourists left the day before. *I thought we had thirteen guests.*

Toya took a deep breath knowing that not all their guests took the time to fill out the comment cards. However, something nagged at her about the empty SUV.

"Sam?"

The man popped into the office.

"Yeah?"

"Can you pull up the security footage from yesterday?"

Sam plopped down in front of his computer. He typed away before turning the monitor toward her. Toya leaned forward watching the tourists follow her through the lobby into the caverns. She waited patiently as Sam sped through the footage until the group exited the caverns. The woman's eyes widened in shock as two of the guests did not return from the tour.

"Uh, Toya. What happened to that couple?"

Toya's heart pounded in fear at the possibilities. Her voice came out in a strangled whisper.

"Sam, call the search and rescue team."

Aiden Wilder coughed harshly as the dim light in the cavern grew slightly brighter. He guessed that it was morning though he wasn't sure if that was good news or not. The man had believed that a rescue would have happened by now. Yet, there was no sign of help coming.

"Aiden?"

Lyric's soft whisper caused the man to cringe. Aiden knew that the woman was weakening by the moment. *I must get her out of here now.*

"Lyric, I'm going to try to get the rocks off you. I'm going to put a rock under you to keep you above water. Can you make it a short time without me?"

The woman's eyes shone with fear.

"I don't have the strength to hold myself up, Aiden. Maybe I can hold my breath if it doesn't take too long."

Aiden didn't like the idea of the weakened woman being under the cold water even for a second, but he knew that they had no other choice.

"Okay. Hold your breath. I'll be right back. Ready?"

Lyric inhaled a deep breath. Aiden released her gently before wading through the water to find a rock big enough to support the woman above the pool. His heart pounded as he panted attempting to hurry. The man rolled a rock that he had moved off the pile earlier. He pushed it on the bottom of the pool until he had reached Lyric. With one arm, Aiden raised the woman out of the water. He cringed as she gasped with water dripping off her face.

"Are you okay?"

Lyric nodded without a word.

Aiden used his other hand and knee to push the rock under the woman. He knew that it would be hard and uncomfortable but waiting for help didn't seem like a possibility anymore.

"I know this isn't a pillow, but I have to try to get you out of here."

Lyric smiled weakly, "I'm fine. Go."

Without wasting any time, Aiden waded back to the rock pile which he could only see in the dim light. His cell phone had died hours ago. *It's the only thing that is going to die.*

The man pressed his cold fingers around the edges of a boulder. He winced at the pain in his hands. Aiden pulled with all his strength. Yet, the rock did not budge. He pushed forward hoping that the giant stone would roll off the other way.

"Come on!"

Aiden's shout echoed off the cavern walls. He growled in fury as his hands grasped another unmoving boulder. The man could feel the fear and desperation fill him. He closed his eyes before shoving his whole body against one of the rocks to no avail. Aiden could feel hot tears of frustration stream down his face. *Lord, please help me! I can't save her alone.*

"Sir, I can help you!"

Aiden's eyes snapped open at the unfamiliar voice. He stared at a muscular man who stood on the rocky shore. The stranger stepped into the water hurrying toward the rock pile. He placed his hands on the same boulder that Aiden was clinging to desperately.

"Let's do it together."

The two men pushed the large rock in unison. A thrill of excitement shot through Aiden as it moved off the pile splashing in the pool of water.

"Good. Let's do the next one."

Aiden nodded at the other man speechless. One after another, the boulders were removed from the woman's body by the joint effort of the two men.

Relief flooded over Aiden as he scooped Lyric up into his arms. The freed woman giggled softly at being released from the rock prison.

"Thank you so much, sir!"

Aiden snapped his gaze toward the stranger who had found them. He frowned at the empty shore. The man glanced around in shock seeing no sign of the heroic helper.

"Where is he, Aiden?"

Aiden shook his head as he trudged through the pool of water carrying the exhausted woman to the shore.

"I don't know. My mother always said to be alert when dealing with other people because we could be entertaining angels unaware."

Lyric touched the man's face with a tender hand. Aiden glanced down at her with a smile.

"God answered my prayers, Aiden."

The man nodded with tears threatening to fall, "Mine too."

Lyric Sinclair stared up into Aiden's face feeling frozen and exhausted. She was glad to be out of the chilly water though she wished that she was in a hot shower warming up. The woman cleared her throat wincing at the pain that came.

"What do we do now, Aiden?"

The man glanced around with a frown.

"I don't know. You can't walk, can you?"

Lyric shook her head.

Aiden sighed, "And I don't think that I can carry you up the slope to the bridge."

"Then what do we do?"

The man set the woman down on the rocky ground. He sat down beside her before pulling her closer. His arm went around her shoulder pleasing the woman. She leaned against him longing to be warm.

"We rest here for now."

Lyric wanted to ask more questions about his plan of getting them back to civilization, but she knew that the man didn't have a full plan yet.

"Okay. Let's rest."

Odessa "Birdie" Raines watched her granddaughter pace back and forth across the living room. It was almost ten in the morning with still no news from Lyric. Birdie wished that she hadn't put the fear and doubt in Harper by mentioning her friend when the young woman had a nightmare. *It could have been something else. I stirred this up for no reason.*

"Harper, why don't we watch a movie? You used to like watching movies when you were a child."

The younger woman froze with a scowl on her face.

"Yes. I enjoyed watching movies with Lyric, but she's not here, is she? No. She is off who knows where doing who knows what."

Birdie sighed, "God knows where Lyric is and what she is doing."

Harper snorted, "Grammy, please. I don't want to talk to you about God."

"Why not, Baby? What is so horrible about talking about God?"

The granddaughter placed her hands on her hips with a snarl.

"Because of God, my father rejected me, and my mother ignored me so that she could drink herself to death. Because of God, Mr. Sinclair who was more of a father than any other person to me died a long painful death. Because of God, my best friend has a brain tumor and is facing death at this moment. I don't want anything to do with God!"

Birdie folded her hands in her lap listening as Harper ranted about the events in her life that had hurt her heart. She waited for the young woman to fall silent. When she did, the older woman took a deep breath.

"Because of God, I became a grandmother to a beautiful young woman. Because of God, I was able to feed and clothe that child when her mother could not. Because of God, I saw a man and his daughter befriend and love that girl. Because of God, I am living with that lovely young woman because she offered me a home when I was losing my own."

Birdie chuckled, "I want everything to do with God."

Harper Raines bit her lip as her grandmother spoke about God as if He was on her side. She didn't know how the older woman could trust Him after all the heartache that she had faced.

"How can you trust Him? He has done nothing, but make you struggle your whole life. How much do you have to endure before you realize that God doesn't care?"

The tight-lipped grimace that came to Grammy's face told Harper that she had gone too far.

"I'm sorry, Grammy, but I just can't see God the way that you do."

The grandmother patted the couch beside her.

"Sit down, child."

Harper opened her mouth to protest. However, she obeyed as Grammy's eyes flared sternly.

"Now, Harper. I am going to tell you something that your mother made me promise never to tell. You need to hear the truth about God."

The younger woman rolled her eyes wanting to dismiss her grandmother. She looked away hoping that the older woman would get the hint.

"Before you were born, your mother was working in a store downtown. Her car wouldn't run so she decided to walk home. A man attacked her leaving her for dead in an alleyway."

Harper frowned at the story that she had never heard before. She turned her attention to Grammy who was staring at her hands.

"Another man found your mother and took her to a hospital. The doctors said that she would have died if she had been left in that alley another hour. Nine months later you were born, and your mother was never the same."

The young woman shrugged, "So what? That proves that God didn't protect her from that monster."

Grammy shook her head.

"You don't understand, do you? That monster had attacked over a dozen women killing all of them. Your mother was the only one to survive. God kept her alive allowing her to physically heal. There was another thing too."

Harper sighed, "What, Grammy?"

The older woman smiled weakly, "The day after the attack, your mother told the nurse that she wanted to thank the man who had saved her and brought her to the hospital. No one knew what she was talking about. The hospital staff swore that she came into the hospital on her own, but your mother said that there was a man who rescued her."

Harper stared at the floor amazed at the disappearing man. She held her breath wondering what it meant.

"Do you know what I believe, Baby?"

"What, Grammy?"

The elderly woman took Harper's hands into her own withered ones.

"I believe that God sent an angel to bring your mother to the hospital before it was too late. I believe that He loved our family so much that He chose to save her and give you to us."

Harper blinked away tears wishing that it was true.

"You may not believe it, Harp, but God loves you and Lyric. He has a special plan for both of you. You just have to trust Him."

The young woman leaned back against the couch thinking about what her grandmother had said. She closed her eyes with a sigh.

"How do I trust Him, Grammy?"

A tender squeeze came to her hands.

"Give Him a chance to work. Wait for His plan to unfold."

Harper allowed the tears to fall.

"Why did Mom never love me?"

Her heart wrenched at her own question. She held her breath as her grandmother remained silent.

"Because she never gave you a chance, Baby. If she had, then she would have seen the same thing that I have since the day you were born."

"And what's that?"

Harper turned her gaze onto Grammy.

"That you, Harper Neveah Raines, are a gift from God. You are the good that He brought from that evil."

Tears fell as the young woman hugged her grandmother. She sobbed as Grammy hummed in her ear. *Please help me to trust You with Lyric. If she is in danger, please save her.*

Aiden Wilder rubbed his hands up and down Lyric's arms hoping that he was providing some warmth to the frozen woman. He knew that being out of the water helped, but the man wished to get her out of the cavern.

A soft moan came from the resting woman. Aiden glanced down at her smiling weakly. He found it amazing that Lyric had claimed that she loved him. The man's love for her had grown over the past few days. He was ecstatic that she loved him too.

Aiden frowned as doubt crept into his happiness. He thought about how adamant the woman had been that he was her employee. The man wondered if the life-threatening crisis had made Lyric profess something that she didn't truly feel. *Maybe she didn't mean to say it. Perhaps her emotions took over. If she really loves me, then she will bring it up.*

Lyric Sinclair rested with her eyes closed enjoying Aiden's strong arms around her. She was glad that she had expressed her love for the man before it was too late. The woman's heart swooned that Aiden had professed his love for her in return. She hoped that they would escape the cavern and begin a life together.

Suddenly, uncertainty replaced Lyric's joy. She frowned at the idea that Aiden had only said that he loved her because she had said it first. *Maybe he pities me because I am sick. I will let it drop. If he loves me, then he will say it again.*

"Hello?"

The two adults sat up straighter at the voice. Lyric smiled weakly in relief at the sight of flashlight beams approaching them. *We're saved.*

CHAPTER 19

ABANDONED LIST

Lyric Sinclair stretched her arms with a yawn as she opened her eyes. She blinked at the brightness of the hospital room. The woman thought about all that had happened the day before. She shook her head in amazement that she was still alive. *It's a miracle!*

"Good morning."

Lyric sat up with a smile as Aiden stood up from a chair across the room. She remembered the last time that she was in a hospital. The fashion designer had fainted during her big fashion show. Aiden was sitting in a chair that day too. *It seems like a lifetime ago.*

"Good morning. Are you okay?"

Aiden smiled warmly, "Yes. How about you?"

Lyric nodded suppressing a wince as her head ached.

"I'm fine. It's nice to be warm again."

The man chuckled, "I know. It's nice to have some light too."

The two adults remained silent for a few moments. Lyric wished that Aiden would repeat that he loved her. However, she accepted that the hazardous situation was the reason that the man had said that he loved her. *It's okay. I can live without him.*

Lyric ignored the fact that she would have died in the cavern if Aiden hadn't been there to help her.

"I guess we are lucky to have escaped without pneumonia and broken bones."

The woman agreed with the man's statement. She was relieved that her legs were only bruised from her entrapment. *It could have been a lot worse.*

"I'll go and see when we can leave. We have a list to finish, don't we?"

Lyric smiled weakly with a slight nod. She watched as Aiden left the hospital room. The woman allowed the smile to fade into the frown that she really felt. She stared down at her bandaged hands which held her cell phone.

Lyric tapped on the screen bringing up her bucket list. She crossed off the cavern tour snorting at how that adventure had turned out. The woman's eyes widened as she read the last item on her list. She was surprised that they were almost finished. *One more thing and we can go home.*

The word "home" brought a sour taste to Lyric's mouth. She knew that once she returned to New York, her focus would have to shift to her health. The woman would not be able to ignore her condition anymore.

Lyric stared at the final item on her bucket list. Her mind shifted to Aiden as she thought about how to accomplish the last task. The woman sighed at the love in her heart which was obviously not reciprocated. She desired to spend more time with the man. Yet, it was too painful. *It's time to let him go.*

Lyric closed her bucket list on the cell phone. She set it on the blanket as Aiden came back into her hospital room.

"The doctor's coming to examine you. If he agrees, then we can leave. What's next on the list?"

The woman swallowed hard. She pasted on a smile hoping that she would look convincing.

"Nothing. We finished it. We can head home now."

Aiden Wilder waited in the hallway while the Missourian doctor examined Lyric. He leaned against the wall thinking through what the woman had said about her bucket list. The man cocked his head in confusion. He was certain that she still had items on the list.

Aiden wondered why they were going home if the journey wasn't over. He frowned as a thought came to mind. *She regrets telling me that she loves me. This is her way of ending our time together.*

The man stood up as the door to Lyric's hospital room opened. He nodded at the doctor who headed down the hallway to the nurse's station. Aiden released the breath that he was holding. *If she wants us to separate, then that's what we'll do. I won't force her to be with me.*

"What did the doctor say?"

Lyric looked up with a smile.

"He said we can leave as soon as the nurse brings the release papers."

Aiden pasted on a smile hoping that the woman would believe that he was happy that their business together would be over soon.

"Great. I guess we can head home." *Then she can get rid of me.*

Harper Raines poked her manicured finger on the accept button of her cell phone as soon as Lyric's picture came up. She jerked the phone up to her ear.

"Lyric, are you okay?"

Silence came to the other end. Harper held her breath dreading that it would be Aiden telling her bad news.

"Why would you ask if I'm okay?"

Lyric's voice brought great joy to the other woman. She released the breath with a sigh.

"I don't know. I had a nightmare last night. I wondered if it was a premonition of something that happened to you."

Her friend snorted, "Since when do you believe in premonitions and visions?"

Harper rolled her eyes. She explained about her grandmother who now lived with her in her apartment. The two women talked for several minutes without pause.

Suddenly, Lyric grew silent. Harper bit her lip worrying about her friend.

"Harper, I'm coming home."

A triumphant smile spread up the other woman's face at the news. She tried to contain her excitement as she spoke.

"So, you finished your bucket list?"

More silence confused Harper. *What's the deal? If she didn't finish her list, then why is she coming home?*

"Yes, Harper. I'm finished."

Odessa "Birdie" Raines listened quietly to Harper's phone conversation with Lyric. From what she could decipher, her granddaughter's friend was on her way home. *Good. Now she can get the help that she needs.*

"Grammy?"

Birdie jerked her attention to Harper who sank beside her on the couch.

"What is it, Baby?"

The younger woman sighed, "Something's wrong with Lyric."

Birdie frowned, "What do you mean? I thought she was coming home to get treatment for her tumor."

Harper stared down at her hands.

"That's just it. Lyric has never been the kind of woman to surrender or back away from a fight. In college, the other design students tried to intimidate her to give up, but she stood firm. Once we started our fashion design line, Lyric took charge making lists and fulfilling every task on them without flaw."

The older woman cocked her head in confusion.

"I don't understand, Harp. Why do you say something's wrong with Lyric?"

Harper shrugged, "Because she is coming home without finishing her bucket list. That's not the Lyric I know."

Birdie nodded in understanding trying to think of something that she could say to help Harper feel more at peace about her friend's homecoming.

"Grammy, will you pray with me?"

Tears came to the grandmother's eyes at the request. She nodded with a smile before reaching for Harper's hands. The two women bowed their heads in unison to seek help from the only One who could give them the peace and wisdom that they needed.

Birdie silently thanked the Lord for bringing her granddaughter closer to Him. She hoped that Harper would have the strength that she needed for the upcoming days.

Aiden Wilder drove the green SUV up the hospital driveway approaching the front lobby area where Lyric was waiting for him to pick her up. He saw her being wheeled out in the wheelchair following hospital protocol. The man had enjoyed watching the woman argue with the orderly about being capable of walking out on her own. In the end, she had surrendered before sitting down in the wheelchair.

Aiden reached for his car door ready to hop out and help Lyric into the car. However, he froze as the woman stood up to walk on her own. The man smirked at her strong stubbornness. He decided to let her have her independence. It was what made the woman tick.

Suddenly, the backseat passenger door opened. Aiden looked over his shoulder in surprise. Confusion swarmed over him as Lyric climbed into the backseat before closing her door. She silently secured her seatbelt averting her gaze from the man.

"Is something wrong, Lyric?"

The redheaded woman stared out her window.

"No. Let's go home." *I guess it is back to master and slave.*

Lyric Sinclair cringed as Aiden began to drive without another word. She hated treating him rudely when he had been such a kind friend, but it hurt too much to look at him. The woman refused to speak to him like nothing was wrong. She didn't want to make a fool of herself. *It's best to go back to the way that we were. I am the employer and he is my employee. Nothing more.*

Lyric's heart twinged at the thought. She knew that it would take a long time before she believed it. The woman focused her attention out the window as Aiden turned on the radio to fill the silence. *Dwelling on what could have been won't help anyone.*

CHAPTER 20

SHARED SORROWS

Aiden Wilder pulled the green SUV up in front of the high-rise apartment building glad that the journey was over. He had been forced to drive for many hours in silence as Lyric sulked in the backseat tapping away on her cell phone. The man climbed out of the vehicle wishing that the woman would invite him inside. However, as Lyric hopped out of the car, it became clear that she had no intention of spending any other time with him. *She doesn't love me.*

"I can help you bring up your luggage."

The redheaded woman shook her head.

"That's okay. I can manage."

Disappointment filled Aiden. *Get over it, man.*

"I can help you bring up your luggage."

Panic filled Lyric Sinclair at the thought of going to her apartment with Aiden. She wanted to make a clean break from the man, but she wasn't sure if that would happen if they went upstairs together. *I need this to be over.*

"That's okay. I can manage."

Lyric cringed as Aiden opened the trunk pulling out her suitcase before he handed it to her. She swallowed the disappointment that came from the man's indifference. The woman reached into her purse pulling out the money that she owed her driver and bodyguard.

"Thank you for helping me, Mr. Wilder."

Aiden took the money with a stiff nod.

"Thank you, Miss Sinclair."

Without another word, the man walked to the other side of the SUV climbing into the driver's seat. Lyric turned toward the apartment building raising her head high to look like nothing bothered her. However, inside her heart was wrenching at the loss of the man that she loved. *It's for the best.*

"Welcome home, Miss Sinclair."

Lyric smiled weakly, "Thank you, Harold."

The elevator door opened with a ding. The distraught woman entered without a word. She noticed that the elevator operator was watching her with a smile.

"Eighteenth floor."

"Yes, Miss Sinclair."

The woman faced the door as it closed. She glanced over at the elderly operator as he pressed the correct button. Lyric frowned as she realized that she didn't even know the man's name.

"I'm sorry, but I have never asked you your name."

The man snapped his gaze to her in surprise.

"It's Leonard, Miss Sinclair."

The woman nodded, "It's nice to formally meet you, Leonard. You can call me Lyric."

Leonard smiled weakly, "Nice to meet you, Lyric."

Lyric stayed silent for a moment waiting for the elevator to reach her floor. When the door opened, she extended a hand toward Leonard. The man's eyes widened before he shook her hand.

"Thank you for always getting me home, Leonard."

"My pleasure, Lyric."

Lyric strutted out of the elevator heading down the hallway to her apartment. She pulled out her key gently putting it into the lock before entering. Her heart froze at the disheveled mess that she had left in the apartment when she had packed and left for her bucket list journey.

Lyric swallowed hard as tears threatened to fall. The realization of her return to reality slammed into the woman. She sighed disheartened that she was back in the real world where she had a brain tumor. The ill woman knew that it was time to face her medical options.

Suddenly, Lyric pulled out her cell phone as the walls seemed to close in on her. She tapped on a contact person's picture eager to fix the growing dread that was rising inside her.

"Harper? Yeah, I'm home. I need a girl day."

"I'll be right there."

Harper Raines tapped her foot nervously in the elevator. She had asked her grandmother to pray with her before she headed to visit with Lyric. The young woman was afraid that she would snap at her careless friend or say something insensitive. Grammy couldn't contain her excitement at leading her in another prayer.

"Eighteenth floor, ma'am."

Harper cleared her throat.

"Thank you."

The fashionable woman clomped down the hallway in her high heel shoes. She took a deep breath before ringing the doorbell of Lyric's apartment. *Don't mess this up, Harper. Stay calm. Be understanding.*

Suddenly, the door swung open to reveal Lyric's smiling face. Harper could tell immediately that the expression was pasted on. The two women hugged before Lyric stepped into the hallway with her purse on her arm.

"So where do you want to go, Lyric?"

"Let's go shopping at that mall that we used to go when we were kids."

Harper's eyes widened in surprise. She had expected the other woman to want to go to a café or shop in one of the exclusive boutiques. Yet, Lyric wanted to go to their favorite childhood place.

"Sounds good. Let's go."

Lyric Sinclair held up a blouse cocking her head in indecision. She liked the turquoise color of the shirt. However, her heart didn't seem to be completely into the shopping experience.

"That's cute, Lyric. You should try it on."

The redheaded woman shrugged, "I don't know."

Lyric hung the blouse back on the rack. She headed toward the exit of the store.

"Let's try another store."

"Lyric Daisy Sinclair, what's up with you? We have been to every store in this mall. You walk in, pick up a couple of items, put them back, and then want to go to another store. Seriously, girl. What's going on?"

The redheaded woman stared out into the mall. She spotted the food court which was a smorgasbord of delicacies.

"Okay, Harper. Let's get something to eat. Then we can talk."

Lyric led the way to the food court eager to stall the conversation that she had been dreading all day. She grabbed a red plastic tray before stepping up to one of the vendors. Though the fashionista was usually focused on healthy choices, Lyric found herself craving different foods than normal.

The two women sat down at a metal table with plastic chairs examining their trays with interest. Lyric was amused to see that Harper had also avoided the healthy foods on this trip.

"Today's theme is deep, fat, and fried."

The duo giggled as they attacked the corn dogs, pizza, pretzels, and fries that waited on their trays. Lyric munched thinking about the dinner that Aiden had cooked for her on their trip. She could almost taste the savory roasted salmon and the rustic golden potatoes. The thought of the heavenly buttered green beans brought a smile to her face.

"Okay, Lyric. What's the smile? I know that you aren't enjoying that corn dog that much."

Lyric snorted, "I don't know. This is an exquisite corn dog."

Harper rolled her eyes.

"Okay, Harper. I was just thinking about my trip."

The other woman squealed, "Yes. Tell me all about your adventures."

Harper Raines sipped her cola as she waited for Lyric to speak about her trip.

"Well, we went to several different places. We went to a farm in southern New York where I milked a cow and rode a horse."

Harper covered her closed mouth attempting to keep the soda from bursting out. She swallowed quickly wincing at the burning that came to her nose.

"You're kidding me? You milked a cow?"

The other woman scowled, "I'm not that sophisticated, Harper. Do you want to hear this or what?"

"Of course. Where did you go after the farm?"

"We went to an amusement park in Pennsylvania where we drove bumper cars and played paintball though I wasn't good at either of them. Then we went on a roller coaster. Aiden hates heights so he was terrified at going on The Widow-Maker. You should have seen his face when we got off. He was so sick. He threw up in a trashcan."

Harper cocked her head in interest as Lyric's face lit up at the mention of the man's name.

"Sounds like fun. What happened next?"

The other woman giggled, "Oh, we went to a circus in West Virginia. The owner, Lady Beatrix, let me bathe an elephant and hold a monkey. It was so magical, but then this great brute named Lynx tried to attack me."

Harper gasped, "What?"

"It's okay, Harper. Aiden stopped him. He fought that giant and almost died. The circus workers helped us. I had to use the first aid kit to clean up Aiden's face. He was pretty beat up, but I don't know what would have happened if he hadn't come to my rescue."

Lyric's excitement shone through her voice and face as she recounted the fight. Harper set her fork down wanting to hear more about the adventures that her friend had endured. *I'm glad Aiden was there. It sounds like he kept up his bargain as bodyguard.*

"Then we went to Florida where we swam with dolphins and flew over the ocean in a hot air balloon. It was amazing."

Harper smiled, "Neat! What else?"

Lyric took a bite of her pizza chewing and swallowing before continuing her story.

"We went to Tennessee to stay in a log cabin in the woods. Aiden cooked an impressive dinner of roasted salmon, golden potatoes, and buttered green beans. It was so delicious!"

The other woman raised an eyebrow in surprise. She found it interesting that the man had cooked a meal for her friend. *He made a romantic dinner for her.*

"What did you do in Tennessee?"

"We went river rafting."

Harper choked on a fry. She gulped down some of her soda relieving the scratch in her throat.

"That's dangerous, isn't it?"

Lyric stared down at her tray. An uneasy feeling filled the other woman.

"Lyric?"

Her friend blurted out, "I fell into the river and almost drowned. Okay? Our guide had to pull me out and Aiden gave me CPR. I am alive because of them."

Harper swallowed hard at the near tragic news. She cleared her throat trying to choose her words carefully.

"Is that why you came home?"

Lyric snorted, "No. I rested for the night and then went ziplining. I wasn't going to let anything stop me from fulfilling my bucket list. Not even Aiden. He tried to talk me out of it, but I wouldn't listen. You know me."

Harper nodded without a word.

"I soared through the air feeling so free. Then Aiden overcame his fear of heights and ziplined too. It was on that part of the trip that I accepted the truth."

"What truth?"

Lyric grew silent. She ate a few bites from her meal before glancing around to watch the other shoppers.

"Come on, Lyric. Tell me."

The redheaded woman blurted, "That I love Aiden."

Excitement filled Harper at the announcement.

"Really? That's great!"

Lyric snorted, "Oh, yeah. Real great."

"What happened next?"

"We went to Missouri for a cavern tour. Aiden wanted to sneak away from the perky guide, so we went off track. There was an earthquake and I fell off a rock bridge into a pool of water below."

Harper's heart tightened at the news.

"And?"

"There was another quake and rocks trapped me in the water. Aiden came to help me. We ended up at the hospital. It doesn't matter anyway. In the cavern, I told Aiden that I loved him, and he said that he loved me."

The other woman cocked her head in confusion.

"Isn't that good?"

Lyric rolled her eyes.

"It would be if he really meant it. He only said it because he pitied me. I had just told him about my brain tumor."

Harper frowned, "How do you know that he said it out of pity? Maybe he really loves you."

The other woman pushed her tray of food away with a sigh.

"No, Harper. I know that he doesn't love me."

Lyric Sinclair raised a hand to stop the protest she knew that her stubborn friend was about to share.

"It doesn't matter anyway. I can't be with Aiden even if he does love me. How can I be with him when I may not be here much longer? Even if I live, what kind of life would it be with me on chemo and radiation? I can't do that to Aiden. I love him too much."

Silence fell over the two women as the seriousness of Lyric's condition came to the surface of their conversation. The hustle and bustle of the mall continued around them.

Harper cleared her throat drawing Lyric's attention back to her friend.

"Have you talked to Dr. Nash?"

The ill woman sighed, "Yes. I called him after I talked to you. He wants to do a needle biopsy tomorrow at the hospital."

Harper gasped, "That soon. What time? I'll cancel my appointments."

Lyric shook her head with a determined expression on her face.

"No, Harper. I'm going alone. There's no need to argue. You keep your day busy and let me focus on the biopsy."

"Okay, Lyric. I'll try, but you need to have Dr. Nash call me with an update if you can't call me yourself." *Hopefully, it will be good news.*

CHAPTER 21

HASTY DECISIONS

Aiden Wilder scratched down mileage and location information for the work log. His mind raced with the adventures that he had endured with Lyric. The man cringed at the thought of the woman that he loved who had rejected him. He stared at the paper as the image of Lyric's pale white face speckled with freckles came to mind. Aiden saw her curly strawberry blond hair surrounding the lovely face.

Suddenly, something hard slammed into the back of the man's head. He yelped in surprise and pain before turning to glare at Desmond. His brother had his arms crossed and a smirk on his face.

"Why'd you do that?"

Desmond chuckled, "Well, I called your name five times with no results. I had no choice, but to whop you. What's on your mind, Aid?"

Aiden shrugged, "Nothing."

"Clearly. Come on, bro. Tell your favorite brother what is bothering you."

The other man snorted, "You're my only brother, Des."

Desmond pulled up a chair straddling it. He stared at his twin with a serious expression on his face.

Aiden turned his chair to fully face his brother. He swallowed hard dreading the lecture that his all-knowing twin would give about not being careful with his emotions.

"I was thinking about Lyric."

Desmond raised an eyebrow.

"Why? The job is over. You don't have to think about that ice queen anymore. You are free."

Aiden's temper flared.

"She's not an ice queen. You don't know the real Lyric, Desmond. She is beautiful and adventurous. Yes, she is stubborn and opinionated, but she is also intelligent with a nice sense of humor. Lyric is more than she appears on the surface."

Desmond Wilder stared at Aiden in shock as his twin brother fiercely snapped at him about Lyric Sinclair. He leaned back from his chair as realization flooded over him. *He's in love with her.*

"Whoa."

Aiden glared at him.

"What?"

Desmond frowned, "You love her."

The power of the statement caused silence to fill the office. The two men froze in their seats. Aiden stared down at the floor. Desmond waited as patiently as he could.

Suddenly, Aiden whispered, "Yes. I love her."

The other brother leaned forward eager to hear the details.

"And?"

"And she doesn't love me."

Disappointment filled Desmond. He knew that the rejection had to hurt his brother's trusting heart. The man wanted to lecture Aiden about not maintaining his distance from the snobby woman. However, he knew that it would be cruel to show his brother the mistakes that he had made while his heart was broken. *I need to be considerate.*

"How do you know that she doesn't love you?"

Aiden shrugged, "I just know."

Desmond rolled his eyes.

"That's not an answer, Aiden. How do you know? Did she say that she doesn't love you?"

The other man sighed, "She said that she loved me, but she didn't mean it."

Desmond cocked his head in confusion.

"What do you mean?"

Aiden stood up with a huff. He began pacing back and forth across the office carpet.

"We were stuck in a cavern alone and she was hurt. It wasn't certain that we would make it out alive. She told me that she was dying with a brain tumor and that this journey was her bucket list. Then she said that she loved me."

Desmond asked, "And what did you say?"

"I said that I love her too. Then we were rescued, and she wanted to go home. She started treating me like an employee again. Trust me, Des. Lyric Sinclair does not love anyone let alone me."

The two men returned to their silence for several moments. Desmond thought about all that his brother said. He wondered why Lyric would return to acting like a snob after professing her love. Only one reason came to mind.

"Aid, she loves you."

Aiden scowled, "What? How do you know?"

"You said that she started treating you like an employee after you were safe again? Well, she probably thought about what happened in the cavern and wondered if you really loved her. Maybe she was waiting for you to show that you really loved her. It is the only thing that makes sense. Trust me, Aiden. Lyric Sinclair loves you."

Aiden Wilder stopped pacing at his brother's words. He held his breath as his mind reeled at the possibility. The man wondered if Lyric was waiting for him to make the next move. *It could be true. Lyric may have thought that I changed my mind or didn't mean it to begin with.*

Aiden spun toward the office desk hurrying over to pick up the keys to the rental SUV.

"Where are you going, Aiden?"

The man headed for the door with his heart racing in excitement and anxiety.

"I'm going to tell Lyric that I love her."

A smile came to Aiden's face as he heard his brother whoop with joy. He jogged out of the building before moving toward the green vehicle. *I will march up to her apartment, ring the bell, and tell her how I feel. Then the rest will be up to her.*

Lyric Sinclair wrung her hands nervously as she waited in the waiting room outside the surgical area. She had filled out the paperwork and completed the blood tests. Now, the woman was trying to remain patient for the nurse to call her back to be prepped. *It will be over soon. Then I can make some decisions.*

Aiden Wilder took a deep breath as he raised his finger toward the doorbell of Lyric Sinclair's apartment. He had practiced what he would say the whole drive through the city. The man's heart raced in apprehension as he touched the doorbell hearing the sound ring out inside the apartment.

Aiden held his breath as he heard movement approaching the door. *Okay, Aid. You can do this. Just tell her how you feel.*

Suddenly, the white door swung open. The man released the breath in disappointment as he saw the woman standing in the doorway.

"Aiden? What are you doing here?"

Aiden frowned, "Harper, I need to talk to Lyric."

The fashionable woman crossed her arms.

"About?"

The man sighed, "Is she here?"

Harper shrugged, "Depends on what you want."

Aiden bit his lip as irritation grew inside him. He wished that the protective friend wasn't at the apartment to provide a barrier between him and the woman that he loved.

"Look, Harper. I am here to tell Lyric the truth."

The woman raised her eyebrows.

"What truth?"

Aiden growled under his breath. He didn't want to tell Lyric's best friend about his feelings before he told Lyric herself. The man lowered his voice.

"That I love her."

Harper Raines stared at Aiden as the man professed his love for her best friend. She had been cleaning Lyric's apartment so that it would be ready for her when she returned the next day from her stay at the hospital. The woman had answered the door disgruntled that the man who had rejected her friend had the nerve to come to bother her. She was delighted by the discomfort that shone on Aiden's face at her resistance.

Harper swallowed hard as her ugly feelings for the man melted away. A smile grew on her face at the truth that Aiden indeed loved Lyric. She knew that the man would be thrilled to hear that the redheaded woman loved him as well. *It's not my place to tell him.*

"Well? Will you let me talk to Lyric?"

Harper replied, "I would if she was here. She's at the hospital getting a biopsy of her tumor."

Aiden frowned, "What? When?"

"The surgery is scheduled for noon."

The woman's eyes widened in shock as Aiden turned on his heel running down the hallway toward the elevator.

"Where are you going?"

Without turning around, the man pushed the button alerting the elevator to return to the eighteenth floor.

"To find Lyric."

Harper leaned against the doorframe blinking away tears that were threatening to fall at the sweet moment. She hoped that Lyric would be bold and return the feelings to Aiden. *Lord, please help her to open her heart even if it will be for a short time.*

The woman shut the door returning to the housework and organization that was her gift for her ill friend. She moved Lyric's cell phone from the table before wiping it with a cloth. Her friend had decided to leave the phone behind since no one was allowed to go to the hospital with her.

Harper thought about Lyric's bucket list. Curiosity filled her at what her friend had accomplished on her journey. She knew what Lyric had told her, but the woman wondered if the list had been finished.

Tapping around on the phone screen, Harper found the bucket list. She smiled at the things that had been marked off. Her eyes fell on one item that was untouched. She smiled warmly at the final task on Lyric's list. *This one might still happen.*

CHAPTER 22

UNCERTAIN HEARTS

Lyric Sinclair adjusted her hospital gown self-consciously as she waited for Dr. Nash to come with the final instructions before the biopsy procedure. She wished that she had her cell phone so that she could check her email or search the Internet. However, the woman had left her phone in her apartment, so she wouldn't have to keep up with it at the hospital.

Lyric took a deep breath trying to calm her nerves. She closed her eyes and pictured the adventures that she had experienced while attempting to fulfill her bucket list. The woman smiled as she thought about the magic of Lady Beatrix's circus. She imagined the fun of bathing Kavi and playing with Misha. A frown replaced the grin as she saw Lynx towering above her. Lyric could see Aiden rushing to her rescue putting his own life in danger.

Suddenly, the woman opened her eyes shaking her head.

"Stop it. You have to forget about him."

Lyric glanced at the clock on the wall. She groaned in impatience as she saw that it had only been a few minutes since she last checked. The woman reflected on her journey again. She thought about the beautiful log cabin hidden in the deep woods. Her heart soared at the lovely bedroom and the fireplace living room area. Lyric recalled walking down the stairs to find that Aiden had cooked her an impressive meal. *It was so romantic.*

"But he doesn't love me. Quit thinking about him."

Lyric swiped the strawberry blond curls out of her face in exasperation. She stared up at the ceiling wishing that Dr. Nash would come in to distract her from her thoughts. The woman reminisced about being trapped in the cavern. She remembered the fear as her head splashed under the water when she was too weak to stay afloat. *Then Aiden came. He held onto me for hours whispering comforting words that gave me hope in that hopeless situation. Aiden was desperate to save me. Why? Because he loves me.*

Lyric snarled at the thoughts. She threw her hands up into the air.

"Aiden does not love me. He's gone. Move on."

Suddenly, a knock came to the wooden hospital room door. Lyric took a deep breath as it swung open. *Here we go.*

Aiden Wilder tapped his hand on the steering wheel of the hunter green SUV. His impatience was growing by the second as he remained trapped in a sea of cars. The man couldn't believe how much traffic was congesting the city streets. He bit his lip in frustration restraining from smashing his hand into the horn.

"Come on. Come on!"

Aiden smirked as the cars in front of him began to inch forward. His pleasure melted in the next instant when he found himself at a stand-still again. The man's heart thumped in apprehension as he wondered if he would ever make it to the hospital. *I must talk to Lyric before she goes into surgery.*

Aiden groaned as the mass of traffic seemed to be closing in. He sighed before praying for help. *Lord, I need to talk to Lyric. Please help me get to her in time.*

Suddenly, the man saw a parking spot on the right of his car. His eyes widened as an idea came to mind. Aiden pulled the SUV into the spot before turning the key in the ignition. He glanced out the window. The man climbed out of the vehicle moving around it to the sidewalk. He clicked the locking button on the key before racing down the street in the direction of the hospital. *I'm going to make it in time. I'm going to tell Lyric that I love her.*

Lyric Sinclair smiled weakly as Dr. Nash entered the room with a clipboard.

"How are you feeling, Miss Sinclair?"

The woman swallowed hard.

"A little nervous actually."

The doctor nodded, "I understand. Let me explain how this is going to work."

The anxious woman gestured for the man to continue.

"Lyric!"

Both adults snapped their gazes toward the closed door. Lyric shook her head certain that she had heard wrong. *Someone shouted something else.*

"Lyric!"

The woman held a hand up to her heart in surprise as she recognized the male voice. She bit her lip sure that it was just wishful thinking. However, Dr. Nash was now looking at her with raised eyebrows.

"Should I see who that is?"

Lyric nodded, "Yes please." *I know who it is.*

The doctor opened the door as a nurse hurried past.

"Sir, please. This is a hospital. You can't be screaming."

"I don't care. Lyric!"

With a giggle, Lyric yelled, "Aiden!"

In the next moment, a familiar man was standing in the doorway panting out of breath. *It is him, but why is he here?*

Dr. Nash stepped toward the doorway.

"I will give you two a few minutes."

Lyric thanked him though her eyes were still on Aiden. The man's hair was disheveled. His shirt had sweat stains on the armpits and collar. *What in the world?*

"Aiden, what are you doing here?"

Aiden Wilder stared at Lyric who sat on an exam table clothed in a blue hospital gown. He smirked knowing that the fashionable woman had to be so shocked by his visit that she had forgotten her informal appearance. *It doesn't matter. She looks beautiful.*

"Aiden, what are you doing here?"

Aiden swallowed hard fearing the rejection that was still possible. He entered the room fully before closing the door. The man approached the redheaded woman who was watching him warily.

"I wanted to tell you something."

Lyric snorted, "It must be pretty important for you to rush here like this. You're lucky that security isn't here to kick you out."

Aiden chuckled, "They still might. I should say this quick then."

"What is it?"

The man took a deep breath. He reached out taking Lyric's cold hands into his own. Aiden could tell that he had surprised the woman again.

"Lyric, I love you."

Lyric Sinclair stared down at Aiden's sweaty hands which were holding her own dry ones. She would have been grossed out, but the shock took her focus.

"Lyric, I love you."

Tears swam in the woman's eyes as her brain processed what Aiden was saying. She blinked the tears away trying to stay firm. Lyric didn't want to believe that what the man said was true. *I don't have time for this. I need to focus on my health.*

"You don't mean that, Aiden."

Aiden squeezed her hands tenderly.

"Yes, I do. I love you, Lyric, with all my heart. I have loved you on our journey and I will love you even if you don't love me."

Lyric sniffed as she glanced away from the man. She swallowed hard trying to control her emotions. *I must be strong. Sweet words can't sway me.*

"I'm probably dying, Aiden."

Silence was the response. Lyric accepted that her words had changed the man's mind. *Good. He won't be tied down to me while I suffer. He will be free to enjoy his life.*

In the next moment, the woman found her hands released. She waited for the sound of the hospital room door opening and then closing. *It's for the best.*

Suddenly, a warm hand touched her chin pulling her face back to the front. Lyric held her breath as her eyes were focused on the man once more.

"Lyric, loving you for even a minute will be more than I deserve."

The touched woman released the breath as the tears threatened to fall again. She wanted to argue with the man telling him that he didn't understand what he was doing. Lyric wished to reject him out of fear and uncertainty. However, she held her mouth shut tightly as a thought came to mind. *You'll never live if you don't take a leap of faith.*

Aiden Wilder waited for a response from Lyric. Time seemed to slow down as the woman struggled with what to say to him. *I knew it. She doesn't love me. I've made a fool of myself.*

The distraught man dropped his hand from Lyric's face before turning to leave the hospital room. His heart ached at the rejection. He didn't know how he would be able to move on.

"I love you too, Aiden."

Aiden spun around in shock wondering if he had heard right.

"What?"

Lyric smiled warmly, "I love you."

The man's heart soared at the words. He rushed forward before wrapping his arms around the woman's waist in an embrace. With a giggle, Lyric's arms went around his neck.

Aiden leaned back keeping his arms around the woman that he loved. A smile flicked around Lyric's lips. The man moved forward at her slight nod.

The couple shared their first kiss knowing that it would not be their last one. *Thank You, Lord!*

Lyric Sinclair's heart swooned as her lips touched Aiden's in their first kiss. She closed her eyes feeling excitement zoom through her body. The woman could feel that she had made the right decision. *We will get through this together.*

Suddenly, a knock at the door alerted the couple that Dr. Nash was returning. Aiden moved back from Lyric before stepping to stand beside her. The door opened to reveal the doctor who was still holding the clipboard.

"May I come in now?"

Lyric nodded with a smile, "Yes, Dr. Nash. This is Aiden. He is my…"

The woman blushed as she glanced over at Aiden who was beaming back at her. She snapped her eyes back to the doctor.

"He's my boyfriend."

Dr. Nash smiled, "It's nice to meet you. I was going to talk to Miss Sinclair about what to expect during the procedure. Will you be staying to hear as well?"

Lyric bit her lip hoping that Aiden would stay with her providing comfort and support.

"Yes. If Lyric wants me to stay."

The woman nodded, "Yes. I want Aiden to stay." *Forever.*

Aiden Wilder listened carefully as Dr. Nash began to explain the process of the biopsy that Lyric was about to go through. He wanted to be as informed as possible about her condition.

"This is a needle biopsy. A tiny hole will be drilled into your skull before a small needle is placed into your brain. The biopsy will be obtained. The incision will be sutured. Then you will be taken into the recovery room. If you are doing well in 24 hours, you will be discharged."

Aiden noticed that Lyric had tensed. He placed a gentle arm around her shoulders hoping to provide her with some comfort. The man was pleased when the woman flashed a reassuring smile in his direction. She released the breath that she had been holding.

Lyric asked, "Then what?"

Dr. Nash explained, "The biopsy will tell us whether your tumor is benign or malignant."

Aiden swallowed hard as he tried to remember everything that he had seen during medical shows on television.

"And we want benign, right?"

Turning toward the man, the doctor smiled, "Yes. Based on the results, we can proceed with proper treatment. Any other questions?"

Lyric replied, "How long will the biopsy take?"

"About fifteen minutes. Then you will be in recovery."

Aiden was surprised as the woman turned to look at him.

"Are you going back to work?"

The man flinched at the question. He shook his head making a decision.

"No. I'm going to be in the waiting room. I'll be with you when you wake up."

Lyric's smile grew at the words.

"Sounds good."

Harper Raines paced back and forth seeking other things that she could do to make Lyric's life easier when she came home.

"We've scrubbed and organized everything, Baby. Why don't you relax?"

The young woman turned to face her grandmother who was sitting at the table with her hands folded.

"I can't, Grammy. I want everything to be perfect when Lyric comes home tomorrow."

Grammy shook her head.

"Overcleaning this apartment won't take the worry away that you are feeling right now, Harp, but you know what will."

Harper opened her mouth to argue that she didn't know what to do to lessen her worry. She snapped it shut as the answer popped into her mind. *Yes, I do.*

The young woman walked over plopping down into a chair at the table.

"Will you pray with me, Grammy?"

The grandmother beamed, "Yes, but you know that you can pray by yourself too."

Harper shook her head.

"I'm not like you, Grammy. I wish I was."

Odessa "Birdie" Raines sucked in her breath wondering if her granddaughter was ready to make a decision.

"Child, you have the same opportunities at becoming a prayer warrior as me. All you have to do is trust the Lord."

Harper opened her mouth no doubt to protest.

"Let me ask you a question, Harp."

The younger woman gestured for her to continue.

Birdie asked, "Do you believe in Jesus?"

The shock on Harper's face was clear.

"What?"

"Do you believe in Jesus? It is a yes or no question. Which is it?"

Her granddaughter shrugged, "Sure."

Birdie shook her head knowing that she was not getting a real answer from Harper.

"What do you believe about Jesus?"

The young woman stared at the table.

"I believe what the Bible says about Him. You know. The stuff that I learned at Christmas and Easter."

Birdie nodded realizing that it was at least something. She thought about her own beliefs in Jesus.

"There is so much more to Jesus than that, Harp. He is the Son of God. He came into the world which we celebrate at Christmas.

Jesus taught people and did miraculous things, but that wasn't the real reason He came. He came to die for us."

Harper looked up at her grandmother.

"I've heard that before, but what does that mean?"

Birdie reached into her purse pulling out her Bible. She was glad that she always brought it with her. The elderly woman thumbed through the worn pages seeking out the information that she needed to help her granddaughter understand the truth of Jesus.

"Romans 3:23 says that all have sinned and fallen short of the glory of God. That means that we have all messed up. We have done things that are against God like lying, disobeying, saying cruel things, and having evil thoughts. Since God is holy, only holy people can be with Him. Our sin makes us filthy, so we can't be with God in heaven."

Birdie smiled as she saw that Harper seemed to be listening to her. The thoughtful expression on the younger woman's face pleased the grandmother. *Please help her to understand, Lord.*

Birdie turned a couple of pages in her Bible.

"Romans 6:23 says that the wages for sin is death, but the gift of God is eternal life through Jesus Christ our Lord. We deserve to die and spend eternity in hell because of our sins. However, God sent Jesus to save us. He did that by dying on the cross like you have learned at Easter."

The elderly woman shut her Bible knowing that she would not need it for the next Scripture.

"John 3:16 says for God so loved the world that He gave His one and only Son that whoever believes in Him, shall not perish, but have eternal life. We have to believe in Jesus and accept Him as our Savior and Lord. That is how we accept this free gift. Then we live a life obeying Him and following His plan." *Now it is up to her.*

Harper Raines listened to Grammy as the older woman quoted Scripture from the Bible and explained it in a way that she had never understood in the past. She stared at the table feeling like all that she had heard about Jesus was true. The young woman assumed what her grandmother was hoping would happen. However, she didn't know if she was ready to decide.

"I will think about it more, Grammy."

The older woman nodded with a smile, "And I will be praying for you, but let's pray for Lyric now." *Yes. Let's pray for Lyric.*

CHAPTER 23

HARSH NEWS

Aiden Wilder thumbed aimlessly through a magazine in the hospital waiting room. He didn't absorb any of the information as he waited to hear how the biopsy had gone. The worried man knew that it was silly to be so impatient for a fifteen-minute procedure. However, he wondered if the process would be as simple and safe as Dr. Nash had said. *Anything can happen when dealing with the brain.*

Aiden dropped the closed magazine onto the waiting room table with a sigh. He leaned back watching the hustle and bustle of the people going about their medical business. The man longed to see Dr. Nash coming to inform him of Lyric's condition. *I just need to know.*

Movement from the side hallway drew Aiden's attention. He held his breath as he saw Dr. Nash marching toward him. The man stood up hoping for good news.

Dr. Nash smiled, "She's fine. The biopsy went well. You can see her in about an hour."

Aiden shook the doctor's hand.

"Thank you so much." *She's okay. Now, we just have to wait for the results.*

Lyric Sinclair squeezed her eyes tightly as light pierced into them. She squinted trying to adjust to the brightness. The woman blinked several times before opening her eyes completely. White walls and a tan curtain came into view.

"Welcome back to the land of the living."

The soft comical voice brought a smile to Lyric's face. She turned her head slowly toward Aiden who was sitting in a chair beside her.

"Hi. It's good to be back."

Aiden reached out taking her hand into his own. His warm smile caused her to blush.

"Dr. Nash said that you did fine. I guess now we wait for the results."

Lyric frowned, "That will be hard. I hate waiting for anything."

The man chuckled, "Don't I know it."

"You're not the most patient person either, Mr. Wilder."

Aiden nodded in agreement which pleased Lyric. He squeezed her hand tenderly.

"True. It was like an eternity waiting for your fifteen-minute procedure to end, but I'm glad that you're okay."

Lyric rubbed a thumb over Aiden's hand feeling blessed to have him here with her.

"I hate to leave, but I have to get back to work. Desmond is chomping at the bit. Will you be okay?"

The woman nodded, "Of course. I'm Miss Independence. I'll probably just sleep anyway."

Aiden stood up releasing her hand.

"I would like to take you home tomorrow."

Lyric smiled, "I'd like that."

The woman swooned as the man leaned over to kiss her goodbye. She hoped that her breath wasn't too bad. However, the worry faded at the passion behind the kiss. *Love doesn't worry about bad breath.*

Lyric tried to suppress a giggle at the thought. She didn't want to make Aiden think that it was the kiss that had caused the laugh.

"See you tomorrow, Lyric."

"Bye, Aiden." *I can't wait.*

Harper Raines moved the flower vase an inch to the left attempting to center it on Lyric's coffee table. She had adjusted the vase several times already as she waited anxiously for Aiden to bring Lyric home. The man had called her with an update about Lyric's biopsy and their new relationship. Harper was thrilled with both pieces of news. *I can tell that You are at work, Lord, and I am grateful.*

Suddenly, the doorbell rang. The young woman suppressed a squeal as she raced excitedly to the door. She swung it open eager to see her best friend. Harper's smile faded at the sight of Lyric who looked pale and weak.

"Lyric, are you okay?"

The other woman smirked, "Sure. Haven't you ever seen a girl without make-up before?"

Harper's smile returned at the teasing tone of her friend.

"Yes, but not you. You look rough."

The two women hugged with laughter resounding through the apartment. Harper led Lyric into the living room anticipating her reaction to the work that she had accomplished.

"Oh, Harper. What have you done?"

"Do you like it?"

The tired woman nodded, "Yes. It looks so clean and organized."

Harper shrugged, "Just like you like it. I thought that you might be too pooped to clean when you came home and we all know that you can't stand a mess."

"That's the truth."

Both women turned to face Aiden who was entering the apartment carrying Lyric's blue overnight bag.

Harper smirked, "Careful, Aiden. You don't want to get on the bad side of this girl."

The man chuckled, "Been there done that. No need to repeat that unpleasant experience."

Lyric opened her mouth in protest.

"I didn't realize that a patient has to endure abuse from her loved ones."

Harper placed a comforting arm around her shoulder.

"Oh, Lyric. That's what loved ones are for. Which reminds me. Welcome to the crew, Aiden."

Aiden beamed, "Thanks. Happy to be here."

The look that was shared between the man and woman caused Harper to remove her hand quickly.

"Well, I have to be going. Call me if you need anything. Oh. Grammy insisted on baking you a chocolate cake as a welcome home present. Save me a slice. Bye, Aiden."

Harper hurried out the door eager to leave the two lovebirds alone. She sighed as she entered the elevator. *I wish I had someone like Aiden.*

Aiden Wilder secured the apartment door after Harper left in a rush. He shook his head in bewilderment before turning back to Lyric. The redheaded woman looked exhausted. *Of course, she is tired. No one can sleep well in a hospital.*

"Why don't you get settled in and rest? I can get started on cooking some dinner."

Lyric raised an eyebrow in surprise.

"That sounds nice, but I don't think you will find much in the refrigerator."

Aiden smirked, "No salmon?"

The woman giggled, "Not in my fridge."

"I'll manage."

The man handed Lyric her blue overnight bag before strolling into the kitchen to see what he could come up with for their dinner. He opened the refrigerator expecting empty shelves and outdated milk. However, the scene before him was the complete opposite.

"Wow!"

"What?"

Aiden turned toward Lyric who was entering the kitchen.

"I think Harper hooked you up."

The man watched as the woman investigated the refrigerator. He was amused to see her emerald eyes widen as she beheld the cornucopia of food that was stuffed inside the appliance.

"That Harper. She is so sweet."

Aiden nodded in agreement, "She sure is. I guess I will have a lot of choices for dinner now. Go and rest, Lyric. I will let you know when it is ready."

Lyric patted his arm tenderly before heading for her bedroom. The man watched her leave feeling blessed to be in a relationship with her. He turned back to the refrigerator with his mind racing at all the possibilities for dinner. *She deserves something special.*

Lyric Sinclair yawn as she woke up from her nap. Her body seemed to have rejuvenated during her rest. She climbed out of bed before moving to her closet to find something fresh to wear.

Suddenly, Lyric froze. Her heart began to race as she remembered that Aiden was in her apartment. The woman swallowed hard. She scanned her clothes trying to find something that wouldn't make her look frumpy. Her eyes fell on the turquoise blouse that she had bought with Harper in their childhood mall. *Perfect.*

The fashionista instantly started to match pants, socks, and shoes to the shirt. She dressed in her outfit checking her appearance in her vanity mirror.

Once satisfied, Lyric brushed her strawberry blonde hair with her silver hairbrush. She grabbed a tube of light peach lipstick swiping it across her lips like an expert. The woman lightly brushed peaches and cream eyeshadow over her eyelids. She smiled at the elegant look that the make-up gave her pale face.

Lyric took several deep breaths before exiting her bedroom. A multitude of aromas wafted into her nose as she entered the open kitchen area. The woman held back a squeal as she saw that the kitchen island had been set with two candlesticks in between two plates. Cloth napkins and real silverware instead of her usual quick plastic utensils were stationed next to the plates. Two tall glasses sat waiting at the top of the dishes. *So lovely.*

"You're just in time. I was about to check on you."

Lyric turned her attention from the beautiful place setting to the chef. Aiden was stirring a pot on the stove. He smiled over at her. The woman returned the smile.

"What have you prepared today, Monsieur Chef?"

The man chuckled for a moment before becoming serious. He spoke with a French accent as he answered her question.

"Today, Madame, we have Creamy Tuscan Garlic Chicken served over linguine noodles. The sauce contains sun dried tomatoes and spinach to give it a fresh taste that is worthy of the finest diners."

Lyric giggled at Aiden's silliness though she had to admit that his dinner sounded delicious. She sat down on a stool at the island while the man took her plate to the cooking area to place her dinner on it. The woman's eyes widened at the elegant display that Aiden had made on her plate as he set it in front of her.

"Wow. Okay, Aiden. You have to tell me where you learned to cook so fancy."

Aiden took his own plate to the stove without a word. He worked on perfecting his dinner before returning to the island.

"So, you don't think that a driver and bodyguard can cook?"

Lyric winced afraid that she had offended the man. However, she relaxed at the wink that Aiden threw in her direction.

"It's not that. It's just that it takes training to cook such complex dishes and then present them so professionally."

Aiden poured iced tea into the drinking glasses before sitting down to their dinner.

"I went to a culinary arts institute."

Lyric's eyes widened at the statement.

"Really? Why aren't you an executive chef somewhere?"

Aiden Wilder cringed at the question knowing that his heart longed to be using his culinary talent to good use. He picked up his knife and fork. The man cut a piece from his chicken thinking about what he wanted to tell Lyric. *She loves me. I can tell her anything.*

"After I graduated, my parents died. Desmond needed help in the family business, so I put my dreams on hold to help him keep his head above water."

Lyric worked on cutting her own chicken. Her face was solemn. Aiden wondered what she was thinking.

"I understand. When my father became ill, I set aside my fashion career to spend time with him. It was hard to start up again after he died. Harper was a great help though."

Aiden took a bite of his dinner feeling satisfied by the creamy sauce that brought the whole meal together. He was glad that Lyric understood him though it made him sad that it was because she had experienced loss as well.

"Do you ever think about restarting your culinary career?"

The man shrugged, "I don't know. Des still needs me."

Lyric nodded as she took a bite. She closed her eyes with a sweet smile on her face.

"This is delicious. I think I like it even more than that heavenly roasted salmon."

Aiden tried to remain humble though inside he was pleased that she liked his food. *Who would have ever thought that I would value her opinion?*

The couple ate their special meal speaking about a variety of subjects getting to know each other. Aiden felt like he could talk to Lyric forever. However, as they finished their dinner along with a piece of Grammy's chocolate cake, the man knew that their night would have to end eventually. He washed the dishes while Lyric scrolled through her television guide seeking something to watch. Finally, with the kitchen clean and the woman content, Aiden headed into the living room.

"I need to head home now so that you can rest."

Lyric Sinclair flipped through the television channels hoping to find something interesting to watch.

"I need to head home now so that you can rest."

Disappointment filled the woman as she stood up from the couch.

"Are you sure? We could watch T.V. together."

Aiden shook his head.

"Maybe another night. You need your peace and quiet now."

Lyric nodded, "I guess you're right. Well, thanks for our first date."

The man stepped toward her with a smile.

"My pleasure. I have to keep you well-fed."

Lyric's heart thumped as Aiden leaned down kissing her. She winced at the garlic breath of the man. The couple moved back with wrinkled noses.

"Whew. Sorry. Maybe garlic wasn't the best idea for our first date."

Lyric giggled, "You'll know next time, Chef Aiden."

"Yes. I will be more careful."

As the man left her apartment, the woman closed the door with a sigh. She was amazed at how sorrowful she suddenly felt. Lyric opened the door desperately.

"Aiden!"

Aiden turned back from where he stood down the hallway.

"What?"

Lyric swallowed hard.

"Will you come back tomorrow?"

A warm smile replaced the worried frown on the man's face.

"Of course. See you tomorrow."

The woman released the breath that she had been holding.

"See you tomorrow."

Odessa "Birdie" Raines hummed to herself as she worked on crocheting a blanket. She had been sitting in Harper's living room listening to the news while working on her special project. The elderly woman hadn't heard from Harper all evening though it didn't worry her since her granddaughter was constantly busy working on the fashion designs for the business that she and Lyric had made for themselves. *So successful.*

Suddenly, Harper's bedroom door swung open. The young woman came out of the room entering the living room. She plopped down on the sofa before focusing her attention on her grandmother.

Birdie continued working though she kept her gaze directed toward Harper. She could tell that something was wrong by the expression on the girl's face.

"Something you want to talk about, Baby?"

Harper shrugged, "I don't know. I know what I need to do, but I don't know if I can."

Birdie frowned in confusion, "What do you need to do, Harp?"

A variety of ideas came to the older woman's mind, but nothing could have prepared her for what her granddaughter said.

"I need to ask Jesus to be my Savior and Lord, but I'm not sure the right way."

Excitement soared through the elderly woman who had prayed for her grandchild her whole life. She wished that she had the energy and ability to do a cartwheel across the living room floor.

Birdie explained, "That's wonderful, honey, but there isn't a right way. You just talk to Jesus and let Him do the work. You tell Him that you know that you have sinned and that you need Him to save you. Speak from your heart, Baby."

Harper Raines couldn't believe what her grandmother was telling her. She was certain that there had to be a formal way to ask Jesus into her life. However, the woman knew that Grammy was an expert in the Bible. *If she says it is that easy, then it must be.*

"You can pray silently if you want, Harp. God can hear you."

Harper thought about it. She realized that she needed to do this aloud in the presence of Grammy for the support and encouragement. The woman knew that it wasn't to show off or prove anything to her grandmother.

With a sigh, Harper bowed her head folding her hands so that her fingers were intertwined like she had seen Grammy do so often. She closed her eyes with her mind racing.

"Lord, I don't really know what to say, but I am going to speak from my heart like Grammy said. I understand that I am a sinner. I have done things that I am not proud of. Things that I know are not pleasing to You. I know that I deserve to die and spend forever in hell because of my own choices."

Grammy whispered, "Yes, Lord. We deserve it."

Harper took a deep breath. She squeezed her eyes tighter before continuing.

"Lord, I believe that You sent Jesus for me. I believe that He died for my sins so that I can be with You. I want to be with You, Lord. Please save me. I can't save myself. I need You and I love You."

"Yes, Lord. We love you."

Harper opened her eyes uncertain on how to end her prayer. She thought about the prayers that she had heard Grammy pray.

"I ask this in the name of Jesus whom I believe. Amen."

Grammy shouted, "Amen!"

The young woman sat back against the sofa. She smiled as a new feeling rose up inside her. Harper knew in her heart that God had answered. *Is it possible?*

"I feel so different already, Grammy."

The elderly woman clapped her hands together.

"Yes, Baby. You are a child of God now. Tough times may come, but you are connected to the One in charge. Praise You, Lord. We thank You."

Tears came to Harper's eyes at her grandmother's joy. She laughed as the same happiness filled her. The woman wasn't sure about the promise of tough times, but she had to admit that having God on her side would make a big difference. *Thank You, Lord! I can't wait to tell Lyric!*

Lyric Sinclair sat in the brown leather chair tapping her foot nervously. She had received a phone call from Dr. Nash two days after her biopsy. The doctor had asked her to come in immediately for her results.

"Don't worry, Lyric. I'm here."

The woman reached a shaky hand out to grasp Aiden's own. She was glad that the man had been willing to go to the doctor's office with her. *I need the support.*

Suddenly, the office door opened. Dr. Nash entered the room moving quickly to sit in the swivel chair behind his desk. Lyric held her breath at the manila folder that the physician was holding in his hand.

"Miss Sinclair, thank you for coming in."

Lyric nodded, "What does the biopsy show?"

Dr. Nash set the folder down on his desk before folding his hands and leaning forward.

"I'm sorry to tell you, Miss Sinclair, that your tumor is malignant."

Lyric's heart raced at the news. She found her hearing muffled as if someone had suddenly wrapped her into a thick blanket of gloom. The woman could feel a firm squeeze to her hand, but she found no comfort in it. She opened her mouth to speak. Yet, no words came. Her mind reeled with options though none of them had a happy ending. *I'm going to die.*

With a shake of her head, Lyric jerked her hand away from Aiden. She stood up waving a hand of dismissal. The woman stormed out of the office desperate to leave the place of doom.

"Lyric!"

Lyric shook her head as she kept walking down the hallway. She refused to stop her departure or talk to anyone about her condition. *There is nothing to say. It's over.*

Suddenly, strong arms surrounded the woman. She was pulled closely against a warm body with a familiar scent. Her eyes closed as she fell into the embrace. Lyric allowed hot tears to fall freely down her face as she grieved in the arms of the man that she loved. *I'm going to die. I'll have to leave Aiden.*

Aiden Wilder's world spun around in chaos as he heard the news that Lyric's brain tumor was malignant. He stared at Dr. Nash inwardly begging that it was a clerical mistake. However, as the horrible news set in, the man accepted the truth. He squeezed Lyric's hand hoping that she would feel comfort and support.

Suddenly, Lyric pulled her hand out of his own roughly. She rose to her feet before stomping out of the office. The man snapped his gaze to Dr. Nash who had lowered his eyes to the manila folder.

Aiden stood swiftly following the fleeing woman.

"Lyric!"

Lyric continued walking toward the exit. She did not even turn back to look at him. Aiden sped up moving in front of the distraught woman. He wrapped his arms around her in a loving embrace. The man pulled her closer hoping that she would accept his support.

Relief filled him as Lyric leaned against him. Aiden held her allowing the woman to release her sorrow. He placed his cheek on the top of her head as her body began to shake. The man closed his eyes hating that the woman that he loved was crying. His heart broke for her though he knew that there was still hope. *Why are You doing this, Lord? Please help us through this. Please show us the way of healing.*

Dr. Nash sat waiting at his desk as Aiden raced after Lyric. He hated the terrible news that he had to give his patient. The doctor had been downhearted when he had read the results of the biopsy. His mind had instantly started going through the possible options for the young woman's condition.

"I'm sorry, Dr. Nash."

The doctor snapped his attention to the doorway as Lyric and Aiden reentered the office.

"I understand, Miss Sinclair. This is shocking news I know."

The couple sat back down in the brown leather chairs stationed in front of Dr. Nash's desk.

"What are my options, Dr. Nash?"

Dr. Nash replied, "It is my recommendation that you begin a combination treatment of chemotherapy and radiation immediately."

The expression on the patient and her boyfriend's faces told the doctor that they were uncertain and reluctant with the type of treatment. *I will just have to convince them that it is the best option.*

Lyric Sinclair's mind filled with memories of her father as he experienced his cancer treatments years ago. She could see the pain on his face as he tried to appear strong after many chemo treatments. The daughter recalled how he had been unable to eat without becoming sick. She remembered how frail he looked when all his hair fell out. *I can't go through that.*

Lyric returned her focus to Dr. Nash.

"Are there any other options?"

The doctor sighed, "I really recommend the combo treatment, Miss Sinclair. Your brain tumor is not in an easily reachable area. The only other option would be surgery, but that could be very dangerous."

The woman thought about the risks of surgery. She preferred them over the tortures of the combination treatment.

"Would you be able to perform the surgery, Dr. Nash?"

Dr. Nash shook his head appearing suddenly uncomfortable.

"No, Miss Sinclair. If you decided that surgery was the way that you would like to go, then I would have to transfer you to another doctor. There is a doctor, Dr. Hayes, who is a surgeon. She specializes in removing tumors that are in sensitive areas."

Lyric bit her lip trying to decide if that was what she wanted. She glanced over at Aiden who smiled weakly at her letting her make her own decision. Seeing the handsome man helped the woman make her decision. *I must have the surgery. If I get rid of this thing, then I can be with Aiden longer.*

CHAPTER 24

DANGEROUS CHOICES

Harper Raines sat on Lyric's couch attempting to remain calm. She had been anxious all morning while waiting for her friend to come back from her doctor's appointment. The woman had wanted to go but changed her mind when Lyric asked Aiden to go with her. She didn't want to create a crowd when her best friend was already nervous.

Now, Harper wished that she had gone as the third wheel. She knew that it would have been better than staying behind worrying. The woman prayed for Lyric as she waited. She was amazed at how differently she felt already with Jesus in her heart. *As soon as I hear Lyric's news, I will tell her about my salvation decision.*

Harper's heart pounded at the sound of the apartment door opening. She stood up wringing her hands as Lyric and Aiden entered the apartment.

"Well? What did Dr. Nash say?"

The distressed expression that the couple exchanged told Harper her answer. She held her breath needing to hear it aloud.

Lyric stepped forward taking her friend's hands into her own.

"My tumor is malignant."

Horror swept over Harper at the news. She squeezed Lyric's hands.

"Oh, Lyric. What does Dr. Nash want to do?"

The sour expression on her friend's face surprised the other woman.

"He wants me to do a combination treatment of chemotherapy and radiation."

Harper sighed knowing how Lyric felt about those treatments. She had been with her friend as her father had suffered in pain. The woman hated the idea of Lyric facing the same anguish.

"Are you going to do it?"

Lyric shrugged, "There is another option. There is a Dr. Hayes who can do surgery to remove my tumor."

A throat clearing caused the two women to turn toward Aiden.

"But Dr. Nash says that the tumor is in a hard to reach area."

Harper frowned, "That sounds dangerous."

The man nodded, "That's what Dr. Nash said. He said that the combo treatment was safer."

A loud snort caused Harper to cringe. She glanced over at Lyric who had crossed her arms.

"Dr. Nash probably has never seen a loved one suffer through those treatments. I have. It is horrible. I have decided to have the surgery."

Harper reasoned, "Lyric, let's talk about this. Many things could go wrong in surgery." *Please let her listen to advice.*

Lyric Sinclair crossed her arms angry that Aiden and Harper thought that she should endure the same torture that her father had when he was ill.

"Lyric, let's talk about this. Many things could go wrong in surgery."

The redheaded woman glared at Harper.

"There is nothing to talk about. I am going to have the surgery. Dr. Hayes is going to remove this tumor, so I will be completely healed."

Movement drew Lyric's attention to Aiden who had stepped forward.

"Lyric, there is no guarantee that Dr. Hayes can remove the tumor."

The woman's temper flared as she moved her hands to her hips.

"It doesn't matter what either of you says. It's my life and I will do as I please."

Lyric stomped into her bedroom slamming the door behind her. She plopped down on the edge of her bed allowing the tears to fall. *Why can't they support me in my decision? Isn't that what love is?*

Aiden Wilder stared at Lyric's bedroom door stunned at her sudden angry outburst. He wondered why she was being so stubborn. *She always has to have things her way. She won't even consider what we say.*

"Well, that wasn't productive."

Aiden smirked at Harper who tumbled onto the couch with a sarcastic roll of her eyes.

"Well, you know how Lyric is, Harper. Very cooperative."

The woman chuckled as she gestured for the man to sit down. Aiden obeyed though he still stared at Lyric's door.

"I don't blame her for wanting to avoid the chemo and radiation. It isn't a kind treatment. We both saw it at work."

Aiden frowned, "What do you mean?"

Harper shook her head.

"It's not my place to say."

The man nodded in understanding. He knew that Lyric would tell him if she wanted to share it with him.

"I think we should support her no matter what she decides, Harper."

"I agree. Maybe you should go talk to her, Aiden."

"Why me? You're her best friend."

Harper sighed, "True, but I don't think she will listen to me right now. Your love is fresh. She might listen to you."

Aiden stood up wondering what he could say to Lyric. He didn't want to anger her any further. The man trudged toward the woman's bedroom. He raised a hand to knock on the door. *Here goes.*

Lyric Sinclair startled at the knock on her bedroom door. She hastily wiped the tears from her face attempting to calm her emotions. The woman adjusted her clothes and swiped her hands through her hair hoping that she looked presentable.

"Come in."

The door creaked open to reveal Aiden. Lyric averted her eyes from the man as he entered the bedroom. She took a deep breath bracing herself for an argument. *I'm not backing down.*

The bed sank down as Aiden sat down beside her. The couple sat in silence for several minutes. *Say something, Aiden.*

"I'm sorry, Lyric. You're right that it is your life and your decision. Harper and I just love you so much that we don't want you to face problems in surgery. However, we have decided to support your decision."

Lyric's frown transformed into a smile at the kind words. She leaned toward the man thrilled when his arm went instantly around her shoulder. Her head laid on his chest comfortably as if it was meant to stay there.

The couple sat in silence enjoying each other's company. Lyric thought about her father who was the reason that she wanted to do the surgery. She wondered if she should tell Aiden about him. *When you love someone, you share everything with them.*

"My father went through chemo and radiation treatments when he was sick. He was in a lot of pain all the time and nothing could make him feel better. He wasted away until death because he couldn't eat, and his body became so weak. Dad is the reason that I wanted to do my bucket list. I didn't want to wait until it was too late like he did."

Lyric fell silent as tears threatened to fall.

"I'm sorry, Lyric. I understand why you don't want to go through that. It would break my heart to see you that way."

The woman smiled weakly, "I know. I would hate for you to see me that way too."

Aiden sighed, "So you are going to do the surgery?"

"Yes, Aiden. I'm going to take a leap of faith."

Aiden Wilder hissed under his breath as his finger touched the hot skillet. He pulled his hand back before putting the burned finger under the water faucet. The man sighed at the coolness that came relieving his pain.

"Watch your temper, Wilder. I'm a Christian now. I don't want to hear any profanity."

Aiden smirked at Harper before returning to his cooking. He was thrilled with the news that the young woman had accepted Jesus as her Savior and Lord. The man had made the same decision as a teenager. He knew the importance of her choice.

"Yes, ma'am. I will keep my words G-Rated."

Girly giggles came from the living room alerting Aiden to the fact that Lyric and Harper were enjoying their conversation. He smiled as he continued cooking their dinner. The man was glad that Lyric had her best friend. He knew that the two women needed each other. *Just like I need Desmond and Lyric. We all must rely on each other.*

Lyric Sinclair's stomach growled as she smelled the detailed dinner that Aiden had insisted on cooking to celebrate Harper's decision to become a Christian. She wondered what the man had decided to cook though she knew that whatever it was, it would be delicious.

"So, does your man know how to cook? Or do we need to get the Chinese take-out menu out of the drawer?"

Lyric chuckled, "Oh, Aiden can cook. He went to a culinary arts institute."

Harper's eyes widened.

"You're kidding."

"No. Aiden is a master chef. You are in for a treat tonight."

The other woman giggled, "Girl, I hope so. Of course, I'm not starving with Grammy around. That woman can still cook great."

Lyric smirked, "Maybe Aiden and Grammy should have a cook-off to see who the best chef is."

A grunt came from the kitchen.

"I don't think so. Those older ladies can cook their aprons off."

Harper and Lyric laughed loudly at Aiden's response.

"Hey, Aiden. What are you making me for my celebration dinner?"

"Well, I thought that we might have chicken nuggets and tater tots."

Lyric held back a laugh at the indignant expression on Harper's face.

"That better be a joke. I can still head home and see what Grammy's making."

"Yes. I'm joking, Harper. I'm making Stilton and pear gnocchi with a salade nicoise."

Harper snorted, "Okay. Now I know you are joking."

Aiden leaned on the kitchen island.

"Actually, I'm not. That's what we are having."

Lyric released her laughter at the shocked expression on Harper's face as she looked at her. She nodded since she was too tickled to speak.

The other woman snapped her eyes back to Aiden.

"Well, what in the world is a salade whatever?"

The culinary genius raised his nose into the air taking on a look of superiority.

"It is a salad with tomatoes, hard-boiled eggs, Nicoise olives, anchovies, and olive oil."

"Ooh, fancy. That sounds worthy of me."

Lyric listened as her best friend and boyfriend continued to banter back and forth. She was delighted that the two adults were getting along.

"Lyric, if you dump this man, send him my way."

"You want to date me?"

Harper smirked, "No. I need a personal chef."

The trio of adults shared a laugh as they prepared to enjoy a luxurious meal together. *Hopefully, this won't be our last.*

CHAPTER 25

FEARFUL ODDS

Lyric Sinclair stood next to Aiden in the elevator as they headed up to Dr. Hayes' office. She swallowed hard hoping to get the nerves to go back down. The woman hoped that the doctor would be able to give her a better idea of what she would be facing in the brain surgery.

The couple exited the elevator as it reached the seventh floor. Lyric read the signs seeing the one that showed them where Dr. Hayes' office was located. She took a deep breath trying to steady her nerves. Aiden took her hand before the couple walked down to the office.

Once inside, Lyric told the receptionist her name. She was told to take a seat and fill out the customary paperwork. The woman sank into a black plastic chair before she started completing the papers. She glanced over at Aiden who had picked up an outdated magazine.

"You might already know everything in that one."

Aiden smirked, "Well, I don't see any sports magazines. I'll have to pretend like this is new."

Lyric finished the paperwork before returning it to the receptionist. She sat back down with her cell phone in her hand. The woman tapped away answering emails from some of her designer friends. She wished that they could understand that she was concentrating on her health right now instead of creating a new fashion line. *They aren't living my life, so they don't get it*.

"Miss Sinclair, Dr. Hayes will see you now."

Lyric stood up following a nurse who had called her name. She glanced back to make sure that Aiden was coming too. The woman was relieved to see that the man was right behind her. *He's with me all the way*.

The door of Dr. Hayes' office was opened by the nurse who gestured for them to enter. Lyric took a deep breath as her eyes fell on a young dark-skinned woman standing beside the desk in a white lab coat.

"Miss Sinclair, I'm Dr. Leona Hayes. Mr. Sinclair."

Lyric suppressed a giggle at the odd expression on Aiden's face. She intervened for the man.

"Actually, this is Aiden Wilder. He is my boyfriend."

Dr. Hayes nodded, "Of course. Nice to meet you both. Please have a seat."

The couple sat down in brown leather chairs that resembled the ones that they had used in Dr. Nash's office.

"Let's get right down to business. Miss Sinclair, I have reviewed your medical records including the MRI and the biopsy. I have studied the location of your brain tumor and I am quite optimistic that I can surgically remove it."

Hope soared through Lyric at the doctor's opinion. She glanced over at Aiden who took her hand with a warm smile.

"Now, I want you to be well-informed about the procedure as well as the possible risks."

The redheaded woman nodded at the doctor, "Yes please."

Dr. Hayes continued, "The surgery that I will perform is called craniotomy. I will open a piece of the skull before I remove the tumor. It is possible that I will only be able to remove part of the tumor. If this is the case, then you will still have to do chemo and radiation treatments."

Lyric swallowed hard at the news. She nodded for the doctor to continue.

"At the end of the surgery, I will return the bone flap from your skull. Then I will suture the wound on your head."

Aiden cleared his throat drawing the attention of the two women to him.

"Have you done this surgery before, Dr. Hayes?"

The doctor nodded, "Yes. I have successfully completed eight craniotomies. All of my patients are able to lead normal lives now."

Lyric smiled weakly, "That's great. What are the risks of my surgery?"

Dr. Hayes' face turned solemn.

"I have to warn you that there are risks with any surgery, but especially when you work in the brain. Risks of a craniotomy can be stroke, seizures, swelling of the brain, nerve damage, or brain damage. Your tumor is located near the right temporal lobe which affects memory and speech. Therefore, there is a possibility that surgically removing a tumor in that area could cause memory loss or impairment in speech."

Silence filled the doctor's office as she grew quiet allowing the patient to process the information. Lyric thought through the list of risks that she was facing by doing a craniotomy. She closed her eyes trying to think over the headache that was forming. The woman rubbed her forehead with her free hand while continuing to hold Aiden's hand with the other.

Lyric opened her eyes to look straight at Dr. Hayes.

"Anything else?"

The female doctor smiled warmly, "No. All I need to know is whether or not you still would like to proceed."

The patient moved her attention to Aiden who was frowning at the massive amount of information.

"Aiden?"

The man sighed, "It's your decision, Lyric. I will support you no matter what."

Lyric nodded with relief, "Thank you, Aiden. Yes, Dr. Hayes. I wish to proceed with the surgery."

Aiden Wilder pasted on a smile as Lyric made her decision. He listened half-heartedly as Dr. Hayes scheduled the surgery before giving the patient some paperwork to help her prepare for it. The man swallowed hard trying to look attentive and supportive. However, inside he was worried about Lyric facing such dangerous risks. *Stroke, brain damage, memory loss. What if she dies? What if she becomes an invalid? What if she forgets all about me?*

Aiden tried to choke down the fear that was rising inside him. He wanted to be brave for Lyric in her time of need, but his concern was like a brick slamming into his face.

"Thank you, Dr. Hayes. I will see you next Monday bright and early."

Aiden forced his legs up out of the chair. He followed Lyric out of the doctor's office toward the elevator. The man's mind raced at the information that had been flung at them by Dr. Hayes. He couldn't believe the level of seriousness that the woman he loved was about to face. *Harper and I should have tried harder to talk her out of it. It won't work now.*

"What do you want to do now, Aiden?"

The man snapped his attention to Lyric who was stepping onto the elevator.

"What?"

The woman crossed her arms with a playful smile.

"I asked what you wanted to do now."

Aiden shrugged, "Whatever."

"How about we go get lunch somewhere?"

The man didn't know how the woman could eat after the avalanche of information that had just crushed them. However, he wanted to keep her happy.

"Sure. Where do you want to go?"

Lyric squealed, "I know exactly where to go."

Lyric Sinclair placed her red tray onto one of the tables in the center of the food court before sitting down across from Aiden. She tried to focus on her smorgasbord of food items that were from several different vendors. The woman knew that something was bothering Aiden. *I can probably guess what it is.*

Lyric looked up from her fries seeing her boyfriend dipping his corndog in ketchup, but never actually taking a bite. She thought about lightening the mood.

"I know that the food court food isn't up to the culinary arts institute's standards, but it isn't too bad. Harper and I love eating here."

The man nodded without a word. He continued dunking his corndog mercilessly into the pool of ketchup.

"Okay, Aiden. Tell me what's wrong."

Aiden snorted, "What could possibly be wrong? You are about to take part in a surgery which could end in a series of dangerous outcomes. Nothing's wrong."

Lyric bit her lip at the sarcasm in the man's voice. She wanted to snap at him angrily. However, the woman knew that harsh words would only make the situation worse. She took several deep breaths while nibbling at her food. *Maybe this is too much for him. Maybe I should let him go.*

"Aiden, I know that this is a lot to swallow. If you want to change your mind about us, then I'll understand."

Silence followed the woman's suggestion. She took a bite of a piece of pizza while she waited for the man's answer. Lyric found it hard to swallow the food as her heart wrenched. *Is this goodbye?*

"I think we should get married."

Lyric choked and sputtered at Aiden's reply. She grabbed her soda taking a large gulp from the straw.

"What?"

Her green eyes darted up to the man's face. Aiden leaned forward.

"Lyric Sinclair, will you marry me?" *Whoa.*

Aiden Wilder gulped as Lyric stared at him with wide eyes. He had been thinking about their relationship since leaving the hospital. The man had absentmindedly followed the woman around the food court picking up items that she chattered on about as being tasty. He had noticed other people milling around selecting their meals. *They all walk around like everything is perfect. They don't know that my world is crashing down.*

Then Aiden had snapped at Lyric about nothing being wrong. He had expected the strong-willed woman to yell back at him. However, she had grown quiet returning her attention to her food. It was in that moment looking at the beautiful woman he was frightened for that Aiden realized what he needed to do.

The man was shocked as Lyric choked on her lunch recovering quickly.

"What?"

Aiden wondered if he should bother repeating his proposal. The fear of rejection plagued his heart. However, he had to know if she would become his wife.

"Lyric Sinclair, will you marry me?"

Lyric's silence was deafening. She stared at him as if he had told a poor joke or passed gas. The man held his breath dreading that the woman might jump up and run away to escape his proposal. However, he released the breath in a huff as Lyric gave him an answer.

"Yes, Aiden Wilder. I will marry you." *Wow!*

Harper Raines swiped her finger across her iPad tablet eager to read the next chapter of Romans. She had been studying the Bible all afternoon while she waited to hear from Lyric about her appointment with Dr. Hayes. The woman had stopped reading every few minutes to pray for the strength and patience that she needed to wait on her friend. *I know that You have a plan for all of us.*

Suddenly, Harper's cell phone vibrated on her lap. She picked it up distractedly until she saw Lyric's picture on the screen. The woman tapped the accept button.

"Lyric, what did Dr. Hayes say?"

A giggle came from the other end. Harper frowned unsure that the doctor could have given any news that would cause the ill woman to laugh.

"Lyric Daisy Sinclair, I have been waiting all day to hear about your appointment with Dr. Hayes. Now tell me why you are so happy." *What in the world has happened?*

Odessa "Birdie" Raines glanced up from her crocheting as Harper demanded an answer from Lyric. Curiosity filled her at the jovial demeanor of the sick woman. She wondered if a miracle had happened. *Lord, have You done something big today?*

Suddenly, Harper jumped to her feet with eyes wide.

"What?"

Birdie frowned at the shocked expression on her granddaughter's face. She watched as a smile spread up the younger woman's face.

In the next moment, Harper shrieked while jumping up and down. The older woman stood to her feet clutching a hand over her heart.

"What?"

Her granddaughter bounced over to her. She grabbed Birdie hugging her tightly as she continued to celebrate.

"Harper Neveah Raines, what in the world are you screaming about?"

Harper pulled back from her grandmother. She beamed with tears of joy in her eyes.

"Lyric and Aiden are getting married." *Lord, what a blessing!*

CHAPTER 26

PERFECT BLISS

Lyric Sinclair entered her fashion studio for the first time since her collapse on the walkway. Confusion swarmed over her at the frantic phone call from Harper. She didn't know what her friend was so upset about, but the fashion designer decided to find out. *It's probably nothing. She gets so hyper about everything.*

Lyric smiled as she thought about Harper's celebration at the news of her engagement to Aiden. She was pleased that her friend hadn't demanded that they wait until they had known each other longer. The young woman felt as if she had been in love with Aiden forever. She couldn't imagine being without him. *But he may have to be without me.*

Lyric shook her head refusing to allow negative thoughts to spoil her happiness over the upcoming wedding. The couple had decided to have a quiet chapel wedding on Saturday afternoon so that they would be husband and wife before the Monday surgery. *It's okay that it is a simple ceremony. As long as Aiden and I are together.*

"Harper?"

Lyric frowned at the dark studio as she entered it expecting to find Harper pacing back and forth wringing her hands.

"Harper! Where are you? What's going on?"

Suddenly, the lights blasted into the woman's eyes. She blinked quickly trying to adjust. When Lyric could see clearly, she gasped.

The fashion studio was lit up with large white lanterns that were hanging on anything they could balance on. White Christmas tree lights were draped over the rafters looking like lit up raindrops. Deep purple flowers were scattered around the studio in crystal vases with intricate designs on them. *Canterbury bells.*

Lyric noticed stacks of purple cloth on a long table. She placed her hand over her heart as she saw a lavender dress on a dressmaker's dummy at the end of the room. Two mannequins holding suits for men were next to the dress. Both suits were velvet fabric though one was black and the other purple like wine.

Lyric's eyes widened at a white gown in the center of the outfits. The white skirt of the dress was bulging in the shape of a round bell. The top of the gown had short poofy sleeves and a modest neckline. *Just like in a fairytale.*

"What do you think?"

Harper's sing-song voice caused Lyric to spin around in surprise.

"Harper Neveah Raines, what is all this?"

The other woman giggled, "The props and costumes of your wedding of course."

Lyric scanned the room again marveling at the beauty. *It's all perfect.*

"How did you know?"

Harper held up her hands like a shield.

"Now, don't get mad, but when you were having your biopsy, I looked at your bucket list on your phone. I saw the last item which was the only one not marked off."

Lyric thought about her bucket list.

"To attend a fairy tale wedding."

Her friend smiled, "After I heard about your engagement and speedy wedding with Aiden, I decided that you should attend a fairytale wedding as a bride."

Lyric frowned, "But how did you get it together so quickly?"

Harper smirked, "Girl, you know I know how to work a phone and a credit card. Besides, I had a little help. Right, girls?"

Squeals and shrieks of excitement echoed off the walls as four ladies came out of the other room where they had apparently been hiding. Lyric hugged the fellow fashion designers who had been her study group in college.

"Monaca, Carol, Jacqueline, and Lolly, I can't believe you are here."

Lolly swished her blond hair before strutting around the studio.

"Honey, you know we couldn't let Harper have all the fun."

Monaca giggled, "That's right. This was a Fashion Dolls emergency."

The group of women laughed as they played catch-up on their lives since college. Lyric blinked away tears of joy as she reunited with her friends.

Suddenly, Harper clapped her hands.

"Ladies! Ladies, we have a lot of work to do."

The women grew quiet awaiting orders.

"Now, the first order of business is for Lyric to try on her wedding dress."

A loud squeal filled the room as the women pushed the bride toward her gown.

Aiden Wilder stared at the glass case flinching at the prices of the rings that were on display. He had hoped to buy an engagement ring and wedding band at the same time. However, the man knew that he would barely be able to afford one. *I wish I was rich.*

"What do you think, Aid?"

The groom glanced over at his twin brother.

"I think I should have been a doctor or lawyer. Then I would be able to buy a ring."

Desmond smirked, "Don't worry, bro. You'll find one that you can afford. Let's keep looking."

Aiden agreed though he didn't think that he would find anything worthy of Lyric. He hated the idea of getting her a chintzy ring when she deserves so much more. *The ring must be perfect.*

"Why don't you just do simple gold bands for the wedding rings? You could both have one."

The man shrugged, "I guess, Des. I would still like to get her something special for her engagement ring."

The brothers searched the jewelry store.

"It's no use. I can't afford any of these rings."

Desmond sighed, "Why don't you look at the rings again, but this time ignore the price tags? Which ring would Lyric like the best?"

Aiden thought that it was useless to follow his brother's advice. *It will just be wishful thinking.*

"Aid?"

The brother grumbled, "Fine."

Aiden walked through the jewelry store staring into each glass case. He shook his head at many of the rings.

Suddenly, the man froze. He spotted a ring that he knew would be perfect for Lyric.

"What did you find?"

Aiden pointed at the ring that held his attention.

"That one. It has a dolphin above a wave with a diamond in the center. Lyric would love that one."

"It's unique."

The groom nodded before cringing at the price tag. *I could spend my whole life working and still never be able to pay for that ring.*

"Have you gentlemen made a selection?"

Aiden opened his mouth to answer. However, his brother beat him to it.

"Yes. We need to buy two plain gold wedding bands and this dolphin engagement ring."

"What? Des, I can't afford the dolphin ring."

Desmond crossed his arms.

"That's why I'm paying for it. It's my wedding gift for you."

Aiden grunted, "Desmond, you can't afford it either."

"Don't fight me on this, Aiden. Harper's gift is the wedding and I am in charge of the rings. You don't want that woman mad at me, do you?"

The other man smiled at the mental image of Harper wagging her finger at Desmond.

"Okay, Des, but I do so under protest."

"Good. And I can afford it. I'm a money packrat. Sir, the bride's rings should be a size seven and the groom's band needs to be a size ten."

The jeweler wrote down the measurements.

"Yes, sir. I will get those on order immediately. When do you need them by?"

Desmond answered, "The wedding is this Saturday though I am sure that the groom would like to give the engagement ring as soon as possible."

"I see. Well, the wedding bands can be acquired easily enough. I am not sure about the engagement ring."

Aiden bit in lip in annoyance. He stared into the case at the beautiful dolphin ring.

"What size is the display ring?"

The jeweler approached the case unlocking it before pulling out the ring gently.

"It is a size seven, but you don't want the display ring."

Aiden nodded, "Yes, I do if it is in good shape."

The jeweler examined the ring carefully.

"Yes. It is still in perfect condition. If you really want it, then I can give it to you for a discount."

The brothers exchanged an excited glance.

Aiden exclaimed, "I'll take it!"

Lyric Sinclair stared at the fluffy white gown in the mirror. She was thrilled that the dress fit perfectly. The woman had never felt more beautiful. *I look like a fairytale princess.*

"It's perfect, girls. Thank you."

Her friends applauded as she twirled in a circle.

Carol reached for a hat box that was sitting on a nearby table. She pulled out a silver tiara which had a long veil of lace on the back of it. Lyric gasped at the beauty of the headpiece. She held her breath as Carol placed it on her head.

"A princess needs a tiara."

The other women cheered excitedly. Lyric smiled at her reflection in the mirror. *Perfect.*

Aiden Wilder concentrated on his shrimp as it seared in the skillet on the stove in his apartment. He refused to take his eyes off it for fear that it would burn and ruin the perfect day. The man had invited Lyric to come over for dinner where he planned to surprise her with her special engagement ring.

"Aiden?"

Aiden smiled at the sweet voice.

"Come in, Lyric. I'll be with you in a minute. I don't want our dinner to run away."

Lyric chuckled, "Knowing how amazing your food is that would be a shame. What are you making?"

The chef replied, "Seared scallops and shrimp which are drizzled with a sweet strawberry-flavored balsamic glaze."

"Wow! I think I'll marry you."

Aiden chuckled as his fiancée moved to his side. He turned his head to give her a kiss before shooing her out of his kitchen. The man continued to cook his special dish hoping that everything would be perfect for their evening together.

Lyric Sinclair closed her eyes swooning over the savory and sweet taste of the dinner that Aiden had cooked for her. She had thought that the last meal was delicious. However, this one was even better.

"Good?"

Lyric snorted, "That word doesn't even come close to what your cooking is. Delicious, divine, heavenly, and scrumptious pale in comparison to this food."

Aiden chuckled, "Then I guess you like it."

"Yes. Put it on the Make-for-Lyric-Again list."

The man took their plates to the sink.

"Are you ready for dessert?"

Lyric smiled, "Sure. What is it?"

Aiden returned to the table before setting a blue velvet box in front of her.

"Something special."

The woman's eyes widened in surprise as she realized what had to be inside the box. She darted her gaze up to Aiden who was waiting expectantly with a smile on his face.

Lyric opened the blue velvet box before gasping. Inside the box was a lovely golden ring with a dolphin jumping over a diamond that was above a wave of water.

"Oh, Aiden. It's like the dolphin we swam with in Florida."

The man reached for the ring before placing it on her left ring finger. Lyric beamed at how well it fit.

"It's perfect. Thank you, Aiden."

The woman leaned forward kissing her fiancée. She stared down at the ring admiring its uniqueness. *I will remember this day forever.*

"You won't believe what those city folks are doing now."

Myra Calhoun rolled her eyes as her husband stood staring out the kitchen window of their farmhouse.

"Huck, step away from that window and leave those folks alone. They have my permission to do whatever they want to make the wedding perfect for that lovely couple."

The farmer snorted as he sat down at the kitchen table sipping his coffee from a ceramic mug.

"Well, I think it's silly to go through all this fuss for a wedding."

Myra glared at her husband.

"We had a pretty fancy wedding too, Huck. Don't you remember?"

Huck huffed, "Well, that was a long time ago."

The farmer's wife smiled as she returned to rolling out the dough for her pie. She thought about when she was a young bride beginning a new life with Huck. *It was exciting and scary at the same time. I hope that Aiden and Lyric have a blessed marriage together.*

Harper Raines darted from each area of the wedding checking to see that everything was ready. She had helped prepare the reception tables and set up chairs in the ceremony area. The woman had helped hang strings of lights and white lanterns from the branches of the trees that were on the sides. *It all looks magical.*

"Harper Neveah Raines!"

Harper spun around to where Grammy was stomping toward her.

"Child, you need to get your rear in gear."

The younger woman rolled her eyes at the ancient expression.

"What do you mean, Grammy? I have been working all day."

Grammy nodded, "I know, but you need to get your dress on, Harp. The wedding is starting in less than an hour."

Harper gasped, "Oh! I lost track of the time."

The maid of honor raced toward the barn that the Calhouns had allowed them to invade as a dressing area. *Lyric will have something to say about my tardiness.*

Lyric Sinclair stood in front of the studio mirror that Harper had insisted on bringing to the Calhoun Farm. She smiled sweetly at the result of her primping. Her eyes brimmed with tears of joy at the enchanting princess who stood looking back at her.

"Oh, Lyric. You look gorgeous."

Lyric turned to Harper who was still dressed in her jeans and tank top.

"Cutting it a little close, aren't we, Harper?"

The other woman giggled as she grabbed her dress before racing behind a divider.

"Yes. Grammy had to help me get my rear in gear."

Lyric rolled her eyes.

"Is that your expression? Or hers?"

Harper snickered, "Hers."

The bride touched her red curls one last time promising herself that she would leave them alone now.

"Okay, Princess Bride. What do you think?"

Lyric smiled at her maid of honor who was dress in her lavender dress.

"Perfect."

Suddenly, sorrow covered the woman as she thought about her father. She wished that he could be there to see how his girls had turned out. The daughter wanted him to escort her down the aisle. *Oh, Dad. I miss you. You would love Aiden. He is a good man.*

"What's wrong, Lyric? You look sad all of a sudden."

Lyric sighed, "I was just thinking about Dad."

The bride regretted the words as soon as she said them aloud. She could see the pain in Harper's eyes. Lyric knew that her father had treated Harper as his own child. *He always loved her. I know that she loved him too.*

"I'm sorry, Harper. I didn't mean to put a raincloud on this beautiful wedding that you have given me."

The other woman smiled weakly, "It's okay. I wish that he was here too. He would be so proud of you."

Lyric hugged her friend thankful to have her at the most important day of her life.

"He'd be proud of you too, Harper. I love you."

"I love you too, girl. Now, let me show you who your escort will be today."

Aiden Wilder swallowed hard trying to get his nerves under control. It was time for him to walk down to take his place near an archway that had been draped with white tulle. The preacher stood waiting holding his black Bible ready to perform the ceremony.

"You got cold feet yet, Aiden?"

Aiden rolled his eyes.

"No, Des. My feet are as hot as ever."

Desmond mumbled, "I hope they aren't as stinky as ever for Lyric's sake."

The groom sighed wishing he could elbow his brother in the stomach. However, there were too many witnesses.

"I should have talked to Lyric about her Prince Charming. I could write a book."

Aiden suppressed a chuckle. He knew that his brother was trying to help him calm his nerves. The man lightly kicked Desmond's leg as music began to play. The twins marched down the center aisle that had been made between the rows of chairs. They reached the end before taking their spots at the right side of the archway.

Aiden nodded at the preacher with a smile. He had known Pastor Jacob Long since he was a child. The preacher had spoken at the Wilder parents' funeral. *He has always been helpful to our family. It is fitting for him to marry me to the woman God has chosen for me.*

As the music changed to a softer tune, Aiden snapped his eyes to the back of the ceremony area. He smiled as he saw Harper's final surprise for the fairytale wedding. The maid of honor was walking toward the center aisle holding a rein which was attached to a pure white horse that Myra Calhoun had forced her husband to loan to the wedding party.

Aiden held back a gasp as his eyes fell on the rider of the horse. He smiled warmly at Lyric who was sitting side-saddle wearing a white gown that would put any princess to shame. On her mountain of red curly hair was a silver tiara attached to a veil. The groom swallowed hard at the beauty of his bride.

"Last chance to run, bro."

Aiden snorted lightly, "Not a chance."

The groom watched as two of the ushers dressed as coachmen stepped toward the horse. Using an ornate footstool, the two men helped the bride down from the horse in a manner that was completely graceful. *She deserves everything to go perfectly today.*

Lyric Sinclair released the breath that she had been holding as her feet reached the ground. She had been nervous about getting off the horse without falling or flashing the guests. The woman smiled at Harper as her maid of honor handed her bouquet of purple Canterbury bells to her.

Lyric took a deep breath as Harper glided expertly down the aisle toward her spot at the front of the ceremony area. Her stomach lurched as the music changed to the bridal processional. The bride met gazes with Aiden who was waiting patiently for her. The warm smile on his face calmed Lyric's fears. She returned the smile with one of her own.

Lyric glided down the aisle keeping her eyes on her groom. She marveled at the peace that came from looking at him. *This is the right thing. We are meant to be together.*

As she reached the end of the aisle, Lyric beamed at Aiden who came to escort her the rest of the way. She placed her arm inside his as the couple moved to stand in front of the preacher. The wedding couple turned to face each other. Lyric held both of Aiden's hands amazed at how much she loved him. *Our love is so strong.*

"Dearly Beloved, we are gathered here today in the sight of God to witness and celebrate the marriage of Aiden Wilder and Lyric Sinclair. We ask God to bless them so that they may be strengthened for their life together. God gave us marriage for the full expression of love between a man and a woman so that husband and wife may cherish and delight in one another; comfort and help each other in sickness, trouble, and sorrow."

Lyric's smile wavered at the reminder of her brain tumor and the struggles that they would face in a couple of days. Aiden squeezed her hands tenderly causing the smile to return. *We are stronger together.*

"The husband and wife may provide for each other in temporal things; pray for and encourage each other in the things that pertain to God; and live together faithfully all the length of their days. Let us pray."

Lyric bowed her head closing her eyes in prayer. She was glad that Harper had decided to make the ceremony center around God. The bride knew that God was the reason that she had met Aiden and fallen in love with him.

"God our Heavenly Father, we know that You are present on this happy day. We ask You to join Aiden and Lyric in the honorable estate of marriage. We ask You to grow their love for You as You grow their love for one another. May they always seek You in times of trials and times of joy. We pray that they will live their lives in a way that pleases You. We ask this in the name of Jesus Christ. Amen."

As the audience answered with their own amen, Lyric opened her eyes feeling that the prayer expressed her own heart.

"Before we proceed to the vows that Aiden and Lyric are ready to share, let me read a passage from the Word of God. Lyric's treasured friend Harper has chosen a passage that is her prayer for the blessed couple. Jeremiah 29:11-13 says, 'For I know the plans I have for you,' declares the Lord, 'plans to prosper you and not to harm you, plans to give you hope and a future. Then you will call on Me and come and pray to Me, and I will listen to you. You will seek

Me and find Me when you seek Me with all your heart.' These verses are a reminder to all of us including Aiden and Lyric that God has a plan for our lives. He knows our struggles and our joys. He knows our triumphs and our failures. The Lord's plans are supreme. We cannot change them. Our job is to trust Him with our past, present, and future."

Lyric blinked away tears which had formed at the words about God's plan. She hoped that His plan was to allow the couple many years together.

"And now, it is time for Aiden and Lyric to exchange their wedding vows."

The wedding couple released their hands so that Aiden could take Lyric's right hand into his own right hand. Lyric held her breath as the man she loved repeated after the preacher.

"I, Aiden, take you Lyric, to be my wedded wife. To have and to hold, from this day forward, for better, for worse, for richer, for poorer, in sickness or in health, to love and to cherish 'till death do us part. And hereto I pledge you my faithfulness."

The bride released her breath quietly with a smile. She took a deep breath as Pastor Long began to tell her what to say.

"I, Lyric, take you Aiden, to be my wedded husband. To have and hold, from this day forward, for better, for worse, for richer, for poorer."

Lyric froze as the next part of the vow was announced by the preacher. Her mind raced with the dangers of her surgery which would take place in a couple of days. Tears streamed down her face at the possible outcomes. The woman flushed in embarrassment at breaking down in front of so many people. She lowered her gaze to the ground.

Suddenly, a gentle hand tenderly wiped the tears from her face. Lyric glanced up at Aiden who was smiling weakly at her in understanding.

The man whispered, "In sickness and health, I will be with you."

Lyric nodded as her smile returned to her face. She took a deep breath.

"In sickness or in health, to love and to cherish 'till death do us part. And hereto I pledge you my faithfulness."

The couple beamed at each other. Lyric's heart swooned with love knowing that she meant every word that she had spoken.

"Marriage is not something that two people invent or construct by themselves. It takes a far wider community of family and friends to make any marriage work. Each of you have been invited here today because you are a part of that community. Therefore, having heard Aiden and Lyric state their intentions through their vows to each other and to God, do you pledge to support their union and to strengthen their lives together, to speak the truth to them in love, and with them to seek a life of love for others?"

Lyric smiled at the affirmative that came unanimously from the guests. She suppressed a giggle at the loud shouts from Harper and Desmond.

"And now, Aiden and Lyric will exchange rings as a symbol of their promise to each other."

Aiden turned toward Desmond who handed him a golden wedding band. He placed the ring on Lyric's left ring finger with her dolphin engagement ring.

"I give you this ring as a token and pledge of our constant faith and abiding love."

Lyric swallowed the excitement that filled her at the promise. She turned toward Harper who stepped forward to hand her a golden wedding band. The bride placed the ring on Aiden's left ring finger.

"I give you this ring as a token and pledge of our constant faith and abiding love."

The couple held both hands as Pastor Long continued the ceremony.

"By the authority committed unto me as a minister of God, I declare that Aiden and Lyric are now husband and wife. What God has joined together, let no one put asunder. You may now kiss your bride."

Aiden leaned forward giving Lyric her first kiss as his wife. She closed her eyes thrilled at their new life that was about to begin.

"Ladies and gentlemen, I would like to introduce to you Mr. and Mrs. Wilder."

The guests applauded and cheered as the newlywed couple faced them before strolling down the center aisle toward the reception area. Lyric gasped at the beautiful table settings that Harper had orchestrated. *So magical.*

Harper Raines entered the wedding reception area with her eyes darting around in search of issues. She nodded in approval at the deep purple tablecloths that covered the tables. The woman liked how the crystal vases full of purple Canterbury bell flowers gave the area a regal appearance. She approached the food table hoping that everything had been placed as she had instructed.

Aiden had suggested some menu items based on his culinary arts training. As Harper looked at the display of food, she could tell that following the man's advice had been wise.

"What in the world, Harper?"

The maid of honor spun around squealing as she saw the bride. She hugged Lyric with a laugh.

"Congrats, girl."

"Thanks, Harp. What all do we have here?"

Harper gestured to Aiden.

The man explained, "We have a buffet of delicacies. First, we have stuffed endive with Roquefort cheese, topped with chopped walnuts. Next, we have roasted new potatoes with dill cream and golden caviar. Then, your taste buds can enjoy wild mushroom tartlets or artichoke mousse puffs. We also have miniature Reuben sandwiches to keep Desmond happy and miniature crab cakes for Harper's appetite."

Harper nodded, "Yes. Those were non-negotiables."

Aiden cleared his throat before continuing his explanation.

"For our pasta lovers, we have ravioli with roasted red-pepper sauce or bow tie pasta with Gorgonzola cream sauce. Of course, for the meat lovers, we have Asian flank steak or Cajun-rubbed turkey breast served with cranberry-mango chutney. I think there is something for everyone."

Lyric giggled, "I would hope so. There's enough here to feed an army. We only have fifty people here."

Harper snorted, "Girl, then we have the privilege of eating the leftovers."

"True. Aiden won't have to cook for a while." *He won't have time with the surgery and taking care of Lyric afterwards.*

Lyric Wilder cherished the bite of artichoke mousse puff. She had been hesitant to try the odd dish. However, Aiden convinced her to try it. The woman had to admit that her new husband knew his food.

"Congratulations, Lady Lyric."

The bride's eyes widened in surprise as a familiar woman approached her table.

"Lady Beatrix, I didn't know that you were here."

The circus owner nodded with a warm smile, "Yes. Mister Aiden sent me an invitation. He said that I vas velcome to come, but that I should leave Lynx at home."

Lyric giggled, "That was probably a good idea. I'm glad that you came."

Lady Beatrix glanced around secretly before returning her attention to the bride.

"I have brought you a gift. I hope that you vill accept it."

The redheaded woman nodded wondering what the present could be that the circus owner was afraid she would reject.

Lady Beatrix reached into a black velvet cloth bag. She pulled out a necklace with a silver chain. The focal part of the piece of jewelry was a blue diamond.

"This necklace vas a gift from my mother. She gave it to me in a very rough time of my life. My mother said that it vas a diamond of hope because it vould always remind me that the future is full of hope."

Lyric shook her head as Lady Beatrix held it out.

"I can't, Lady Beatrix. Your mother gave it to you. It is too precious."

The circus owner nodded, "Yes, Lady Lyric. It is precious. My mother told me that she vas not giving it to me forever. This gift is meant to be given to someone else in need when they have fallen into dark times. Though today is happy, you have dark times coming. Please accept it."

Lyric took the necklace tenderly thanking the other woman. She placed it around her neck marveling at the beauty of the diamond. The bride touched the diamond feeling more like a princess than ever. *My fairytale wedding has been perfect, but will I still get my happily ever after?*

CHAPTER 27

SEEKING MIRACLES

Lyric Wilder yawned as she stepped silently through her apartment. She held her shoes in one hand while carrying her purse in the other. The new wife needed to be leaving for the hospital, but she didn't want to wake her husband up. She knew that he was tired from their busy wedding weekend. *He can come later. He should rest.*

"Lyric?"

Lyric froze with a cringe. She slowly turned back toward the queen size bed with a frown. Aiden was sitting up in bed staring at her with disheveled hair.

"I'm sorry, Aiden. I was trying to be quiet."

"Why?"

Before the woman could answer, her husband's eyes grew wide.

"Wait! You have to be at the hospital at 7:30 this morning."

Lyric nodded as she opened her mouth to protest. However, she knew that it would be useless as Aiden threw the blanket off himself climbing out of bed.

"Just give me a few minutes. I'll be ready."

The wife smiled warmly, "Take your time. It's still early."

Lyric sat down on the edge of the bed suddenly feeling tired. She tried to tell herself that it was only because it was so early in the morning. However, the woman wasn't convinced. She knew that her nerves and her condition were influencing her body. *It will all be over soon.*

"Are you ready?"

Lyric pasted on a smile as she rose to her feet. She nodded slightly before leading the way to the door. The couple entered the elevator together finding Leonard already at work operating it.

"Good morning, Leonard."

The elderly operator beamed at the couple.

"Good morning, Lyric and Aiden."

The woman had introduced her husband the day before much to the delight of both men. Once in their apartment, Aiden had said that he instantly liked the older man.

"Today's the day?"

Lyric sighed, "Yes."

Leonard reached a withered hand over to the nervous woman patting her on the arm.

"It will be okay, honey. God is bigger than your tumor."

The woman nodded, "Thank you, Leonard. You're right. We will trust Him."

Aiden added, "Yes, we will." *I wish that I felt as confident as I should.*

Aiden Wilder sat in the hospital waiting room with his new wife as they filled out a new stack of paperwork. His mind raced with the what-ifs of the surgery's outcomes. The man tried to keep his focus off the negative. However, he kept coming back to the problems that could go wrong. *I wish it was me. If I died, I know I would go to heaven. What about Lyric?*

Aiden tensed at the question. He glanced over at Lyric who was finishing the last form. The man's love for the woman drove his mouth.

"Lyric, are you a Christian?"

The redheaded woman snapped her attention to him.

"What? Why are you asking me that?"

Aiden winced at the tone of his wife. He wondered if he had offended her.

"I'm sorry, Lyric. I was just asking because we don't know what will happen today."

Lyric's glare softened at the words. She nodded lowering her eyes to her lap.

"I understand. Yes, Aiden. I accepted Jesus as my Savior when I was a teenager. I haven't been living completely like He wants me to, but I firmly believe that I still belong to Him."

The woman took a deep breath causing the man to frown.

Lyric continued, "If I die, Aiden, I know that I will go to heaven to be with my Lord and see my Dad again."

Aiden swallowed hard at the idea of his loving wife dying. However, he had to admit to himself that knowing she would spend an eternity in heaven brought him hope.

"That's great. Me too. Of course, you are going to be fine. I just wanted to make sure."

The woman leaned her head on her husband's shoulder.

"I know."

The couple remained silent for several moments before Lyric spoke again.

"I'm glad that I got a brain tumor."

Aiden tensed at the announcement. He frowned down at the woman who sat up at his reaction.

"Why?"

Lyric explained, "Because if I didn't have a brain tumor, then we would have never fallen in love. You would have still seen me as a spoiled snob."

"I wouldn't have called you a spoiled snob."

The woman chuckled, "Maybe not to my face, but that had to be how you saw me. Anyway, we wouldn't have completed my bucket list if I had remained healthy. It's like God gave me this tumor so that you and I would find each other."

Aiden nodded in understanding. He had to agree that the two adults would never have spent time together if it wasn't for the tumor that prompted Lyric's bucket list. The man hated that she might suffer, but he was grateful that they were together.

"I'm glad that we met too, but I am looking forward to many more years together after the tumor is gone."

Lyric leaned toward the man planting a kiss on his lips. Aiden returned the kiss hoping that it wouldn't be their last one.

"Why don't we say a prayer before the nurse preps you for surgery?"

The woman nodded, "Good idea. Will you lead us?"

Aiden agreed taking his wife's hands into his own. The couple bowed their heads closing their eyes.

"Heavenly Father, we thank You for the many blessings that You have given us. We thank You for choosing us to be husband and wife. We know that You have many things in store for us yet. Lord, we pray that You will give us the peace and comfort that only You can give us in this time of uncertainty. We pray for wisdom and guidance for Dr. Hayes and her team as they do the surgery today. Please help Lyric to come out of the surgery healed and whole. We are trusting You with our lives. In Jesus' name. Amen."

The couple remained still holding each other's hands even after the prayer ended. Aiden opened his eyes to look at his wife. He smiled reassuringly as Lyric met his gaze. *It's going to be okay.*

"Mrs. Wilder?"

Both adults snapped their attention to a nurse who stood waiting with a clipboard.

"We're ready to prep you for surgery."

Lyric stood up with a sigh. Aiden followed eager to provide her with further encouragement.

"Mr. Wilder, you will have to stay out here. Dr. Hayes will be sending updates about her condition in surgery."

Aiden nodded, "Okay. I'll see you after, sweetheart."

Lyric smiled weakly, "You bet."

"I love you."

The patient smirked, "You better. I love you too, Aiden."

Harper Raines' high heel shoes clacked on the tile floor of the hospital hallway. Her heart pounded in apprehension as she thought about Lyric being in surgery. The woman had planned to be at the hospital before her friend went back to be prepped. However, she had overslept. *Lyric's been in surgery for at least an hour by now if they started on time.*

Harper reached the surgical waiting room only to find that it was empty. She glanced around expecting to see Aiden standing by a window or pacing at the side of the area. However, the man wasn't anywhere to be seen. *Where is he?*

The confused woman approached the nurse's station seeing a volunteer in a pink smock.

"Excuse me, ma'am?"

The older woman smiled sweetly, "Yes, dear."

"I'm with the Lyric Wilder family. Do you know where her husband went?"

The volunteer nodded, "Yes. He went to the chapel after getting an update about the progress of the surgery."

Harper's heart thumped anxiously at what could have driven the man into the chapel during the surgery. *It can't be good.*

"Where's the chapel?"

After listening to the directions of the hospital volunteer, the young woman stomped toward the area of the hospital where the chapel was located. She took a deep breath at the chapel door before opening it and entering the dim room.

Harper calmed on seeing the stain glass window of Jesus that was at the front of the sanctuary. She squinted in the limited light searching for Aiden. The woman saw the man sitting in a pew with his arms on the one in front of him. His head was on his arms.

Harper hated to disturb him. However, her concern for Lyric trumped her manners. She marched up to the pew where Aiden was praying.

"Aiden?"

The man jerked his head up with wide eyes. He relaxed on seeing the woman.

"Harper, you're here."

Harper nodded, "Of course, I'm here. What happened to Lyric? Why did you come in here? Did something bad happen?"

Aiden held up his hands attempting to calm the woman.

"The doctor said that she had a reaction to the anesthesia. They were trying a different kind. I decided to come in here and do some extra praying for her."

Harper swallowed hard as she tried to relax. She didn't like that her friend had already had problems during her surgery.

The woman sighed, "Well, scoot over. God's going to be getting triple prayers."

Aiden raised an eyebrow.

"Triple?"

"You bet. Grammy is on her knees in her bedroom right now. She said that she will not stop praying until I call her."

The two adults bowed their heads in silence each sending their own pleas up to the Lord. *She's going to be fine. You have a plan for her and it doesn't include death. I hope.*

Odessa "Birdie" Raines ignored the ache in her legs as she knelt beside her bed. She had started praying for Lyric and her doctors as soon as Harper ran out of the apartment a couple of hours ago. The elderly woman knew that God had big plans for the Wilder couple. She couldn't imagine Him taking that girl away when she had the energy and ability to make a difference in the world. *You must have a plan for her, Lord. Please help us to accept it.*

Suddenly, Birdie's cell phone began to ring. She glanced at the screen wondering if Harper was calling so soon. The woman answered the phone without stopping to see the name of the caller.

"Hello?"

"Hello, Birdie. It's Tillie."

Birdie smiled at the voice of her friend.

"Oh, Tillie. I'm so glad that you called. I have a job for you."

Tillie replied, "Oh? What would that be, hon?"

"There is a precious young lady named Lyric who is having surgery today to get rid of a brain tumor. She needs some prayer warriors."

The other woman cackled, "And you want me to spread the word to the girls?"

"Yes."

"Okay, Birdie. I'll get the prayer chain going. I'm sure that Ada, Nellie, Cora, and Harriet will be eager to pray for this young lady."

As the two women ended the call, Birdie returned to her prayers. She knew that there would now be a whole group of warriors sending their prayers to the gates of heaven. *You're going to do big things, Lord. I just know it.*

Aiden Wilder leaned back against the pew in the hospital chapel. He had been praying for over an hour before an idea came to mind. The man pulled out his cell phone tapping on a memo screen.

"What are you doing?"

Aiden smiled weakly, "I'm going to make a list of things that Lyric and I can do when she is well."

The husband glanced over at Harper wondering what the woman thought about his idea.

"That's sound great, Aiden. Lyric would love it."

Aiden nodded in agreement as he began typing on his phone. A smile spread up his face as he added several adventurous items to his list.

"There you are. I've been looking for you."

The man jerked his head around at the sound of his brother's voice.

"Des, what are you doing here?"

Desmond rolled his eyes.

"Duh, Aid. I'm checking on my brother and sister-in-law. How's Lyric?"

Aiden sighed, "She had a reaction to the anesthesia, so they gave her a different one. The last call was about half an hour ago. She was doing better with the meds and the surgery had officially started."

"How long will it last?"

Harper answered, "Anywhere between three and five hours. We have a long wait ahead of us."

Desmond sat down in the pew behind his brother.

"Well, good thing I am here to help pass the time with you." *Yes. This should be interesting.*

Harper Raines hung up her cell phone before heading back toward the chapel. She had stepped out into the hallway to call her grandmother with an update. The woman was beginning to worry about Lyric's surgery. *Five hours passed an hour ago. What is going on?*

"Excuse me, ma'am. You are with the Wilder family?"

Harper nodded at the hospital volunteer.

"Dr. Hayes would like to meet with you in the consultation room."

"Let me go get the rest of our group."

At the volunteer's nod, Harper clacked down the hallway as quickly as she could. She entered the chapel out of breath.

"Guys, Dr. Hayes is ready to talk to us in a consultation room."

The two men hopped to their feet before following the woman back to where she had left the hospital volunteer. The older woman led the group to a private consultation room where she had them sit at a table.

"Dr. Hayes will be here in a few minutes." *Oh, Lord, please give us a miracle.*

CHAPTER 28

SHAKEN FAITH

Dr. Leona Hayes took a deep breath as she entered the consultation room where the Wilder family was waiting. She had updated families on the progress of surgery many times, but this time it was more difficult.

Leona sat down at the table suppressing a flinch at the hopeful expressions on the three adults' faces. She had met Lyric's husband Aiden, but she didn't know the other two though she could guess that the other man was Aiden's brother since they looked so similar.

"Mr. Wilder, let me start by saying that Lyric survived the surgery."

The husband released the breath he had been holding before exchanging a glance with the other two people. Leona had learned in her years of experience to start with good news before sharing the negative.

"I was able to completely remove the brain tumor."

Smiles were the response to the doctor's success. *Now the hard part.*

"In order to fully remove the tumor, I had to go deeper than I originally thought. There may have been some damage."

The mood of the room dropped at the news. Leona waited for a moment to give the family time to process the information. *It's going to be a lot to swallow.*

Harper Raines stared at the table trying to understand what Dr. Hayes had told them. She had felt such hope at the news that Lyric survived the surgery. However, the happiness was crushed by the thought that there might be some brain damage.

The young woman asked, "How bad?"

Dr. Hayes sighed, "We won't know the extent of the damage until she wakes up. It was in her temporal lobe so there is a possibility of memory loss or speech impairment. There is also a chance that she may have no brain activity at all."

Harper sucked in a startled breath at the thought that her best friend may be in a vegetative state for the rest of her life. She blinked away tears that were threatening to fall. *Oh, Lord. How can You allow this to happen? Lyric is so young. She has so much to live for now. Please restore our hope.*

Sudden movement drew Harper's attention to Aiden. The man was standing almost towering over Dr. Hayes who had leaned back in surprise.

"I need to see her."

The doctor nodded, "I understand. She is in recovery now. You can see her in her hospital room in a few hours."

Aiden mumbled under his breath before storming out of the consultation room. Harper glanced over at Desmond who had a solemn expression on his face. Aiden's brother nodded slightly before excusing himself from the room.

"I'm sorry."

The soft words of Dr. Hayes surprised Harper. She glanced over at the doctor who was staring at the file folder in front of her.

"Don't worry, Doc. I don't think God is finished with Lyric yet."

"Aiden!"

Desmond Wilder raced to catch up with his brother. He knew that Aiden had to be as distraught as he was with the possible condition of Lyric. The man reached a hand out touching his twin's shoulder trying to stop him.

"Aiden, wait. Let's talk about this."

Aiden stopped walking but didn't turn around. He snorted before crossing his arms.

"Talk about what? You want to talk about how I have lost my wife? Or maybe you want to talk about how Lyric may wake up not knowing me at all?"

Desmond winced at the harsh tone of his brother.

"We don't know that anything has happened to her, Aid. She could still wake up fine. We have to hang on to hope."

Aiden shook his head.

"Just leave me alone, Des."

The other man lowered his hand from Aiden's shoulder. He stood still watching his brother stomp into the chapel. Desmond hoped that the man would find peace and comfort from God. *Please bring Lyric back to us for Aiden's sake.*

Aiden Wilder sank down into a pew in the hospital chapel. His heart was broken at the thought of Lyric having any damage. The husband was thrilled that she had survived the dangerous surgery. However, he couldn't breathe as he pictured his wife never being able to function on her own. *What if she doesn't know me? What if she doesn't remember all that we have done together?*

Aiden leaned back in the pew. He glared at the stain-glass picture of Jesus. The man's temper flared the more that he thought about Lyric's condition.

"Why did You do this to her? She trusted You!"

Aiden's voice echoed through the chapel.

"We both trusted You. You were supposed to heal her. You were supposed to bring her back to me, so we could start our life together. What kind of life will we have now? What will I do if she doesn't know me?"

Tears flowed down the man's face as his fury transformed into sorrow. He lowered his eyes from the window staring at the floor. Aiden slouched his shoulders in disappointment and exhaustion. *Why?*

"It sure is hard when His plan doesn't line up to our own."

Aiden snapped his head up at the voice. He turned toward a pew across from his own. A woman with silver hair tied up in a bun sat looking at him. She was dressed in a black dress with a silver cross necklace hanging around her neck. *Where did she come from? She wasn't here when I came in.*

"I'm sorry to intrude, sir. I just wanted you to know that you are not alone."

Aiden nodded, "Thanks. Sorry if I disturbed you."

The woman shook her head.

"I am not disturbed by a man with a broken heart. Have you lost someone, dear?"

The man sighed, "I don't know. I mean she is alive, but we don't know what damage her brain surgery may have caused."

The woman stood up before walking over to Aiden's pew. She sat down next to the man.

"Who is she?"

Aiden mumbled, "My wife. Her name is Lyric. We just got married on Saturday. Now, who knows what will happen?"

The woman replied, "God knows."

The husband averted his gaze before crossing his arms. He didn't want to talk about God. *He let me down.*

"God loves Lyric more than you do. He has a plan that no one can destroy. You need to trust Him even in this dark uncertain time."

Aiden sighed keeping his gaze on the stain-glass window of Jesus. His heart softened slightly at the words.

"Don't give up, Aiden. Lyric needs you to be strong."

The man frowned at the use of his name knowing that he had not introduced himself. He snapped his eyes toward the woman surprised to see that no one was sitting beside him. Aiden stood up spinning around to seek out the mysterious woman. His eyes widened at the empty chapel. *Where did she go? Did I just imagine her?*

Aiden turned back to the picture of Jesus. He smiled weakly before sitting back down. The man bowed his head closing his eyes. *Lord, I don't know what just happened here, but I think I got the message. I will trust You with my future with Lyric. Please help me to be strong for her.*

Harper Raines sat in a waiting room chair wiping silent tears that kept falling as she thought about Lyric. She hated the helplessness that she felt. The woman was usually so strong. Yet, here she was brokenhearted and unable to help her friend or her husband.

Harper thought about searching for Aiden and his brother, but she didn't know what she could say to make the man feel better.

"Are you okay?"

The woman looked up at Desmond who had his hands in his pockets.

"I think so. How's Aiden?"

The man frowned with a shrug. He sat down in the chair next to her.

"I don't know. He told me to leave him alone. Then he went in the chapel. I heard some yelling. I decided to leave him in peace."

Harper nodded, "Good idea. Maybe he just needs to vent. God understands."

"What do you mean?"

The woman explained, "Well, God knows everything, so He knows how we feel. He knows our frustrations and our fears. Maybe it will help Aiden to tell God how he feels aloud."

"That's very insightful, Harper. Thanks. I feel a little better now myself."

Harper glanced over at the man expecting to find him mocking her. Instead, Desmond was staring at her with a serious expression on his face. *Such a handsome face.*

The man smiled warmly at her causing the woman's face to feel warm. She returned the smile with one of her own.

Desmond grinned, "So we have a little time before we can see Lyric. Do you want to go to the cafeteria with me? I'll buy you whatever you want."

Harper chuckled, "Careful. I've been known to rack up a bill."

Chapter 29

Shocking Discoveries

Aiden Wilder sat beside Lyric's sleeping body in her hospital room. He held her hand gently hoping that the woman would wake up ready to continue their life together. The man smiled weakly at the lovely pale face and curly red hair.

"You've made it through the surgery, Lyric. Dr. Hayes said that she removed the tumor. It can't hurt you anymore."

Aiden rubbed Lyric's hand.

"Now we just need you to wake up. We need you to spring up in bed and start telling us what to do."

The man stared at the unconscious woman for several minutes.

"I love you, Lyric. Wake up so I can show you."

Lyric Sinclair's eyes fluttered as she struggled to wake up. She winced at the bright light that flashed into her vision. The woman blinked several times to adjust her eyes.

"Lyric?"

The male voice caused Lyric to frown. She stared at a man with black hair and green eyes who was sitting beside her. The woman lifted her head trying to figure out who he was. Her mind remained blank.

Lyric noticed that something was keeping her hand from moving. She glanced down seeing a hand grasping her own. The woman jerked her hand away while sitting straighter in bed.

"Who are you? What are you doing in my room?"

Her shriek caused the man to lean back against his chair with a frown on his face.

"Lyric, what in the world? Girl, you could wake the people in the morgue."

Lyric turned her attention to the woman's voice. She sighed in relief.

"Harper, thank goodness. Call security."

The woman stared at her friend who was cocking her head in confusion.

"What for?"

Lyric pointed at the strange man in the chair.

"Duh, because there is an intruder in my room."

Harper crossed her arms without making any move toward getting help.

"Harper, get help!"

The other woman sighed, "Calm down, Lyric. You know him."

Lyric shook her head.

"No. I've never seen him before. Call the police."

Aiden Wilder clenched his teeth disappointed that Lyric did not recognize him. He was glad that she was able to talk and function, but he had hoped that she would remember everything too. The man sat quietly slightly jealous that his wife knew Harper. *It makes sense. They have known each other much longer.*

"No. I've never seen him before. Call the police."

Aiden interrupted the woman's outburst.

"It's okay, Lyric. We're married."

The redheaded woman grew instantly quiet. She glared at the man.

"Who is married? You and Harper?"

Aiden shook his head. He opened his mouth to respond, but Harper beat him to it.

"No, girl. You're married to Aiden."

Silence filled the room as Lyric appeared to be considering what her friend had said. Aiden watched as she flicked her eyes between Harper and himself.

"What kind of sick joke is this, Harper Neveah Raines?"

Aiden sighed at the red flush that was covering the pale woman's face. He could tell that she was getting angrier.

Harper threw an exasperated look at the man.

"Lyric, a lot has happened. We need to talk."

The redheaded woman scowled, "Fine. Get rid of this stranger and we can talk."

Aiden nodded without a word. He stood up from the chair resisting the urge to kiss his wife. The man went out into the hallway hoping that Harper would be able to convince Lyric of the truth. He walked toward the nurse's station with a heavy heart. *She doesn't know me. Get a grip, Aiden. It could be a lot worse.*

"Can I help you, Mr. Wilder?"

Aiden replied, "Yes. Please tell Dr. Hayes that Lyric is awake."

The nurse's face lit up.

"How is she?"

The husband shrugged, "Better than she could have been."

Harper Raines sat down in the chair that Aiden had abandoned.

"Okay, Lyric. What is the last thing that you remember?"

The redheaded woman folded her hands onto her lap with a sigh.

"We are preparing a big summer fashion show. It is two months from now."

Harper raised an eyebrow in surprise. She liked that her friend was only missing a few months of memories. *It could have been a lot more.*

"We already did the fashion show, Lyric. It was a couple of months ago."

Lyric frowned, "Really? Why don't I remember that?"

Harper explained, "You had a brain tumor. Dr. Hayes did a craniotomy to remove it. It has affected your memories."

The patient nodded, "I guess that makes sense."

"Lyric, we need to talk about Aiden."

Lyric asked, "Who?"

"The man you kicked out of this room."

"Oh. I don't want to talk about him. When can I go home?"

Harper wanted to force her friend to hear about her husband. However, she knew that there would be time later for that. The friend didn't want to upset Lyric so soon after she woke up.

"We will have to check with Dr. Hayes."

As a nurse entered the hospital room, the two women grew silent.

"I'm here to check your vitals. Dr. Hayes will be here in a moment to talk to you. Is there anything that you need, Mrs. Wilder?"

Harper cringed at the dark glare that Lyric shot at the nurse.

"I am not Mrs. Wilder. I'm Miss Sinclair." *This may take a while.*

"Yes, ma'am."

Desmond Wilder sat up straight in the waiting room chair as he saw Aiden coming down the hall toward him. He held his breath waiting for an update. The man tensed at the scowl on his brother's face. *It's not good news.*

"Well?"

Aiden walked past the other man facing a window. He crossed his arms. Desmond stood up approaching his twin.

"What happened, Aid?"

His brother shrugged, "She's fine except that she doesn't remember me at all. She knows Harper, but I am a stranger. I'm an intruder."

Desmond remained silent as he saw Aiden's hurt expression through the reflection of the window.

"What do I do, Des?"

"Just be patient, Aid. Give her time to remember you."

Aiden nodded, "I'll try."

Harper Raines bit her lip as she approached the Wilder brothers. She dreaded telling Aiden what Lyric had told her. The woman felt horrible for the man whose wife didn't remember him at all.

"Hey, guys."

Desmond and Aiden spun to face her.

"I talked to Lyric. She thinks it is pre-fashion show. I tried to talk to her about you, Aiden, but she's not ready to discuss it. And she wants to go home."

Aiden smiled weakly, "That's something."

Harper shook her head.

"Actually, she wants to stay there alone."

The husband turned back to the window. Harper exchanged a concerned glance with Desmond.

"Fine. I'll move back in with Desmond tonight. The apartment will be all hers again by tomorrow."

Harper cringed at the hurt tone of the man.

"Thank you, Aiden. Don't give up. She just needs time." *We all do.*

Dr. Leona Hayes smiled with pleasure at the good condition of her patient. She was thrilled that there had been no severe brain damage. The doctor was slightly concerned with the minor memory loss, but she knew that it could have been a lot worse.

"Dr. Hayes, when can I go home?"

Leona replied, "If you are doing well, then you can go home in three days."

The patient sighed, "Okay. I guess that is soon enough."

"Good. Now rest up. We will get an MRI in a little bit to make sure that everything looks all right."

The doctor headed for the door.

"I will check in with you soon, Mrs. Wilder. I mean, Miss Sinclair."

Lyric Sinclair flipped through the channels on the television searching for something to watch. She sighed in boredom. The woman had returned from her MRI only to find that Harper had left to get some work done at the studio. She wished that she could go back to work creating beautiful outfits to make the world more beautiful. However, Lyric knew that she was stuck in the hospital until her three days were up. *Then I will be back to my busy life.*

Lyric left the television on a cooking channel before picking up her cell phone. She tapped on the screen to get to her memo app. The woman frowned at a list that had all the items marked off. She wondered when she had typed it. *What is this list? Weird items.*

Lyric shook the curiosity away as she opened a new memo. She began to type a list of things that she wanted to accomplish once she was free from the hospital. The woman blinked away tears that came to her eyes as she struggled to remember the past couple of months. *Nothing. I just want my life back.*

CHAPTER 30:

RETURNED LIFE

Lyric Sinclair strutted toward her high-rise apartment building. She was excited to be out of the hospital and back home. The fashionista entered the building eager to take a hot shower and put on an outfit worthy of her superiority. She held her nose in the air as she stepped inside the elevator.

"Welcome home, Lyric."

Lyric scowled at the elderly elevator operator. She couldn't believe that he dared to call her by her first name.

"It's Miss Sinclair to you. I'd prefer you don't talk to me at all. Take me to the eighteenth floor."

"Yes, ma'am."

The redheaded woman stared at the doors as the elevator headed for the eighteenth floor. She frowned as a dark feeling fell over her. Lyric glanced over at the elevator operator who had his eyes lowered to the floor. She regretted speaking to him in such an ugly tone. Yet, the woman couldn't bring herself to apologize.

As the elevator opened, Lyric marched out with mumbled thanks. She reached her apartment door. After fumbling with her keys, the woman unlocked her door and entered her apartment for the first time since her surgery. She froze at the sight of it. Everything was as it should be with all items in their proper place. However, Lyric couldn't help, but feel like something was missing. She glanced around wondering if she had been robbed. Yet, nothing was missing. *It must be my imagination.*

Lyric took her suitcase into her bedroom. She frowned as a strong feeling came over her. The woman knew that something was different, but she still couldn't put her foot on it. She began to unpack hoping that she would feel more comfortable once everything was completely in place.

Lyric opened her closet to place some shoes inside. She froze at an empty side of the clothes rack. The fashionista had always kept a full closet. *Why is there an empty spot?*

The woman touched the clothes that were hanging on the rack. She pulled them aside taking inventory. Lyric grabbed a hanger that held a turquoise blouse. She had never seen the shirt before. *Where did this come from?*

Suddenly, the doorbell rang. Lyric hung the blouse back on the rack before heading for her front door. She looked out the peephole before opening the door with a smile.

"Harper! Come in."

"Hey, girl. Are you getting settled?"

Lyric stepped aside letting her friend enter the apartment.

"I was just unpacking."

"Great! Take a girly talk break."

The redheaded woman plopped down on the sofa next to Harper happy that her best friend had come to visit. She noticed that the other woman was holding a present in her hands.

"What's that?"

Harper handed the package to her.

"Open it. It's a welcome back gift."

Lyric tore the paper off the present wondering what her friend had chosen as a homecoming gift. She frowned as she saw that it was a photo album.

"What's this?"

Harper rolled her eyes.

"It's a photo album. I filled it up with pictures of your wedding. I thought it would help you remember."

Lyric cringed at the words.

"I told you that I didn't want to do this."

Harper sighed, "Lyric, you love this man. You willingly married him. What's your plan? To ignore your husband for the rest of your life?"

The redheaded woman tossed the photo album on the coffee table before rising to her feet.

"I appreciate your concern, Harper, but this is none of your business. Now, if you will excuse me, I have things to do before I go to work tomorrow."

Harper stood up.

"Lyric, I think you need to rest for a few days. You don't want to overdo it."

"I am bored out of my mind, Harper. I must do something. What better way to bring me back into my life then to design a new autumn line."

The other woman threw her hands up into the air before heading for the door.

"Okay, Lyric. You're the boss. See you tomorrow."

Lyric nodded feeling in control of her life once more. She thought about how to get her errands done the next day. *I need to hire a driver.*

Aiden Wilder tapped away on the video game controller as he attacked the trolls on the television screen. He was enjoying the destruction of the wicked creatures who dared to try to steal his happiness. The man knew it was silly to vent his frustrations on imaginary trolls. However, he still felt satisfaction at the conquest.

Suddenly, the phone rang. Aiden continued to attack the trolls ignoring the sound. He glanced over at Desmond as movement caught his eyes. The twin brother scowled at the gamer.

"Trolls make you deaf, bro?"

Aiden snorted, "Yes."

Desmond picked up the phone answering in his professional manner.

"Hello? Yes, ma'am. We have a driver available for tomorrow. Your name? Oh. Yes. That will be fine. Yes. I will have a driver there at nine o'clock in the morning. Thank you. Goodbye."

Aiden blasted a troll delighting in his anguished yelp. He glanced over at Desmond who was staring at him without a word.

"Don't even think about it, Des. I am not working tomorrow."

The other man crossed his arms with a smirk.

"Oh? I think you might want to once you hear the information."

Aiden snorted, "Not a chance. There is nothing you can say to change my mind."

Desmond chuckled, "It's a job for Lyric Sinclair."

A troll destroyed Aiden's knight as the man found his focus shift. He dropped the video game controller onto his lap as he snapped his attention to Desmond.

"You're joking."

"Nope. Lyric needs a driver for some work that she is doing tomorrow. She wants to be picked up at nine o'clock outside her apartment building. Sure, you don't want the job?"

Aiden leaned back against the couch dazed by the information. He hadn't been allowed to see Lyric in three days due to her aversion to him. The man missed her so much already. He wondered if she would let him drive her around. *It might help her remember me.*

"You changed my mind, Des. I definitely want this job." *It's the chance of a lifetime.*

Lyric Sinclair tapped her foot angrily as she waited for the driver that she had hired. She shook her head at the incompetence of the man that she was paying to drive her around the city. The fashionista checked her watch grumbling under her breath about how it was almost nine o'clock.

Suddenly, a limousine pulled up to the curb in front of her. Lyric placed a hand on her side ready to give the man a piece of her mind. She stomped forward as a man came around to open her door. The woman froze as she recognized the driver.

"You! What are you doing here?"

The man smiled warmly, "I'm your driver for the day. You don't remember me, but my name is Aiden Wilder."

Lyric snorted, "Like that matters. Very well, Mr. Wilder. You will have to do."

The man tensed at her tone.

"Well? Open the door, Mr. Wilder. You are wasting my time."

Mr. Wilder opened the door waiting until she was settled before closing it. Lyric tapped on her cell phone hoping that the man wouldn't feel it necessary to talk to her. *I have no interest in what he has to say.*

As the limousine moved through the city, Lyric occasionally glanced up at the driver. She remembered how Harper had told her that the man was her husband. The woman noted that though he was a handsome man, she couldn't see herself settling for someone who drove cars for a living. *I have my standards.*

Lyric frowned at the feeling of guilt that came over her at the thought. She didn't understand why her heart ached whenever she shared her beliefs about people. It was almost like she regretted thinking or saying such cruel things. However, the woman had never felt bad about such things before. *What has changed?*

Aiden Wilder bit his lip in annoyance as he picked up Lyric at her apartment building. He had hoped for some kind word or expression from the woman that he loved. Yet, she treated him like a stranger. *Worse. Like I am beneath her.*

Aiden stared ahead as he drove through the busy morning traffic. He couldn't believe that his sweet Lyric had returned to her snobby self. His heart longed to speak to her and remind her of her true beautiful self.

"I'm sorry that I was so ill-tempered back there."

Aiden glanced into the rearview mirror.

"Apology accepted. Thanks."

The driver returned his focus to the crammed road. He thought about what else he could say.

Lyric cleared her throat.

"So, how did we meet?"

Aiden smiled weakly, "You hired me to take you on a road trip."

The woman snorted, "Oh, yeah? Where did I have you take me?"

"Lots of places. You had a list on your phone of things that you wanted to do. It was after you found out that you had a tumor. You called it your bucket list." *Please help her to remember me.*

Lyric Sinclair frowned at the mention of a list on her phone. She pulled up the mysterious list that had things marked off. The woman stared at the list wondering if she had really gone to so many odd places.

"Tell me about the road trip. Where did we go? What did we do?"

The driver nodded, "Of course. We had quite an adventure. We started by going to the Calhoun Farm which is thirty miles out of the city. Myra and Huck Calhoun let us explore their farm. We milked their cow and rode their horses."

Lyric wanted to deny the information knowing that she had never been much of a farm girl. However, her eyes fell on the first two items on her list. *Milk a cow. Ride a horse.*

"What was next?"

Mr. Wilder stopped at a stoplight before he answered.

"We went to an amusement park in Pennsylvania. We did the bumper cars and paintball. Then you made me ride on this scary roller coaster called The Widow-Maker. I got sick afterwards."

Lyric smirked at the information. She could see herself amused by the wimpy man as he vomited after the roller coaster. The woman glanced down at the cell phone screen. *Ride The Widow-Maker.*

"What did we do after the amusement park?"

Silence came as the response. The woman stared at the driver as he moved through the stoplight continuing their journey through the city.

"Well? What came next?"

Mr. Wilder replied, "We went to a circus in West Virginia. Lady Beatrix, the owner, let you bathe an elephant and play with a monkey."

Lyric frowned as two names came into her mind. *Kavi and Misha.*

"Then this giant man attacked you and I fought him."

The woman's green eyes widened in surprise.

"What?"

Mr. Wilder continued, "Lynx was his name. He hit you before I attacked him. He almost choked me to death before the circus workers stopped him. You used the first aid kit to tend my wounds."

Lyric swallowed nervously at the frightening information. She was grateful that the giant man hadn't been allowed to continue hurting her. The woman wondered how big the man was who had been able to subdue Mr. Wilder. *He's muscular himself.*

Lyric glanced down at her cell phone. She read the next two items on the list. *Bathe an elephant. Hold a monkey.*

"That was brave of you to stand up to a giant for me."

Mr. Wilder nodded, "It was worth it."

The woman blushed at the compliment. She cleared her throat.

"Where did we go after the circus?"

The driver passed a car safely before answering.

"We went to Florida. There we were able to swim with dolphins and ride in a hot air balloon. It was in the balloon that you told me about your father."

Lyric frowned at the mention of her father. She wondered what private information she had told the man who was her employee.

"You told me what he said at the pool when you were a kid."

The woman smiled warmly, "You'll never live if you don't take a leap of faith."

"Right. You also helped me face my fear of heights."

Lyric averted her gaze to her cell phone screen. She read the two items that were accomplished in Florida. *Swim with dolphins. Fly in hot air balloon.*

"We're at your studio."

The woman glanced out the window at the building. She saw that the limousine was parked at the curb.

"Are you ready to go in?"

Lyric looked down at her list.

"No. Tell me where we went after Florida."

The fashionista could see the smile that crossed Mr. Wilder's face in the mirror. She wanted to snap at him for his unprofessionalism. However, Lyric didn't want to have to apologize later for her words.

"Well?"

"Well, we went to a log cabin in Tennessee. We went river rafting and zip-lining."

Lyric's eyes widened at the adventurous activities. She double checked them with the list on her phone. *Go river rafting. Go down a zip line.*

"Then we went to Missouri to explore the caverns." *That's on the list too.*

The woman read the last item on the list.

"Where did we go for the fairytale wedding?"

Mr. Wilder sat silently for a moment. His smile faded into a frown.

"Back in New York."

Lyric cocked her head wondering about the fairytale wedding that was marked off the list.

"Whose wedding was it?"

Mr. Wilder opened his driver's door with a sigh.

"Ours."

The man hopped out of the limousine slamming his door. Lyric stared at the screen wondering about the wedding. She shook her head as she prepared to exit out her door. Mr. Wilder opened her door holding out a hand to help her out of the limousine. The fashionista took it with mumbled thanks. She adjusted her purse on her shoulder before gliding toward the fashion studio entrance. *Time to get my mind off things.*

Aiden Wilder watched his wife strut toward the fashion studio front door. He bit back the frustration and disappointment that came from the woman's lack of reaction to the memories that he had shared with her. The man had hoped that she would suddenly remembered their life together. He had longed to hear her say that she recalled loving him. Yet, nothing came from the reciting of their adventures. *Be patient. I must be patient. Don't give up. Be strong.*

"Aren't you coming?"

Aiden nodded slightly before following Lyric toward the building. He liked being near her though it broke his heart that she had returned to her spoiled self. *I love her too much to stay away. I just wish that she remembered that she loves me too.*

Harper Raines entered the driving services building. She marched toward the front desk noticing Desmond sitting with his feet up on his desk reading a sports magazine.

"You look busy."

The man lowered the magazine with a smirk.

"Good morning, ma'am. How may I help?"

Harper waved a hand of dismissal.

"You think you are so funny. Is Aiden here?"

Desmond snorted, "You mean you don't know?"

"Know what?"

The man stood up with a chuckle before taking on a professional air.

"Well, ma'am. A Miss Lyric Sinclair called to hire a driver. Mr. Aiden Wilder mistook her as Mrs. Lyric Wilder and instantly jumped at the chance to spend some time with her. He was supposed to pick her up at her apartment building this morning at nine."

Harper's eyes widened at the news. She was surprised that Lyric hadn't mentioned it to her when she talked to her last night. The woman crossed her arms at Aiden's cleverness. She hoped that the more time they spent together, the more memories would return to Lyric about the man.

"Lyric didn't tell me. Do you think Aiden will be able to cope with being around her? She seems to have gone back to her not so pleasant demeanor."

Desmond's smile fell into a frown.

"Oh. That's not good. That might be hard on Aiden. He's already struggling with Lyric not knowing who he is. If she is treating him like a lowly employee, then he may not react well."

Harper nodded, "I agree. Maybe I should head to the studio and keep an eye on Her Majesty."

"Good idea. I'll text Aiden often to make sure he is okay."

The two adults smiled at each other as they started their agreed upon plan. Harper left the building thinking about how handsome and kind the man was. She shook her head. *No time for that. I must keep an eye on Lyric.*

Aiden Wilder gritted his teeth in frustration at the last order that his customer had demanded. His stomach lurched at how much Lyric was acting like her former self. The man hated that the kind woman had reverted into a pampered princess. His heart ached as he watched his wife flitting around the studio. *I miss her.*

"Hanging in there?"

Aiden snapped his eyes to the woman standing beside him.

With a weak smile, the man replied, "Yes, Harper. It's killing me to see her like this. She became so much more before the surgery."

"I know. It hurts me too. She just needs time to remember."

Aiden nodded though in his heart he didn't want to wait. He wanted his wife to remember their beautiful life together immediately.

"Don't lose hope, Aiden. Our Lyric is in there somewhere."

The man shot a smile at Harper.

"You're right, Harper. She's not completely gone. Thanks for the pep talk."

"Any time. Now, I'm going to go check on Miss Nose-in-the-Air."

Aiden nodded as Harper glided over to where Lyric was examining some designs. He winced at the lovely smile that the redheaded woman gave to her best friend. *I wish she would smile at me like that.*

Lyric Sinclair smiled at Harper as her friend started helping her with designing an autumn line of clothes. She knew that together the almost sisters could come up with some best-sellers. The fashion designer maneuvered through her design program on the computer adjusting her sketches. *These must be perfect.*

Lyric unconsciously touch the chain of the necklace around her neck as she concentrated on the sketches. Her fingers reached the bottom of the necklace finding an unusually large stone. She knew that she had always been accustomed to wearing petite jewels on her jewelry.

The confused woman glanced down while raising the stone, so she could see it. Her eyes widened at the beauty of the blue diamond. She wondered where she had gotten the necklace. *I don't remember buying it. I doubt I could afford something so extravagant anyway.*

Suddenly, Lyric had a mental picture of a plump woman with shiny black hair and olive skin. The stranger wore a leathery red dress with black leggings and boots underneath. Lyric frowned as the woman's name came to mind. *Lady Beatrix.*

Lyric held her breath as she could hear the woman speaking to her in a strange accent. *This necklace vas a gift from my mother. She gave it to me in a very rough time of my life. My mother said that it vas a diamond of hope because it vould always remind me that the future is full of hope.*

"It was a wedding present from Lady Beatrix."

Lyric snapped her attention to Mr. Wilder who had approached with a covered coffee cup. She reached for her latte which the driver handed to her willingly. The woman dropped the necklace returning to her work on the computer.

"Thank you, Mr. Wilder."

"You're welcome, Lyric."

Lyric opened her mouth to chastise the man. However, she changed her mind as the use of her name by Mr. Wilder seemed comfortable. *Why is that? Could he really be my husband?*

"Do you have plans tonight, Lyric?"

The woman frowned, "Why?"

"I would like to cook you dinner."

Lyric snorted, "Oh, really? Do you even know how to cook?"

Silence followed the woman's insult. She grimaced realizing that she had been rude again. Lyric bit her lip wondering what the driver would say in reply.

"Why don't you let me cook for you and find out?"

The fashionista prepared to decline the invitation. However, as she looked into the man's green eyes, she changed her mind. Her heart thumped nervously as she stared into his handsome face. *Maybe I should spend a little time with him.*

"Very well, Mr. Wilder. You can cook dinner for me at my apartment tonight."

"Great. I'll go grocery shopping after I drop you off."

Lyric shrugged, "Whatever. If you want to waste your money, go for it."

The man turned to return to the wall where he had been stationed for the day. His slumped shoulders showed the woman that she had hurt Mr. Wilder's feelings. Lyric didn't know why, but she felt an urge to apologize.

"I'm sorry, Mr. Wilder. I'm sure that it will be fine."

The man turned back with a slight smile.

"It's Aiden."

The woman sighed, "Fine. Aiden. I'll be ready to go home at around five o'clock."

Aiden nodded, "Whatever you say, Lyric."

Aiden Wilder pushed the metal shopping cart down the aisles of the grocery store. His mind raced with ideas of what he could cook to impress his wife. Though he had cooked for her before, it was the first time that Lyric would remember. *It must be perfect.*

Aiden stopped at the meat section remembering what his culinary professors had always taught him. *Choose the meat first and then fill in the blanks.*

The man leaned on the cart looking at the endless choices. He wondered what would show Lyric his love for her.

Suddenly, Aiden's eyes lit up. He knew exactly what to cook for his wife. His heart soared with hope at the thought of Lyric remembering everything based on the memories that the meal would prompt. *This must work.*

Lyric Sinclair pretended to stare at her cell phone as she kept a close eye on the man who was cooking in her kitchen. The variety of sounds and smells made the woman wonder if Aiden really knew what he was doing. She found herself curious at the prospect that the lowly driver had culinary skills. *Let it go, Lyric. He's probably making beanie wienies and mac and cheese.*

"Dinner's ready."

Lyric set her phone down on the coffee table before strutting over to the kitchen island. She raised her eyebrows at the fanciness of the table setting. The woman sat down wondering what else she could expect from the dinner. She gasped as Aiden set down two plates filled with food.

"Wow. What is this?"

The man replied, "Tonight, our chef has prepared roasted salmon, golden potatoes, and buttered green beans."

Lyric picked up her fork marveling at the perfection of the meal. She used her knife to cut a piece of salmon. The woman blew on it gently before taking a bite. She closed her eyes savoring that smoky fish that filled her mouth with flavor.

"How is it?"

Lyric opened her eyes trying to control herself.

"It's good."

The two adults ate quietly for several minutes. The woman tasted the potatoes enjoying them as well. She took a bite of the buttered green beans amazed by the taste. *These are delicious. I feel like I have enjoyed this meal before, but when?*

Lyric's mind searched for the answer to her question. She continued eating in hopes that a memory would come. The woman frowned suddenly as she saw Aiden in a kitchen in a log cabin. She recalled sitting together eating the same meal while teasing each other.

Lyric looked up at the man sitting in front of her. He was eating his own meal without noticing her. *He's cooked this for me before.*

"Did you make this meal for me before? In a log cabin?"

Aiden snapped his eyes to her before a smile grew on his face.

"Yes. It was when we were in Tennessee before the river rafting."

Lyric swallowed hard. She sipped her iced tea trying to think of what else she could say. The woman found herself becoming attached to the man from her limited memories. She set her glass down gently. *Harper agreed that he is my husband. Could she be serious?*

Aiden Wilder dried the last few dishes placing them expertly in the correct cabinets. He was thrilled that Lyric had remembered the meal at the log cabin. The man felt hope that his wife was beginning to remember him. *I just need to keep waiting on You, Lord.*

"Thank you for dinner. It was very satisfying."

Aiden smiled warmly, "You're welcome, Lyric."

The man watched as the woman sank onto her couch. She reached for her cell phone which was on the coffee table. Aiden cocked his head as he noticed a white photo album also on the table. He picked it up thoughtfully.

"What's this?"

Lyric shrugged, "Harper gave it to me."

"May I look at it?"

"I don't care."

Aiden gritted his teeth at the uncaring response of his wife. He sat down on the other end of the couch. The man opened the album amazed to find photographs from their wedding and reception. He turned the pages slowly examining each picture that showed the beauty of that day. *It was perfect. Then everything went wrong. If only, we could return to that day.*

Lyric Sinclair checked her email on her cell phone. She was vaguely aware of Aiden sitting down on the couch with the photo album that Harper had given her. The woman noticed that the man was pouring over each page at a slow pace. She glanced over to see what held Aiden's attention.

Lyric saw a picture of herself dressed in a regal white gown. On her head was a beautiful tiara with a veil. She saw Harper standing next to her in a lavender dress. The two women in the photograph looked so happy.

Aiden turned the page no doubt unaware that the woman was looking at the pictures too. Lyric leaned slightly to see the next page better. She saw herself dancing with Aiden under a string of white lights. The glowing smile on both of their faces proved one thing. *They love each other.*

"Let me see that."

Aiden passed the album to her before he scooted closer. Lyric blushed at the closeness of the man. She focused her attention on the album. The surprised woman turned each page slowly studying the pictures for details. She couldn't remember anything from the day.

Lyric took a deep breath. She waited a moment hoping for the courage to ask a question that was now plaguing her.

"Are we really married?"

Something touched her hand. Lyric glanced over to find Aiden's hand caressing her own. She held her breath at the feeling of love that rushed over her.

"Yes, we are."

Fear filled Lyric at the variety of emotions that swarmed over her. Tears came to her eyes as she realized that she had lost much in the surgery. The woman wondered what else she had lost.

Suddenly, Lyric threw the album across the room while jerking her hand away from the man. She stood up overwhelmed by the truth. The frightened woman backed away from Aiden who had stood up as well. She shook her head at him as he opened his arms approaching her.

"No! You must leave! Now! I want you to leave!"

The man lowered his arms with a nod.

"Okay, Lyric. I'll leave. It's okay."

Lyric watched Aiden exit her apartment. She stared after him for several minutes marveling at the ache in her heart at his departure. The woman stormed into her bedroom. She removed her diamond of hope necklace shakily before opening her jewelry box to place it inside.

Lyric froze. She noticed a blue velvet box resting beside the jewelry box. The woman picked up the box opening it carefully. Her eyes widened at two rings. One was a simple golden wedding band. The other ring was clearly an engagement ring. It had a dolphin jumping above a golden wave with a diamond in the center of it. *So beautiful.*

A flash of a memory came to Lyric's mind. She saw herself swimming in a pool with Aiden. Then a dolphin interrupted the couple. The woman clenched her eyes shut tightly trying to cause the memory to disappear.

"No!"

Lyric screamed as she slid her hands across her vanity. She knocked the boxes off causing the jewelry to fly in all directions. The woman opened the drawers throwing her clothes all around the bedroom. She fell to her knees with a shriek.

"Why? Why did You let this happen? What else have You taken from me?"

Tears streamed down Lyric's face as she screamed at God. Her heart wrenched in pain at the loss that she had experienced.

"Dad always told me to trust You but look what You did to him! Now, You've failed me. I don't know anything about Aiden. He is my husband and I don't even remember falling in love with him. How could You betray us like this?"

Lyric sobbed as she laid down on the soft carpet. She could find no comfort for her broken heart. The woman grieved for all that she had lost. She wailed for the things that she didn't know.

After what seemed like hours, Lyric grew quiet. She allowed the tears to dry on her face. The woman's body was exhausted. She slowly moved to her feet before climbing into her bed. Pulling a blanket over herself, Lyric closed her eyes falling instantly to sleep.

CHAPTER 31:

FAMILIAR MOMENTS

Lyric Sinclair opened her eyes as bright sunlight flashed into them. She stared at the ceiling recalling the outburst that she had had the night before. The distraught woman sat up slowly knowing that she should be heading for the fashion studio. *There is much to do.*

Lyric climbed out of bed wincing at the mess of clothes and jewelry that she had scattered on the bedroom carpet. She shook her head throwing a hand of dismissal at the disorganization before entering her bathroom. *Who cares if it is a mess?*

Lyric went about completing her morning routine as she prepared for the day. Her mind raced with things to do to complete the sketches for the autumn line of clothes. The fashion designer decided to call a taxi cab instead of bothering Aiden. She thought that a day away from the man who apparently was her husband would help her. *I just need time to think.*

Sitting in the taxi cab, Lyric typed away on her cell phone updating her autumn line list. She was pleased with what she had accomplished the day before. The fashionista knew that there was still a lot to do before summer ended.

Suddenly, Lyric had a mental image of waking up wet at the side of a river. She saw Aiden leaning over her with a relieved smile. The woman gasped as she saw herself sit up and hug the man with whispered thanks. *He saved me.*

"Are you alright, ma'am?"

Lyric's emerald eyes darted to the cab driver who was looking in the mirror at her.

"Yes. Thank you."

The woman returned her attention to her phone. She quickly swiped the screen bringing up the bucket list with the marked off items. *Maybe if I look at the list, I will remember more things.*

Lyric read the list. She closed her eyes trying to picture the places. The fashionista frowned as nothing came to mind.

"We're here, ma'am."

Lyric paid her cab bill before climbing out of the yellow car. She strutted toward her fashion studio thinking through her list.

Suddenly, a memory slammed into the woman. Lyric saw herself trapped under a pile of rocks in a dim cave. She was being held above the water by Aiden. The woman remembered telling the man about her brain tumor and the bucket list trip. She closed her eyes as the trapped Lyric whispered to Aiden. *I love you, Aiden.*

"Lyric? Are you okay?"

The redheaded woman opened her eyes at the familiar voice. She smiled as she saw Harper hurrying toward her.

"I'm fine, Harper. I was just remembering something."

"What?"

Lyric sighed, "That I love Aiden."

Harper Raines crossed the parking lot as she advanced toward the fashion studio. She glanced around enjoying the beautiful sunshine. The woman saw Lyric standing near the building, but she was not moving. Her friend's eyes were closed.

"Lyric? Are you okay?"

Relief filled Harper as Lyric opened her eyes with a smile.

"I'm fine, Harper. I was just remembering something."

The other woman felt a wave of excitement rise inside her at the idea that her friend was beginning to get her memories back.

"What?"

With a sigh, Lyric replied, "That I love Aiden."

Harper clapped her hands excitedly.

"Lyric, that's wonderful. You should tell him how you feel."

The redheaded woman adjusted her purse on her shoulder. She averted her eyes to the concrete.

"Lyric?"

"I don't think I'm ready, Harper. I need more time."

Harper put an arm around her friend's shoulder. She smiled warmly as the two women headed toward the studio entrance.

"That's okay, Lyric. Aiden will understand." *I hope.*

Aiden Wilder paced back and forth in the office mumbling to himself. He had thought that Lyric believing that they were married would make him happy. However, the man was disturbed by the woman's reaction. *She threw me out. She didn't want anything to do with me. It's all over.*

Aiden's annoyance faded into sorrow at the thoughts. He sank into a swivel chair feeling burdened by his emotions.

"Thank goodness you sat down. I thought you were going to wear out the carpet."

Aiden rolled his eyes at Desmond who was leaning against the wall near the doorway.

"What's going on, Aid?"

The brother shrugged, "Nothing. Just some stuff with Lyric. I don't want to talk about it."

Desmond pulled up a chair in front of his twin. Aiden held his breath certain that the man was going to attempt to comfort him anyway.

"Aiden, you're fired."

The other man snorted, "Very funny, Des."

"I'm not joking, Aid. You have put your life on hold long enough for me. It's time for you to return to the wonderful world of culinary arts."

Aiden crossed his arms scowling at his brother.

"Des, I can't just leave you here alone."

Desmond scoffed, "I'm a grown man too, Aid. You don't have to worry about me anymore. Leave this job of rich snobs. Go out there and follow your dreams."

Aiden smiled weakly at his brother's words. He had to admit that it sounded great pursuing his love of cooking. However, the man still didn't like the idea of leaving his brother to continue the family business alone.

"Please, Aiden. I can't watch you continue to be unhappy. You have to do something for yourself for once."

Aiden stood up hugging Desmond who rose to his feet as well.

"Thanks, brother. I'll miss you."

His twin snorted, "Don't go overboard, brother. We still live together for now."

Aiden chuckled, "True. I still have to put up with you some."

Lyric Sinclair moved the mouse of her computer clicking on the parts of the design program that would help her with perfecting her autumn line of fashion. She sighed as she found that her heart really wasn't in her work. The woman couldn't get her mind off Aiden. She kept replaying the scene where she told the man that she loved him. *Does he love me too?*

Lyric shook her head trying to refocus. She stared at the computer screen rolling her eyes at the mistakes that she had made while she was daydreaming about Aiden.

The fashion designer clicked on a light blue color placing it on a dress she was designing. She frowned as her mind wandered to a new memory.

Lyric saw herself sitting on an exam table in the hospital. She was wearing a light blue hospital gown. The woman gasped as she saw Aiden talking to her. She closed her eyes allowing tears to escape as she recalled what the man had said to her. *I love you, Lyric, with all my heart. I have loved you on our journey and I will love you even if you don't love me. Loving you for even a minute is more than I deserve.*

"He loves me."

Harper shouted from across the studio.

"What did you say, Lyric?"

The redheaded woman stood up searching for her purse.

"Lyric? What's going on? Where are you going?"

Lyric laughed feeling joy feel her. She knew that there were still missing pieces, but she felt like she had discovered the two most important ones.

"I love Aiden and he loves me. Where am I going, Harper? I'm going to find my husband."

As Lyric ran as best she could in her high heel shoes, she could hear her friend rejoicing behind her.

"Hallelujah, sister! Go and get him!"

Lyric hurried toward the curb before raising a hand to hail a cab. She tapped her foot impatiently as she waited for a taxi driver to notice her.

"Lyric Wilder. That name definitely has a ring to it."

Horror filled the woman as she glanced down at her left ring finger. She frowned at the emptiness that she found there. *I can't see Aiden until I have my rings.*

Lyric hopped into a taxi cab that stopped in front of her. She instructed the driver to take her to her apartment building. The woman's heart thumped nervously as her mind planned. *First, I find the rings. Then I find my husband.*

Desmond Wilder scribbled down information into his log book. He missed having his brother around already, but he knew that he had made the right decision. *It was time to free him.*

"Hello?"

Desmond glanced up at the familiar voice. He smiled as he saw Lyric standing in the doorway.

"You look almost like Aiden."

The man stood up with a snort.

"I always thought that I was the more attractive Wilder brother. I'm Desmond."

Lyric nodded glancing around.

"Is Aiden here?"

"No. He doesn't work here anymore."

The downcast expression on Lyric's face tugged at Desmond's heart. He could tell that the woman was disappointed at not finding Aiden.

"Aiden went to a job interview."

"Where?"

Desmond smiled, "He is interviewing for the executive chef position at The Electric Café."

Lyric nodded, "I see. Well, he cooks good enough for that place. Thank you."

Desmond watched the woman leave. He wondered why she was looking for Aiden. The brother hoped that it was because she now remembered her husband. *If only.*

Lyric Wilder sighed as she exited the driving services building. She was disappointed that Aiden wasn't there. The woman had longed to talk to the man who was legally her husband. She wanted to tell him that she remembered their love for each other. Yet, Lyric's courage disappeared at the thought of going to The Electric Café. She didn't want to make a public display. *This must be between him and me.*

Lyric hailed another taxi cab eager to get back to the fashion studio for some advice from Harper. She knew that she could talk to Aiden later. The woman was certain that the man's brother would tell him that she came by the business. *Maybe he will find me when he is ready.*

Harper Raines took a sip from her cappuccino cherishing the flavor. She used a pencil to add to the sketch that she was designing for their autumn line. The woman had always loved sticking with pencil and paper instead of computers when it came to drawing her designs.

Suddenly, sunlight blasted into the studio. Harper snapped her attention to the doorway. She frowned as she saw Lyric trudging in with her eyes lowered to the floor. The redheaded woman was dragging her purse with a deep frown on her face.

"Lyric? What's wrong?"

Harper bit her lip waiting for her best friend to respond. *Surely, Aiden didn't reject her after waiting all this time.*

Lyric continued walking until she reached her artist desk. She set her purse on the floor with a thud.

"Aiden wasn't at work. He is off interviewing at The Electric Café. I didn't want to talk to him in front of a lot of people, so I came back here."

Harper frowned, "I'm sorry, girl. I'm sure Aiden will find you later to talk. That man loves you something fierce, Lyric. He won't let you go now. Just be patient."

Lyric Wilder sat down in her red leather desk chair. She pushed the power button on her computer bringing it to life. The woman sighed as she clicked on her design program determined to continue her sketches.

"Come on, Harper. We have work to do."

"Lyric."

Harper's harsh whisper caused the fashionista to flick her attention to her friend. She saw that the other woman was staring toward the entrance door. Lyric followed her gaze swallowing hard when she saw what had captured Harper's focus. Her emerald green eyes widened as she saw that the front door was open. Standing in the doorway was Aiden. *He couldn't have found out that I was looking for him. It is too soon. What is he doing here?*

CHAPTER 32:

UNBREAKABLE LOVE

Lyric Wilder held her breath as Aiden stepped fully into the studio. She wrung her hands under the desk fearing what the man had come to tell her. *He's probably tired of waiting on me. He wants to move on. He wants a divorce.*

"Lyric, can I talk to you?"

The nervous woman nodded, "Of course. What is it?"

Aiden glanced toward Harper.

"Oops!"

Lyric snapped her gaze to her friend who was leaning over the trashcan.

"Oh, dear. I dropped my cappuccino into the trash. I'm going to go down the street to get another one."

The redheaded woman rolled her eyes knowing that Harper had dropped her coffee on purpose. She shook her head knowing that it was unnecessary to make an excuse for her absence.

"Smooth, Harp."

The other woman grabbed her purse clomping toward the studio exit.

"I don't know what you are talking about, Lyric. See you two later."

Lyric took a deep breath as she focused on Aiden. The man looked amused at Harper's exit as well. He turned back toward her with his smile fading.

"I came to see you because I have some good news. You were the one that I wanted to tell first."

Lyric blushed at the compliment. She was touched that the man thought about her first.

"What's the news?"

Aiden beamed, "I interviewed for an executive chef job at The Electric Café. I barely got out of the restaurant before I got a call that I got the job."

Lyric recalled the dinner that he had made her the other night. She had to admit that the man was a wizard in the kitchen. The woman was thrilled that he had been hired for a job that he wanted. She longed to hug him in celebration. However, Lyric didn't feel like they were at the point of embracing yet.

"Congratulations."

Aiden Wilder's happiness deflated like a balloon at Lyric's monotone congratulations. He had hoped that the woman would be as happy as he was about restarting his culinary career. However, the man could tell that his wife didn't even care that he was one step closer to following his dreams.

"Well, I just wanted you to know about the job. Bye."

Aiden stomped out of the studio grumbling to himself. *I shouldn't have wasted my time coming down here. She doesn't know me. She doesn't care about me. I've had enough.*

"Aiden, wait!"

Lyric's voice caused the man to stop walking. He turned around to face the woman who was clacking across the parking lot toward him. Aiden crossed his arms unsure of what Lyric wanted.

"What is it, Lyric?"

Lyric stopped in front of him attempting to catch her breath.

"Listen, Aiden. I was looking for you earlier, but your brother said that you were at the interview."

Aiden cocked his head in curiosity.

"Why were you looking for me?"

The redheaded woman took a deep breath making the man wonder what she was going to say.

"I wanted to tell you that even though I don't remember you completely, I do remember two things."

Aiden's heart began to pound nervously. *What does she remember?*

"What?"

Lyric smiled warmly, "I remember that I love you and you love me."

The man released the breath he was holding in relief. He had longed for his wife to remember their love for each other since the surgery. *Thank You, Lord!*

"Aiden, if you are willing to wait on me, I would be willing to get to know you again."

Lyric Wilder stared at her husband waiting for the man to decide whether he was willing to start over. She hoped that Aiden would love her enough to give their new relationship a chance.

Aiden reached his hands toward Lyric. She placed her hands into his own. The man rubbed a finger over her left ring finger where her dolphin engagement ring and wedding band were stationed.

"Yes, Lyric. I love you too much to give up on us now. Let's get to know each other again."

Without allowing her brain to ruin the moment, Lyric pulled her hands away before wrapping them around the man's neck. She was thrilled when her husband completed the embrace by putting his arms around her. *We get a fresh start.*

Harper Raines leaned against the window of the coffee shop watching Aiden leave the studio. She could tell by the man's stance that he was upset. *Oh, Lyric.*

The woman held her breath as she saw Lyric rush out of the studio stopping the man. She watched as the couple talked. Harper wished that she could hear what they were saying. *I should have picked a closer place to spy.*

Suddenly, Aiden took Lyric's hands into his own. Harper suppressed a squeal. However, as the couple hugged, the woman released her joy.

"Yes!"

The woman glanced around at the other customers who were watching her with odd expressions on their faces.

"Sorry. I just love happy endings."

Harper pulled out her cell phone. She dialed it before tapping her foot impatiently.

"Hello?"

"Desmond, it's Harper. Aiden and Lyric have found each other again. I just saw them hugging."

The loud whoop of joy from the other end of the line brought a giggle from the woman.

"You want to celebrate tonight, Harper? I know a great place to get some barbecue ribs."

Harper smirked, "Desmond Wilder, you sure know how to treat a girl. I'm in." *Maybe those two won't be the only ones to have a happy ending.*

Lyric Wilder straightened her turquoise blouse nervously as the doorbell to her apartment rang. She fluffed her strawberry blonde hair before gliding to the door. Taking a deep breath, the woman opened it. She smiled at Aiden who was dressed in a dark blue shirt with a red tie.

"You look handsome, Mr. Wilder."

The man winked causing the woman to blush.

"So, do you, Mrs. Wilder."

Lyric stepped back inviting the handsome man into the apartment.

"I hope you don't mind, but I ordered in."

Aiden frowned, "I was hoping to cook for you."

The woman smirked, "You did. I ordered it from The Electric Café."

"Oh. Then I bet it will taste delicious."

Lyric giggled, "So modest."

The couple sat down at the kitchen island to eat their dinner. Lyric savored the food and the conversation with the man that she was falling in love with all over again.

"I wanted to show you something, Lyric."

The redheaded woman cocked her head in curiosity.

"What's that?"

Aiden pulled out his cell phone.

"It's something that I made while you were in surgery. I thought about deleting it the other day, but now I'm glad that I didn't."

Lyric leaned forward to see what was on the man's cell phone screen. She frowned as he purposely held it out of sight.

"Why can't I see it?"

Aiden smirked, "Because it is a secret. It's our new bucket list."

"What do you mean?"

The man pocketed his phone.

"It is a list of things that I want us to do together. It's a new trip full of adventures."

Lyric sighed, "Well, what is on it?"

"If you will go with me, then I will show you."

EPILOGUE

NEW LIST

Lyric Wilder smiled as the cool English air caressed her face. She couldn't believe that she was getting ready to tour the Windsor Castle with her loving husband Aiden. The woman had been traveling the world with the man one secret bucket list item as a time. She had to admit that the adventures had brought the couple closer.

A tender squeeze to her hand drew Lyric's attention to Aiden. She rubbed his hand with her other one lovingly.

"This place is amazing, Aiden."

"I know. I have always wanted to look out of a castle window with a princess."

Lyric rolled her eyes at the man who was waggling his eyebrows at her.

The woman giggled, "Well, Prince Charming, it is the next logical step after a fairytale wedding."

Lyric stared up at the massive castle that towered over the couple and the other tourists. She loved that she was sharing this experience with her husband. The woman had begun to remember things little by little over the last few months. She had visited with Dr. Hayes before leaving on their world trip. The doctor had given her a good report that the tumor had been completely removed and no other treatments were necessary. Lyric was thrilled since she didn't want anything keeping her from enjoying her new life with Aiden.

As if things couldn't get any better, Lyric's best friend Harper and Aiden's brother Desmond had recently gotten engaged. The thought of helping her sister-friend design a wedding brought great joy to the recovered woman. She had so many ideas for the dresses and suits. *Maybe we can make it into a fashion show.*

Lyric leaned her head onto her husband's shoulder cherishing the beauty of the next item on the Wilder bucket list. She smiled warmly as Aiden kissed the top of her head.

The man whispered, "Are you sure you want to go up that high?"

Lyric smirked knowing her husband's fear of heights. She knew that he was better than he used to be, but the wife was sure that he wasn't completely fearless yet.

"I'm sure. You'll never live if you don't take a leap of faith."

ABOUT THE AUTHOR

Carrie Rachelle Johnson believes in chasing your dreams. She has always wanted to be an author and hold her own published books in her hands. Carrie constantly follows God's inspiration in her writing finding the path where He takes her amazing and unpredictable.

When she is not writing, Carrie enjoys watching movies, spending time with her loving family, and chatting with fellow authors or readers online. She also enjoys teaching elementary students and serving the Lord in her family church.

Carrie is the author of The Glory Chronicles series and Magnolia Ruby Mysteries. She would love to hear from her readers. Be sure to check out Carrie Rachelle Johnson on Facebook, Carrie's website at https://carrierachellejohnson.wordpress.com, or feel free to email her at carrierachellejohnson@outlook.com!

CPSIA information can be obtained
at www.ICGtesting.com
Printed in the USA
LVHW082150030919
629858LV00017B/1387/P

9 781982 093976